THE SINISTER HEART

Unmarriageable

Book 2

Mary Lancaster

Books from Dragonblade Publishing

Dangerous Lords Series by Maggi Andersen
The Baron's Betrothal
Seducing the Earl
The Viscount's Widowed Lady
Governess to the Duke's Heir

Also from Maggi Andersen
The Marquess Meets His Match

Knights of Honor Series by Alexa Aston
Word of Honor
Marked by Honor
Code of Honor
Journey to Honor
Heart of Honor
Bold in Honor
Love and Honor
Gift of Honor
Path to Honor
Return to Honor

The King's Cousins Series by Alexa Aston
The Pawn
The Heir
The Bastard

Beastly Lords Series by Sydney Jane Baily
Lord Despair
Lord Anguish

Legends of Love Series by Avril Borthiry
The Wishing Well
Isolated Hearts
Sentinel

The Wicked Marquis
The Wicked Governess
The Wicked Spy
The Wicked Gypsy
The Wicked Wife

Unmarriageable Series by Mary Lancaster
The Deserted Heart
The Sinister Heart

Highland Loves Series by Melissa Limoges
My Reckless Love
My Steadfast Love
My Passionate Love

Clash of the Tartans Series by Anna Markland
Kilty Secrets
Kilted at the Altar
Kilty Pleasures

Queen of Thieves Series by Andy Peloquin
Child of the Night Guild
Thief of the Night Guild
Queen of the Night Guild

Dark Gardens Series by Meara Platt
Garden of Shadows
Garden of Light
Garden of Dragons
Garden of Destiny

Rulers of the Sky Series by Paula Quinn
Scorched
Ember
White Hot

Hearts of the Highlands Series by Paula Quinn
Heart of Ashes
Heart of Shadows
Heart of Stone

Highlands Forever Series by Violetta Rand
Unbreakable
Undeniable
Unyielding

Viking's Fury Series by Violetta Rand
Love's Fury
Desire's Fury
Passion's Fury

Also from Violetta Rand
Viking Hearts

The Sins and Scoundrels Series by Scarlett Scott
Duke of Depravity

The Unconventional Ladies Series by Ellie St. Clair
Lady of Mystery

The Sons of Scotland Series by Victoria Vane
Virtue
Valor

Men of Blood Series by Rosamund Winchester
The Blood & The Bloom

CHAPTER ONE

O N A MOONLESS night, the familiar inn looked somehow strange and unwelcoming. Had Cecily been of a fanciful nature, she might have described it as menacing. Fortunately, she was the most practical and sunny natured of young women, so she merely took her aunt's arm and led her inside.

The wall of noise and smells hit her at once, for the door from the entrance hall to the public taproom was wide open. However, at least it also enabled the innkeeper to catch sight of his noble customers, too, for he hurried toward them at once, shouting to his underling to take his place, and closed the door behind him.

"Your ladyships," he exclaimed, bowing low. "What a pleasant surprise. I'm sure we've had no word of your coming."

"No, you wouldn't have," Cecily's aunt, Lady Barnaby, said dryly. "It was not our intention until an hour ago when one of our wretched horses went lame. We've had to toil our way to you, the nearest shelter. We require a bedchamber each, and your private parlor."

The innkeeper, who rejoiced in the name of Villin, looked dismayed. "Your forgiveness, ma'am, but I have only the one bedchamber in the whole of the inn, and the parlor is taken, too."

"Drat," Lady Barnaby said crossly. "I suppose we would not care for the coffee room at this time of night either. Well, our hands are tied. We shall take your one bedchamber and whatever dinner you can find for us."

At that moment, the parlor door opened and the innkeeper's wife came out carrying an empty tray. Beyond her plump, comely person, Cecily glimpsed several men bathed in the somehow mysterious glow from scattered candles. Most were seated around a table in the middle of the room, but one man stood by the fire, leaning carelessly against the mantel shelf. Although his dress looked to be that of a gentleman, he wore it extremely casually, with his cravat loose and his coat unbuttoned. Neither did the coat fit with fashionable snugness across his broad shoulders. Clearly, it was made for comfort rather than appearance.

He seemed to be ignoring the men at the table, who, from her one hasty glance, gave Cecily a vague impression of tense malevolence. While they drank and talked with quiet intensity, the gentleman scowled at the hearth, his expression dark and brooding. His lean jaw was shadowed with stubble. His raven-black hair, too long for fashion, fell carelessly forward over his high forehead. In all, he looked a little like one of Lord Byron's heroes, and was handsome enough besides, to make Cecily's heart skip a beat.

As though he heard the anomaly, he glanced up, unerringly straight at Cecily. His lips curved. Some dangerous light glinted in his eyes like fire. And then Mrs. Villin closed the door on the room and Cecily breathed again.

"Here's my wife who'll show you to your bedchamber," Villin said with relief. "And my daughter will bring you up some dinner in just a few minutes."

"Thank you," Cecily said, glancing once more toward the parlor door.

"Bless your ladyships, what a pleasant surprise," Mrs. Villin said, handing her husband the empty tray. "Just a shame we're so busy tonight, for we didn't expect you. Visiting at Audley Park, were you?"

"Yes," Cecily replied, following her upstairs. "We attended Miss Maybury's wedding to Lord Dunstan."

"How wonderful," Mrs. Villin exclaimed with genuine pleasure. "And were the duke and duchess there, too?"

"Indeed, they were," Cecily replied, "but they have already returned to Lincolnshire. We were heading to London when one of our horses went lame and forced us to stop. So, is it the gentlemen in the parlor who have taken all your bedchambers?"

"Some of 'em," Mrs. Villin said, leading them across the landing to the door at the end of the passage. "Here we are, my ladies. I'm sorry you have to share, but I hope this will do for you."

Cecily and her aunt cast a quick glance around it. Though a little sparse of furniture, it was a large room with a huge bed.

"It looks very comfortable," Cecily assured her. "By the by, I'm sure I know one of the gentlemen in the parlor, but his name eludes me,"

"Oh, no, my lady, you won't know any of *them*." Mrs. Villin sounded shocked by the very idea.

"Why ever would I not?" Cecily asked, amused.

"You're a young lady," Mrs. Villin stated. "I'll have your bags sent up and Lily will bring you dinner presently."

As she bustled away, Lady Barnaby took off her bonnet and cast it on the bed before sinking onto the one arm chair in the room, and peeling off her gloves. She fixed Cecily with her sternest gaze. "What, pray, is your interest in the gentlemen downstairs?"

One could never keep anything from Aunt Barny.

"Curiosity, dear aunt, curiosity," Cecily replied. "Didn't you wonder what they were doing there so solemnly? In the middle of nowhere?"

"Be reasonable, my dear. The Hart cannot be in the middle of nowhere when the taproom is so full of locals."

"Yes, but *they* weren't local," Cecily argued. "In fact, I've never seen such an odd set of men sitting at one table before. Did you not notice? One of them looked like a bank clerk, and the others looked largely villainous. As for Childe Harold by the fireplace …"

"Childe Harold?"

"The hero of Lord Byron's poem," Cecily said impatiently. "I give you my word, he looks exactly like him."

"Then I'm not surprised Mrs. Villin was so reticent! Drat, how are we to cope without the maids?"

Their maids, with the baggage, had been sent on ahead to London before the accident occurred.

"We must 'maid' for each other," Cecily said flippantly. "It's quite fun having no entourage. We can pretend to be damsels in distress."

"I am most certainly a matron in distress!"

The innkeeper's pretty young daughter, Lily, brought them dinner a little while later. Since the inn's cooking was wholesome and tasty, Lady Barnaby's mood improved somewhat.

"I daresay we shall be back in London tomorrow," she observed. "And our first caller will inevitably be Torbridge."

Young Lord Torbridge, son and heir of the Marquis of Hay, was Cecily's most persistent admirer. She wrinkled her nose, acknowledging her aunt was no doubt correct.

"So, have you made up your mind?" Lady Barnaby inquired. "Will you accept him?"

"Aunt, he hasn't even offered yet." She stabbed her fork into a piece of beef with unnecessary force.

"But if he did?" her aunt persisted. "I think you like him better than any other gentleman."

It was true, there was something appealing about Torbridge, though she couldn't put a finger on exactly what. He was a high sticker in areas of propriety, which didn't normally attract Cecily. On the other hand, he was very good natured about it, and he did make her laugh. He was just a little different from most of her suitors, who were either too pleased with themselves or too obviously fortune-hunters.

"You are nearly one-and-twenty," Lady Barnaby pointed out.

"Torbridge is a good match, and you would be a marchioness one day. Alvan would be happy."

But would I? In truth, she rather liked her life as it was, carefree and amusing, with her aunt's sudden journeys to make her life interesting. But she knew it couldn't go on forever. Her family duty was to marry well.

She sighed, refocusing on her aunt whose hand pressed to the base of her throat.

"Oh dear—heartburn?"

"I ate it too quickly," Lady Barnaby mourned. "And my wretched medicine is with the baggage!"

Cecily stood. "I'll get them to send up a glass of milk," she said sympathetically. "That usually helps."

"Oh, don't go downstairs, Cecily. That nasty taproom is much too busy."

"It's quieter now," Cecily assured her. "I can barely hear them. Besides, I would rather not stand at the top of the stairs and shout. I feel that would draw more unwelcome attention!"

Aunt Barny was clearly in too much discomfort to argue, so Cecily left their chamber and ran lightly downstairs. She meant to go directly to the kitchen rather than look for their hosts in the public taproom, but as luck would have it, Lily was crossing the hall toward the parlor, a heavy tray laden with food and wine in her hands.

"Lily, might I trouble you—"

"One moment, my lady, if you don't mind," Lily said apologetically, knocking on the door with the corner of the tray.

The door opened almost at once to reveal the man Cecily thought of as Harold. To her surprise, he took the tray from Lily, then his gaze flickered around the hall as though he somehow sensed another presence.

Cecily refused to shrink into the shadows, but he didn't appear to notice her, merely vanished with the tray. To Cecily's annoyance, Lily followed him inside.

Tempted to sit on the stairs to wait, Cecily drummed her fingers on the bannister instead. However, the first person to emerge from the parlor was not Lily, but Harold.

He seemed about to close the door when he caught sight of her. Immediately, she looked in the other direction, as though he was of no interest to her. Which, of course, he wasn't, except for his imagined resemblance to her favorite literary hero of the moment.

After a pause, she risked a glance back toward the door. He still stood there, watching her. He did not bow, simply began to walk toward her, his pace slow and somehow predatory, like a large, stalking cat. Her heart lurched with alarm, but it was not in her nature to show fear, so she simply regarded his approach with what she hoped was haughty disapproval.

His dark, hooded gaze dipped, unhurriedly taking in the rest of her before returning to her face.

A faint smile played around his lips as he raised his hand to his heart. *"The very instant that I saw you, did my heart fly to your service. How may I assist such patient beauty?"*

His voice, deep and beguiling, seemed to slide under her skin. If he had looked an attractive man at a distance, close-up, he was devastating—large, physically overwhelming, and yet his black eyelashes were long and thick, such as any woman might envy. His deep, heavy-lidded eyes glinted, at once teasing, tempting, and distracting.

But fortunately, her mind still worked. *How may I assist such patient beauty?* "By not quoting words from Shakespeare among your own," she said shortly. "As you go about your business."

His smile widened, adding a sardonic twist to his humor. "I don't pretend they are my own. I merely borrow to make up for my deficiencies. As for my business, do you mean mine does not connect with yours?"

She raised one eyebrow, a devastating trick that had brought grown men to their knees. "How could it when we have never met?"

The stranger appeared to be immune. "I conduct business with many people I have never met."

She curled her lip. "*I* do not conduct business at all."

He tilted his head. Although his eyes never broke contact, she had the impression she had surprised him.

Lily emerged from the parlor, giving Cecily the excuse to step around him. As she did so, she caught the faint whiff of brandy on his breath.

"Lily, might I trouble you for a glass of milk for my aunt?" she said briskly.

"Of course, m—"

"Thank you," Cecily interrupted, and whisked herself upstairs. When she glanced down from the landing, Lily had vanished, presumably into the kitchen, but the stranger still stood at the foot of the stairs watching her. Her heart seemed to twist. She couldn't work out whether the feeling was pleasant or not, but it certainly churned her up.

What in the world had that been about?

"Something strange is going on in that parlor," she told her aunt. "And I am convinced Harold is at the root of the business. Whatever it is."

"Mind your own, Cecily," her aunt said, swallowing painfully.

Cecily frowned. "My own what?"

"Business," Aunt Barny said dryly. "Oh, is that my milk, do you think?" she added hopefully as footsteps hurried across the landing.

"Come in," Cecily called to the knock, and Lily entered bearing a large glass of milk, which she took straight to Lady Barnaby.

"Thank you, Lily," Cecily said gratefully as her aunt sipped the milk. "Tell me," she added quickly as the girl turned to go. "Who is that rude man who spoke to me downstairs?"

Lily glanced about her with something very like fear. "Oh, my lady, you don't want to go talking to him. It's not at all suitable."

"Why, who is he?" Cecily asked again, even more intrigued.

Lily lowered her voice. "Lord Verne."

Lady Barnaby all but choked on her milk. "Verne?" she spluttered. "*Verne?* Under this roof?"

"The sinister baron himself," Cecily said, more comforted than alarmed by this news. "But he's a friend of Alvan's, is he not?"

"That's as may be," Aunt Barny said with dignity. "Gentlemen know many people they do not introduce to their sisters."

"Well, aside from his nickname, which I'll allow does suit him, I can't see what the fuss is about. I daresay he behaves no worse than any other nobleman."

"Apart from murdering his way to the title," Aunt Barny said indignantly. "To say nothing about the devil worship, the orgies, and the vanishing women! Who may be no better than they should be, but who do not deserve to disappear without a trace."

"Well, I'm sure no one deserves that," Cecily agreed. "But if you ask me, it all sounds like a hum."

"Really?" Lily was looking at her closely. "You don't believe any of it? *Really?*"

In truth, she hadn't thought about it beyond teasing her aunt. Besides, her natural instincts were to defend someone the world denounced. But some of the rumors at least surely had substance. There was something downright dangerous about the man, and the company he kept must be shady to say the least.

"Why, have tonight's women vanished already?" she asked flippantly.

"I wouldn't go downstairs again tonight," Lily advised with an anxious tug at her apron.

"He has not threatened you, has he?" Cecily asked, outraged at last.

Lily laughed. "Oh, no, my lady, no one threatens me. But I saw how he looked at *you*."

"How?" Lady Barnaby demanded, scowling.

"Like the cat with the cream," Lily said bluntly.

For some reason, Cecily flushed. "I've no need to go down again."

Lily nodded as though satisfied. "Is there anything else you need?" she asked Lady Barnaby.

"No, I thank you," Aunt Barny said with a sigh and Lily took herself off.

The milk appeared to help Lady Barnaby's heartburn, so Cecily helped her prepare for bed, and had her own clothes loosened in return. But though her aunt fell into almost instant sleep, Cecily felt too restless to go to bed just yet.

Instead, she wrapped a shawl about her shoulders, then took the one candle still lit and went to the window seat, where she opened one shutter and looked out into the shades of darkness over the inn yard to the nearby cliffs and the gently rippling sea.

Although the inn was off the main turnpike, it had a beautiful location. But Cecily didn't have long to enjoy the view before she was distracted by movement in the yard. Three figures emerged from the inn. Something about their brisk pace made them seem unlikely late-night revelers being sent home at last. One of them carried a lantern, whose weaving light swung upward, allowing her a glimpse of Lord Verne's saturnine countenance.

Cecily sat up straighter, resting her forehead against the glass. The men with him had surely been in the parlor, too. One of them threw a cloth over the lantern, deliberately shading its light—which was bizarre behavior on so dark a night. In quick suspicion, though of what she was not sure, Cecily unfastened the window and opened it a crack.

But the men did not seem to speak to each other as they walked under her window toward the gate. They halted, and Lord Verne offered his hand to one of the men. Finally, he did speak, and by the luck of some freak breeze, she heard him say, *"Au revoir. Bonne chance."*

Among educated people of his class, it was not uncommon to hear such phrases in French. But as the other man, surely of a quite different degree, took the outstretched hand, he replied in the same language. *"Merci, monsieur. Au revoir."*

The hair on Cecily's neck seemed to stand up in alarm. Simple schoolboy French and yet surely there was no need, no reason for it to be spoken in this place at this time? Something about it was just *wrong*.

Of course, the man could be a French émigré, driven from his own country by the revolution, who had lived here for years. They were not all aristocrats. But everything about this situation pointed to something much more sinister. The secretive meeting in the private parlor of an inn so close to the sea. Lord Verne's rather odd words to her, which she suddenly interpreted as an accusation of spying on him... as if that was his business, too.

Her heart rebelled against the idea of him being a spy, let alone one who aided his country's enemy. For one thing, he was Alvan's friend. For another... despite his forward manners and the legion of accusations against him, there had been something about him she liked.

Well, she refused to like Bonaparte's spy. They said the monster was about to invade Russia, as if he was not satisfied with the huge swathe of Europe he already controlled, but he would never give up on Britain, who alone had always stood against him.

Below, the men had parted, two leaving by the gate and vanishing into darkness on foot, Lord Verne returning to the inn. Hastily, she drew the shutter back across the window, in case he noticed her observation.

What was she supposed to do about this? Tell Alvan? Or Lord Liverpool, who was now prime minister since poor Mr. Perceval had been shot and killed only a few weeks ago.

What if it was not a disgruntled merchant who shot Mr. Perceval? What if he was acting for the French? What if Verne is somehow involved, smuggling assassins and spies into the country?

Here, she pulled herself up, forced to smile at her wild imaginings, which were quite a leap forward from a few innocuous words spoken in French! Alvan and Liverpool would laugh at her, and quite rightly. All the same, what if she was right that *something* bad was going on? How could she then live with herself for not having told?

Told what? demanded her sensible self. She had nothing to tell anyone, for she didn't *know* anything.

Cecily turned, gazing thoughtfully at the bedchamber door. This was the inn where her brother Alvan had first met Charlotte Maybury and confronted armed intruders. There was something about the house that seemed to inspire recklessness. But everyone agreed the Villins were good people, and she was sure they would let nothing bad happen to her.

Besides, where was the danger is just listening at the parlor door, to overhear what was said? The taproom was quiet. She suspected the inn staff—or most of them—had gone to bed already. If Verne or his cohorts caught her skulking, she did not doubt her ability to distract them. With flirting, if necessary. She was a past master of that art, learned in the ballrooms and drawing rooms of London, where she often encountered gentlemen whose intentions were not strictly honorable. Even her abduction last month by one of the most pathetic creatures she had ever encountered had taught her she could deal with any situation, and in this case, forewarned was surely forearmed.

With decision, she picked up her candle and walked to the door. Halfway there, she paused for footsteps sounded on the stairs and then in the passage. She heard a couple of murmured goodnights and knew a moment of disappointment. If they were Verne and his remaining companions from the parlor, then they were speaking now in English. And she had no more chance of overhearing their evil discussions.

The trouble was, she had only glimpsed the men in the parlor. She wasn't sure how many there had been. Judging by the amount of supper Lily had taken them, quite a lot.

After a brief hesitation, Cecily resumed her plan, opened the, door and crept downstairs.

CHAPTER TWO

LORD VERNE POURED the remains of the brandy into his glass and gazed moodily into the amber liquid. His business concluded, he had no reason to stay. And none to go, either. Except a comfortable bed at the end of his ride. It probably beat falling into oblivion in the armchair and being discovered so by the Villins in the morning.

Irritated, he knocked the brandy down his throat and delved into his pocket for money which he left on the table beside his empty glass. If the final bill came to more, they knew where to find him.

As he strode to the door, the faintest of rustling beyond it gave him warning. He jerked open the door faster than was seemly and saw a girl in a paisley shawl with her back to him, moving toward the stairs. The same outrageously beautiful girl he had found before in much the same place.

Well, he thought, watching the graceful swing of her hips with undisguised lust. *Here is a useful loose end to clear up.*

"Can it be *impatient* beauty this time?" he said aloud.

She paused, and as he'd hoped, she turned her head and raised one haughty eyebrow. "Sir?"

"Come, let us talk before I go."

Jem, one of the inn servants, emerged sleepily from the taproom, as though drawn by their voices.

Perhaps reassured by his presence, the lady took her foot off the step and turned to face him. "What is it you wish to say to me?"

Her eyes were clear and unafraid, brilliant even in the dim light of the hallway. He liked that courage. If she was an enemy, she was a worthy one. She was also the loveliest creature he had ever laid eyes on, with delicate, perfect bone structure, creamy skin and lush, rosy lips just ripe for kissing. From her dusky hair to her little kid boots, she radiated vitality. And temptation.

"Or are you tongue tied?" she marveled. "Without Mr. Shake-speare's contributions?"

Verne smiled. "Why, no, I'm merely awaiting a moment of priva-cy. Jem, saddle my horse, if you please, and fetch him round to the door."

"Yes, m'lord." Jem tugged his forelock and hurried off to do Verne's bidding.

For an instant, something flashed in the girl's beautiful eyes. It might have been consternation, but she veiled it with commendable speed, merely tilting her chin and spreading one hand in invitation to speak. Her eyes laughed, her smile challenged. She was mocking him and yet flirting at the same time and the effect was devastating.

Men must fall at her feet like nuts shaken from a tree.

"Well, my lord?" she urged flippantly. "Speak now or forever hold your peace."

"My lord," he repeated. "It seems you have the advantage of me."

"Of course I do, Lord Verne."

He, too, had a devastating smile, used with cynical deliberation over the years. He employed it now. "So, you know my name. Why are you not afraid of me?"

"Because I know you will not hurt me."

"Nothing is further from my mind," he agreed. "But you cannot possibly know it. You are a lady who takes risks." He let his gaze settle on her lips. Her tongue darted out, moistening them, either with nervous anticipation or provocation—it was impossible to tell which. Slowly, he raised his eyes once more to hers. "Come with me."

"Sir," she said with exaggerated shock. Clearly, she had been expecting such a blatant offer. "I cannot possibly leave my aunt."

"You have already left her," he pointed out. "What difference does another few feet make?"

She blinked, and he let another smile play around his lips. He had thrown her off-balance. Not quite so sophisticated, then, as she pretended. The knowledge aroused him further and he pressed his advantage.

"What did you imagine?" he mocked. "That I was inviting you to my evil lair to have my wicked way with you? I merely ask you to take the air with me, and wish me well on my journey. With Jem as chaperone, even your aunt could not object." He strolled to the front door. "You have not told me your name."

There was a pause, but she did follow him. "Cecily," she said at last.

He let her precede him out the door. "Cecily," he repeated softly as she passed him, close enough to feel his breath on her cheek. She shivered, and he knew she felt the same tug of attraction, quite separate from their mutual suspicion.

Jem came into view with a lantern, leading his saddled horse.

"What did bring you here to the Hart?" he asked, following her.

"One of our horses went lame." She turned to face him, so suddenly that he halted just a little too close. He could smell her skin, sweet flowers and fresh, clean herbs, and behind it, something sultry and exotic that inflamed him. "And you?"

"What about me?" he asked without interest, too fascinated by the shape and texture of her lips.

"Why did you come to the Hart?"

"I don't remember," he said. "I don't care anymore."

She smiled, a siren's smile that deprived him of breath. "Why not?"

She knew the answer, damn her.

Reaching out without looking, he took the reins from Jem with one hand and tossed him a coin with the other. "Thanks, Jem. You can go to bed now." Without pause, he aimed his words at the girl. "Why not? Because I can only think of you."

He gave her no time, simply dipped his head and tasted her lips.

They opened wide in shock and he took full advantage, kissing her with deep, blatant sensuality. And God, she tasted divine, her lips warm and soft and sweet. She yielded as his arm closed around her, but he didn't fool himself that it was more than astonishment. She wasn't immune, but neither did she respond like the temptress she was pretending to be. He wasn't surprised.

He slipped his tongue into her mouth, heard her gasp, and then he released her lips and, without warning, threw her into the saddle. Instinct made her cling on rather than slide back down. Before she could think of it, he leapt up behind her, held her firmly in one arm, and kicked the horse into a gallop.

APART FROM THE time she had been abducted—not a remotely amorous situation—Cecily had always been in control. In certain social circumstances, she liked the fun of flirting, especially with witty men who made her laugh. And, if she was honest, she rather enjoyed her power in keeping her admirers at arm's length. From instinct, observation and quick thinking, she had always been able to evade rakes and ruiners, and if she had occasionally allowed a secret kiss, from sheer curiosity, it had been on her terms. Something quick, disappointing, and ultimately forgettable.

She had never encountered a man like Lord Verne, and she had certainly never been kissed like *that*. She hadn't known a man's mouth could be rough and tender at the same time. Exciting and sweet, it was an assault on her senses as much as her dignity. His earthy yet clean male scent enfolded her, thrilling her.

Although astonishment had at first stopped her fighting back, her fury was swiftly drowned in a surge of heat and fear and secret pleasure. She recognized the smell of brandy on his breath, tasted it in his mouth, and for the first time, wondered if he were foxed. She didn't want him to be.

And then, somehow, she was on the horse, his arm like steel around her and she was galloping away into the night. Into the unknown.

This was carelessness. This should not happen to a lady *twice*. Stupidly, she had forgotten the lesson she had learned only a month ago—don't stand too close to a dangerous man. She could have been forgiven for not understanding the threat of her first captor, but *Verne*... she had sensed his danger at once, but like a child touching a flame, she could not resist. She had been too sure of her own control. And of his. He was her brother's friend. Now for the first time, she seriously doubted he was affected by such trivial considerations.

"You can't do this," she said intensely. "Take me back to the inn at once."

"I'll take you back in the morning," he said without apparent interest. "Or you can go yourself in a couple of hours." His eyes glittered as they briefly focused on her through the darkness. "If you still want to."

Instinctively, she pulled away, but his arm tightened at once, holding her immobile. She could not even hit him, for he held one of her arms imprisoned next to her body, and the other was trapped between them.

But there was a more immediate danger. He was galloping at full speed in the dark, without a light of any kind, apart from the sliver of moon which occasionally emerged from the clouds.

"My horse knows the way," Verne said, insanely casual, "and will slow when he has to."

"I don't believe you," she said flatly. From the deeper blackness ahead, they were leaving open fields and about to enter a wood. "My one hope is that you are knocked from the saddle by a very large branch."

"It will make no difference. He'll still take you to Finmarsh. I shall merely limp in a little later."

She stared at his averted face. Impossible to see his expression in the dark. "Then your servants have orders to imprison any lady who happens by your... er... lair?"

"Oh, I barely have any servants. But where else would you go?"

As he had promised, the horse slowed, swerving to avoid branches in its path while it continued at a fast trot that bumped her against her captor unmercifully.

She eyed him with dislike. "I would rather take my chances wandering blindly around the countryside than enter your house."

"Liar."

"*I'm* the liar?" she gasped in outrage. "Do I need to point out that you promised *not* to abduct me to your *evil lair?*"

"No, I didn't. I merely asked if you thought that was my intention."

A surge of fresh fear drowned her natural outrage. "You are making a huge mistake," she managed. "Take me back before my aunt raises a massive hue and cry."

"Oh, I doubt she will do that."

Another fear hit her like a blow in the chest. "Oh, dear God, you have not hurt her?"

His gaze came back to her, just as the pale moon cast a shred of light across his face and vanished. She thought he was frowning. "Of course, I have not. When would I have had the time, let alone the inclination?"

"Your inclinations baffle me, sir," she retorted.

"I'm inclined to talk to you," he said. "Well, if we are being honest, I'm inclined to do a lot more, but I will settle for the talk if you wish it."

"I have no desire whatever to talk to you!"

"Then why were you skulking outside my parlor door? And watching me, I suspect, from your bedchamber. I presume it was *your* shutter twitching?"

God, he had seen even that. She began to think the rumors about him were true, that he was some kind of sorcerer.

"I may have looked out at the sea," she said with dignity.

"I like you," he said unexpectedly, just as the horse picked up pace again.

"That's a matter of indifference to me since I most certainly dislike you!"

His breath caressed her ear, making her shiver with more than fear. "That isn't the impression you gave me earlier."

Her body flamed with uncomfortable memory. "You are mistaken. Take me back or let me go."

"After our talk," he insisted.

"If I tell you who I am, will it make any difference?"

"At this point? No. Later, it probably will,"

Later? Another surge of fright kept her silent, though even then she wondered why she wasn't more afraid *all* the time. He was a much scarier proposition than Cornell, despite the fact he did not wave pistols around. Nor had he bound her. But there was no Charlotte to rescue her this time. She was depending still on his friendship with Alvan... and her probably silly belief in her own ability to twist men around her little finger. He was just a slightly more difficult victim, surely?

"Plotting?" he asked sardonically.

"Worrying," she answered honestly. For even if she could somehow keep him at bay, if it ever came out she had spent a night under his roof without so much as a maid, her reputation would be ruined beyond repair.

She felt his attention on her, had the impression he was frowning. Certainly, there was a long pause before he said, "Play by my rules and neither of us need worry."

"Oh, for heaven's sake, I don't even know what that means!" she raged. "*Will* you just let me down or take me back to the Hart?"

He laughed. "No."

There was no more talk between them until, suddenly, they rode over a hill and there below stood a dark, sprawling and forbidding house. Beyond it, the dark earth seemed to glisten, as though it were built on the edge of a marsh.

Cecily's heart beat so hard it seemed to rise up her throat. But she had one chance, and she meant to be ready to snatch it. Without urging, the horse picked its way down the hill to a path that met what looked like the main drive to the house. A faint light burned inside, showing in the glass above the door.

The horse came to a halt right in front of it. Cecily tensed. But he did not dismount first. She did not mind much, for she doubted the horse would have obeyed her had she tried to flee on its back. Verne shifted her by the waist and let her slip to the ground.

And this was the moment she'd been waiting for. As soon as her feet touched the ground, she darted like a hare for freedom. To her relief, she heard no hoofbeats behind her. Perhaps, he had decided just to let her go...

He hadn't. Within seconds, his arm slammed around her waist, spinning her back round the way she had just come.

"Don't be such a bad guest," he complained. "We agreed to talk first."

"*You* agreed!" She struggled against his compelling grip. "*I* have nothing to say to you."

"Well, don't run off here. There's a lot of dangerous marsh, and if you don't know the land, you can easily come to grief."

For the first time in her life, she felt utterly helpless and without choices. All she could do was try to keep the galloping fear at bay.

As he urged her back to the house, a manservant with a lantern emerged from the front door. He didn't look remotely surprised to see his master with his arm around a strange female, which told Cecily rather more than she wanted to know.

"See to Jupiter, will you?" Verne said cheerfully and swept her through the open door, across a large, shadowed entrance hall to a door on the right.

He closed it behind them and finally released her to turn up the lamp already lit there, and light more candles from the spills on the mantelpiece. She watched him in silence, trying to quell the trembling of her limbs.

She appeared to be in a comfortable library. The walls were lined with books from floor to ceiling, while armchairs and sofas were scattered around the room. The remains of a fire still glowed in the grate.

Surely, not an hour since, she had been safe at the Hart with her aunt, making up stories in her head about this man and French assassins. Now, it seemed, if she had not been right all along, he was something much more immediately dangerous.

As he dropped a log on the almost burned-out fire, she realized she was cold, and held her shawl tighter about her shoulders. But she refused to draw nearer. She wasn't even sure her trembling legs would carry her.

He straightened and turned to face her.

Oh yes, he was devastating to look at. Darkly handsome, mysterious, forbidden… and terrifying. Every rumor she had ever heard about him rushed on her with a vengeance. Murderer, Satanist, seducer—to call it no worse.

With slow deliberation, he walked up to her. She tilted her chin in instinctive defiance, but he only took it between his finger and thumb and gazed down at her. The glitter in his black eyes might have been brandy, or it might have been lust. Behind it lurked a tinge of humor she was in no condition to appreciate.

His thumb moved on her skin, softly caressing. "What is your name?"

She swallowed. "I am Cecily Moore."

CHAPTER THREE

T HE APPRECIATION IN his eyes intensified. "Fustian," he remarked. "But it's a clever ploy."

She cast her eyes to heaven and irritably tried to brush his fingers away. But unexpectedly, they tightened. A frown had formed on his brow and he searched her face more seriously.

"My God, you could be," he uttered. "You look just like Alvan offended by the bad smell of an imbecile under his nose."

"I can certainly sympathize with the feeling," she retorted.

Laughter hissed between his teeth and turned into a groan. He let her go. "Oh well, who needs friends, anyhow?" He strode toward the cabinet, unstopped a decanter, and sloshed amber liquid into two glasses. He knocked the contents of one straight down his throat before refilling it. He walked to a sofa, "Come, sit down," he invited. "You had better tell me everything."

She stared at him. "Everything about what? That you wantonly abducted the daughter of a duke, ruining the sister of your friend? Did I miss anything out?"

"Yes," he said ruefully. "*Only* friend. Dash it, am I really so bosky that I can't tell the difference between a hussy and a high-ranking lady?"

"Apparently."

He looked at the glass he hadn't yet drunk from. "Well, you'd better come and take this from me then, or the shock may compel me to drink both. Don't be frightened," he added impatiently. "I won't touch you."

"I am not remotely frightened," Cecily returned at once. "But I have no desire to come anywhere near you."

"Can't blame you for that," he admitted. His eyes settled on her once more. "But we'd better think of a way out of this."

"Give me a horse," she commanded.

"Don't be silly. You'll never find your way back to the Hart in the dark. And you certainly don't want to risk being seen with me—or my servants—in the middle of the night."

"But it was an acceptable risk on the way here?"

"When I didn't know who you were," he said, frankly, "yes."

"It should make no difference at all who I am!" she exclaimed, starting impetuously toward him.

"No, it shouldn't," he agreed. He held up the glass to her. "Here. It will warm you, if nothing else. What the devil—I beg your pardon—what *on earth* were you doing at the Hart?"

She snatched up the glass and sipped the fiery liquid. "I told you."

"So that explains no servants. It might even explain why Lady Cecily fetched her aging aunt a glass of milk. Only it doesn't explain why she was roaming about the inn at midnight, listening at my parlor door. With her clothing awry."

Cecily blushed fierily. It had never entered her head that he would notice such a thing beneath her shawl. But they had been very intimate both before and during the ride.

She sat down abruptly. "I was preparing for bed," she said with dignity. Then, throwing caution to the wind, she added, "When I saw you and your friends below and heard you speaking French. I was trying to set my suspicions at rest because I knew you to be a friend of my brother's."

"Do *you* not speak French?" he asked in surprise.

"Of course, I do."

"I didn't listen at *your* door."

"No, you merely abducted me and ruined me!"

His eyes darkened. "Don't tempt me." He dragged his fingers through his unruly hair. "How bad is this? Are you contracted to anyone?"

"No."

He cocked an intelligent eyebrow in her direction. "About to be?"

"No," she said with a little less certainty. The very proper yet amiable face of Lord Torbridge swam before her eyes and was dismissed. "Probably not."

"You can't tell me there is no one. A girl of your charm and beauty, to say nothing of wealth and breeding, must have suitors haunting your front door."

"I do not care for any of them," she said loftily.

"Then why did you hesitate?"

She sighed. "Well there is a gentleman my aunt is disposed to favor for me, and in truth, I like him better than anyone else, but he has not offered, and I am not convinced I would accept him if he did. You may take it that I am not engaged nor likely to be, though why that should make any difference to this current mess—"

"There's a way out of this for you," he interrupted. "I just have to think what it is. Where is Alvan?"

"Halfway to Lincolnshire at the very least."

"No use, then. The only relatives either of us have within spitting distance are your aunt and my late brother's mother-in-law…"

Cecily couldn't imagine he was on good terms with the latter, since the world believed he had murdered her daughter. He stared moodily into the flames, apparently deep in thought. Then, in one of his sudden, shocking movements, he finished his brandy and stood, striding to the desk by the window.

He wrote busily, without pause, for a minute or two, then blotted the paper and folded it while he crossed the room and threw open the door.

"Daniel!" he bellowed.

Cecily didn't know whether to laugh or invite him to use the bell instead. Perhaps it didn't work. While he waited for "Daniel," he paced back and forth in front of the open door until hurried footsteps sounded, and the servant she had seen outside appeared looking a trifle breathless.

"My lord?" he said without apparent surprise.

Verne shoved the folded paper into his hands. "See that this is given to…" He swung on Cecily. "What's your aunt's name?"

"Lady Barnaby," she replied, warily.

"To Lady Barnaby at the Hart Inn," he told the servant. "It is to be delivered into her hands *first thing*. Make sure Villin understands that."

"Yes, my lord. I'll send the boy."

"Good, then send Shilton to me."

Since she was well brought-up, Cecily did not argue with him in front of the servant, but as soon as the door closed again, she said uneasily, "What are you writing to my aunt? I don't want her worried. I would rather write to her myself."

"It's done now. We just have to hope she's more sensible and discreet than either of us." He walked back to the decanter, swiping up his glass on the way. As he poured more brandy, he glanced at her, holding up the decanter invitingly. She showed him her glass which still held at least half of what he had given her previously.

"I shouldn't be drinking brandy," she observed. "It isn't ladylike."

He shrugged impatiently. "Who makes such stupid rules? Besides, you've clearly drunk it before for it didn't make you choke."

"Julius gave me some one day because he had no tea and nothing to eat. My aunt was scandalized." She thrust aside the memory of visiting her younger brother in Oxford, and glared at her companion. "Though that is nothing to how she'll feel about… *this*! You are not even related—" She broke off, brightening with the sudden thought.

"Oh, but perhaps we are related! Surely, if we go back far enough, there must be some connection between your family and mine? We could be distant cousins."

"I doubt it. And even if we are, it must be very distant indeed! Certainly not close enough to weigh against my reputation, let alone the circumstances of your arrival, should that ever come out."

"If it ever comes out, I suppose Alvan will feel compelled to fight a duel with you," Cecily said with satisfaction. "He will probably kill you."

Verne cast her a crooked half-smile. "I'm sure we all hope he may. Unfortunately, Alvan favors less comfortable methods of punishment. He is not really a dueling man."

"As it happens, he fought a duel with the last man foolish enough to abduct me," Cecily said with dignity.

Verne eyed her with fascination. "How often does this happen to you?"

"Twice in my life. The last was in broad daylight, and it could only have been a couple of hours before Alvan confronted him and challenged him on the spot."

She was trying to frighten Verne, if she could, but his face expressed more entertainment than fear. In fact, he sat back on the sofa beside her.

"I'm very glad to hear it. Did Alvan shoot him?"

"Well, he shot the man's driver, who was a terrible villain and clearly didn't understand the terms of a duel. But his accuracy scared C—this man—so much that he begged Alvan for mercy."

Verne was grinning openly now. "What did Alvan do?"

"Hit him," Cecily said with relish. "Twice."

"I wish I'd been there."

"You will be," Cecily said sweetly, and Verne laughed, just as a maid came into the room.

Although she looked very sleepy, she was fully dressed. A stickler might have noticed her cap was not quite straight and the hair beneath it escaping untidily. Cecily thought she had been asleep in her clothes, which was odd for a maidservant. But then, this was a very odd household.

"This is Shilton," Verne said, standing. "She is a lady's maid. Shilton, this is Lady Cecily who will be staying with us for a few days,"

"A few days!" Cecily repeated in outraged astonishment.

Verne ignored her. "Are there any guest bedchambers made up?"

"Just Miss Jane's, sir."

"Well that will do for tonight. Tomorrow, we'll need more. Show her ladyship to Miss Jane's chamber and give her what help she needs."

"Yes, sir," Shilton replied. She didn't look remotely interested. Cecily could only suppose such requests in the middle of the night were common.

"Good night, my lady," Verne said, with the greatest civility he had yet shown her. He even held out his hand compellingly.

She wanted to ignore that hand. She already knew its strength and its hardness. It was also surprisingly shapely for a man's, the fingers long and tapering. She could walk past it and out of the room. But they were playing a part he seemed to think would ultimately save her reputation. She couldn't see how, but with reluctance, she placed her hand in his. His fingers curled around it with gentle firmness and he bowed over it with more elegance than she had imagined he possessed.

"Good night, my lord," she returned, slipping her hand free, and walked out the room. For some reason, her heart was beating too fast again.

Following Shilton upstairs, Cecily was finally struck by the oddity of a lady's maid employed in what she had assumed was a bachelor establishment.

"Shilton, who is your mistress?" she asked curiously.

"Lady Verne, my lady," the maid replied, without turning. "She's dead."

Cecily shivered. Shilton must mean the Lady Verne who was sup- posedly murdered along with her husband, the current baron's elder brother. She wished she could remember the story, but she had never paid much attention since she did not know the people concerned. Until now.

"Then what ladies reside here now?" she asked.

"None, at present. Save your ladyship."

At the top of the stairs, Shilton led her along a passage to the right, which, in the darkness, was undeniably eerie. The pale flames of the candles they each carried, flickered up the walls, occasionally illumi- nating alarming faces in portraits.

Shilton opened a door and went in. With quiet efficiency, she set down her candle by the door, and lit a spill from the flame. She walked around the room, lighting candles until it was well illuminated.

"Don't you have a nightrail, my lady?" Shilton asked.

"No. I have nothing with me."

"Miss Jane's garments will be too small."

"It doesn't matter. I shall sleep in my chemise for once. Who is Miss Jane?"

"My lady's daughter."

From the emphasis, Cecily took her to mean the late Lady Verne's daughter. "The present lord's niece?" she hazarded. It did not look like a child's room. There were no toys or children's books. Perhaps Miss Jane did not stay very often. Or perhaps she was grown-up.

Shilton nodded, pulling back the bed clothes. She turned, and looked Cecily up and down.

Cecily sighed and threw her shawl on the bed. "There is not much for you to do," she said defiantly, showing the maid her semi-unlaced gown and stays.

Shilton advanced and wordlessly unpinned her hair before helping her step out of her clothes. "I'll clean the gown," she said briskly, shaking it out and then closing the curtains while Cecily used the chamber pot and then thrust her hands into the bowl of cold water on the wash stand. "If your ladyship will wait a few minutes, I'll bring you warm water for washing."

"There's no need," Cecily said hastily. "Bring it in the morning instead, if you please. I only want to sleep."

Shilton walked to the bed and held up the covers commandingly. Obediently, Cecily climbed in and lay down. Shilton walked around the room, blowing out all the candles again until she came to the one by the door which she picked up. By its solitary light, she looked drawn and haggard, almost tragic.

"Good night, my lady."

"Good night, Shilton. And thank you."

Without a further word, the maid left, closing the door softly behind her.

Considering whose house she was in and how she had got there, it seemed Cecily had got off very lightly. He even seemed determined to save her reputation. However, she lay awake for some time, listening to every sound in the house, wondering if the bedchamber door would creak open.

CECILY WOKE TO disorientation and the distant neighing of horses. It took a moment before she recognized her surroundings, and the bizarre events of last night rushed back. She did not feel rested, for her sleep had been uneasy, scattered with moans and cries that might have been part of her troubled dreams.

At least Verne had not come near her. Not that she had truly expected him to after he had sent for the maid to look after her, but the possibility had always been there. Thinking about it now, it struck her that his aim of seduction had seemed almost secondary. He had never revealed exactly why he had abducted her, except that he had mistaken her for a "hussy," which seemed monstrously casual.

And yet, he did not seem a monstrous person. Whatever he had done or would do, she had found him secretly rather likeable. Which perhaps was not surprising when Alvan counted him among the very select ranks of his friends.

A knock at the door heralded the arrival of the maid, Shilton, bearing a jug of warm water. This morning, she looked much neater. She was a comely woman, something over thirty years old, but even in daylight, Cecily had the odd impression that darkness remained in her eyes. They were… haunted.

She went through the motions of her duties almost mechanically, as if her mind was constantly somewhere else. But she had cleaned and pressed Cecily's traveling dress to perfection and she dressed her with gentle precision before brushing and pinning her hair.

"Where is his lordship?" Cecily asked abruptly.

"Don't know, my lady. He went out, but left orders for breakfast."

Drat the man. "Do you know when he will be back?"

"No, my lady. We never know."

Cecily sprang to her feet. Did he expect her to kick her heels here while waiting for him to turn up and explain whatever drunken plan he had made for the rescue of her reputation? Well, she wouldn't. She would simply ride back to the inn and brazen it out. No one knew her in this neighborhood, and surely she could rely on the Villins' discretion?

"Thank you," she said abruptly to Shilton. "Is there—" She broke off as the faint rumble of carriage wheels reached her ears and hastened to the window instead. But her hope it was Verne returning swiftly vanished in recognition.

This was her aunt's carriage. With an exclamation, she bolted from the bedchamber, and ran along the passage. She charged down the staircase and across the gloomy entrance hall. Here, she more than half-expected the front door to be locked so she could not escape, but it flew open at her impatient tug.

Lady Barnaby had stepped down from the coach and was moving purposefully toward the front door when Cecily launched herself down the steps and into her arms.

"Oh, my dear!" Aunt Barny gasped. "My poor, sweet child! What has that man done to you?"

Perversely, Cecily found herself defending him. "Why, nothing, of course! Apart from abducting me in the first place, which seems to have been mostly a matter of mistaken identity. But now he knows who I am, there is no question of him harming me."

Lady Barnaby drew back. "Beyond what has already been done," she said wrathfully. "Where is the miscreant?"

"I don't quite know," Cecily admitted. "But apparently there is breakfast." She glanced back at the carriage horses, frowning as they were driven away to the stables. "They're not our horses."

"No, the blacksmith is sent for, though, so they'll be sent on."

"What did he say in his letter to you?" Cecily demanded, while her eyes were drawn at last to the state of the house. The center and the right of the building looked perfectly normal, if slightly neglected. But the wing to the left was merely a shell. Most of the roof had gone, and she could see only daylight through the glassless windows. Some of the stone was blackened, and Cecily finally remembered the full horror of the unofficial accusations against her host—that he had murdered his brother and sister-in-law by setting fire to their private apartments. That their daughter had escaped the blaze was considered something of a miracle.

Even as she shivered with distress, Cecily thought it was also a miracle that the rest of the house had survived apparently undamaged.

"I beg your pardon?" Cecily said to her aunt, drawing her toward the front door. She remembered she had asked about Verne's letter to her, but had not even heard the reply.

Lady Barnaby scowled. "He says you and he are to be married."

CHAPTER FOUR

C ECILY STOPPED IN her tracks, one foot on the front step. "He says *what?*"

"It's not what I wanted for you," Lady Barnaby said grimly, dragging her onward and into the house. "But I see no other solution. It won't stop him receiving a piece of my mind, to say nothing of the worst dressing-down he's ever endured in his miserable life."

She came to a halt in the hallway, glaring across at her host, who stood by the stairs in riding dress, a sardonic smile on his handsome face. Cecily's heart bumped.

"I look forward to it, ma'am," he said with an elegant, yet somehow insolent bow. "Welcome to Finmarsh. I'm Verne."

"I know who you are," Aunt Barny said regally, drawing herself up to her full height. "I shan't sully my lips with *what* you are, for I suspect you know very well!"

"Better even than your ladyship," Verne assured her. "But you must be hungry after your early start. Please join me for breakfast."

Cecily and her aunt exchanged bemused glances but followed him across the hall to a sunny room at the back of the house, where a decent breakfast was set out on a sideboard. Politely, he poured them coffee, helped them to choose from the dishes available, and ushered them to seats at the table. Then, he fetched a cup of coffee for himself and sat opposite them.

"Have at me, if you must," he invited Lady Barnaby. "But I guarantee you will say nothing I have not heard before, or indeed told myself before. Besides, I understand that in all probability, Alvan is already on his way to shoot me. So, unless you feel it your duty to spend this time castigating me, we could use it more profitably by discussing how to minimize the damage."

Cecily and her aunt both gazed at him in fascination.

"I'll take that as assent."

"Don't," Lady Barnaby said at once. "For marrying my niece will not save her from scandal. It will only add to her troubles, especially if conducted in such a sudden, secretive way."

"You are quite right," he agreed.

"Besides," Cecily put in, for it was important for this to be clear, "I have no intention of marrying you."

"No indeed," he said with unflattering fervency. "I'm sure it's the furthest thing from both our minds. I don't mean we should *actually* marry. Just put it about that we are engaged. Name the date for a couple of months hence, and then at some point before that, you can cry off. No one will be surprised."

"And how do you explain how my niece met you, let alone consented to this engagement in the first place?"

Verne shrugged. "Your horse went lame in my neighborhood, did it not? I stepped in to help."

"And we just happily stayed here without a hostess?" Aunt Barny said in disbelief.

"No indeed," he said in mock shock. "You both stayed last night at the Hart, and then drove over to Finmarsh this morning as invited. Many people will have seen your carriage with its coat of arms."

Lady Barnaby appeared to accept that with a thoughtful nod.

"As for a hostess, I'm almost sure my late brother's mother-in-law will be here by teatime. She may bring an army of female servants, but in case she does not, you would be well advised to send for your own people and your baggage. I understand they went on to London. If you send now, they might just make it here by nightfall."

Lady Barnaby closed her mouth.

Cecily said, "You have done this many times before, haven't you? Averted scandal at the last moment."

"Actually, no. I've never troubled before. But then, contrary to popular belief, it hasn't been entirely my fault in the past."

"Is that an apology?" Cecily asked.

He shrugged. "I'm trying to make the only one that matters. Words don't make any difference to your situation."

"Neither will a fake engagement," Cecily argued. "I thank you for your trouble, but if we are pretending, I have been with my aunt all this time, I have no need to engage myself to anyone."

"Actually, you do," Aunt Barnaby said treacherously. "We have no reason to be here without an engagement, or at least a sudden attachment."

"Our lame horse," Cecily reminded her.

"We'd be on our way already if he had chosen to help us yesterday."

Cecily jumped to her feet. "Then, what are we waiting for? Let us go at once!"

Verne regarded her with some amusement, sitting back in his chair with his coffee cup cradled in both hands. "It's as well my feelings are not easily hurt."

"Actually, it isn't well at all," Aunt Barny said crossly. "I wish it happened to you more often. But he is right, Cecily. Word of our presence here will get out, and anything quick or secretive will only make matters worse. We will have to brazen out the engagement."

"Look on the bright side," Verne advised. He finished his coffee and set the cup down in its saucer. "Alvan may still come and shoot me, and think how much fun that will be. We could marry on my death bed and all this crumbling grandeur could be yours." He rose to his feet. "I'll leave you to think about it."

His bow was more of a nod. Then he sauntered toward the door and went out.

"You would think he got engaged every day," Cecily marveled, loud enough for him to hear.

The closing door paused. "Oh no," he said provokingly over his shoulder. "Of course, you are my first, and my last."

Lady Barnaby scowled after him. "He isn't taking this seriously."

Cecily, who believed to the contrary, spent some time arguing with her aunt over Verne's scheme. Every instinct cried out against it, though she found it difficult to name her reasons, save for her dislike of dishonesty. Used to winding her aunt round her little finger, she was appalled to find her immovable in this. What's more, she declared that Alvan would agree with her.

"Well, Charlotte will agree with me," Cecily raged. "And we both know where that will lead."

"Not in this case," Lady Barnaby said implacably. "Whatever it does to his friendship with Verne, he will understand it is the only way."

"It is *not* the only way and I refuse to do it!"

"You needn't be afraid of him," Aunt Barny said. "*I* am here. And I'm sending for the maids and *two* more coachmen *and* grooms. And I shall write to Alvan later, once I have consulted further with Verne."

Cecily, unable to trust herself to speak with any civility whatsoever, left the room to seek some air. She stomped around the outside of the house, through slightly overgrown formal gardens, a kitchen garden, and stable yards. She encountered very few servants, either because there weren't any or because they were all busy, and the peaceful exercise did soothe her nerves a little. However, she had only her shawl against a sharpening wind, so she decided against walking further, merely completing her circuit of the house, past the ruin of the north wing.

The damage was worse from the back, with many stones tumbled to the ground and moss and ivy growing over the remains. The interiors open to the elements were blackened and unrecognizable as a baron's apartments.

She paused, both drawn and repelled by the scene of such tragedy. A blackened door on the first floor opened as she watched. The maid, Shilton, took a step inside, then halted unmoving.

Cecily watched, curiously. The woman remained perfectly still yet somehow tense for several seconds and then she spun around and vanished from sight, closing the door behind her. Thoughtfully, Cecily walked on, taking a wide route around the corner to what was left of the side of the house.

In front of her, several yards nearer the building, stood Lord Verne himself, gazing upward. The wind blew his wild hair back from his face. Somehow, he looked both untamed and world weary. Childe Harold, indeed.

She thought quite seriously about creeping past him. She didn't think he would notice her. But this was no more in her nature than the proposed fake engagement. Besides, there was something in his stance that provoked both curiosity and compassion. He was almost universally vilified, shunned by his peers, and isolated from society. But he still lived with the tragedy of his loss.

After only a moment's hesitation, she walked up to him until they stood side by side, gazing at the ruin.

"Can it not be repaired?" she asked.

"Oh, just about anything can be repaired if one has the will."

"What happened?"

His head turned toward her, as though the question surprised him. "Surely everyone knows I set my brother's house on fire, thereby murdering him and his wife and inheriting his title and estates."

"I don't believe that." She met his gaze and found a baffled if fascinated expression there.

"You don't know me well enough to exonerate me."

"No, but Alvan does. My brother would not remain friends with a man who could do such a thing."

Verne swung away, as though he could not be still. "Guilt takes many forms," he said obscurely. "Come, let us get out of this wind. I hope you have come around to my proposal."

She took a couple of running paces to keep up with him, and he shortened his stride abruptly. "I don't wish to lie to people," she said. "It seems beneath contempt."

"Perhaps it is, but do you really imagine those same people wouldn't be joyfully sharing lies about you anyway? Lies that would do you considerably more harm."

Ruefully, she had to concede the point. "But it is not even believable that you and I should form such a firm attachment so quickly!"

"Who is to say it is quick? I'm sure the world knows Alvan has never dropped me. We could easily have met before. Besides, you are known for both kindness and waywardness, so I really doubt the world will be terribly surprised to hear you have made such an unsuitable choice of husband. But I'm sure they will be highly sympathetic when you dismiss me."

She frowned in consternation, but unexpectedly, his elbow brushed hers in a light, friendly nudge.

"Don't take it all so seriously," he advised. "There is nothing to lose here, and we might even have a little fun with our masquerade."

She eyed him uncertainly, and his lips curved into a rather wicked smile. "I did not mean that kind of fun, although, I would be most happy to oblige—"

"You will oblige me by keeping your distance," she said hastily.

"Oh, I shall not overstep the mark," he mocked. "But you might also consider if we are to carry this off, you need to pretend a *little* affection. You need not hang on my every word or swoon with love every time I enter a room, but you should at least look pleased to see me and laugh at my jokes."

"Why, who is to see?" she demanded.

"I expect the Longstones—my sister-in-law's family—this afternoon."

"Why, what did you tell them?" she asked dubiously.

"That if they wished to meet the lady I plan to marry, they should present themselves here today."

She pounced. "So, you did not use the word betrothed?"

"No. As I said, we should not make any of this seem too rushed."

"But I cannot lie to these strangers and tell them we've known each other for years!"

"All we need say is that Alvan and I are friends. They can make what they will of it. I shan't tolerate a catechism, and I'm fairly sure you are adept at diverting questions you do not wish to answer."

She let that go, since it was alarmingly accurate.

They had rounded the corner to the front terrace and were now approaching the main door.

"You don't need to do this," she said abruptly.

He appeared to think about it. "No one needs to do anything. But I am more than happy to carry this out. For many reasons."

She searched his averted face until he glanced down at her.

"What?" he demanded.

"I am curious to know your other reasons."

"They come under the category of entertainment," he said carelessly as they climbed the steps to the front door. "As I said, I see no reason why we can't both have a little amusement before you break my black and unworthy heart."

WITHOUT ACTUALLY AGREEING to the false engagement, Cecily found she was going along with the idea. Shilton showed her to a different bedchamber next to the one to be occupied by her aunt.

"Even so, we shall not stay unless Mrs. Longstone arrives to act as hostess," Lady Barnaby said firmly.

But it seemed Verne understood his connections very well, for not long after midday, a carriage arrived and disgorged an elegant gentleman, a plump, middle-aged lady, a younger, much more languid lady, and a child of about eight-years-old.

Cecily watched with her aunt from her new bedchamber window. To her surprise, Verne walked out to meet them, and the little girl flung herself at him with cries of, "Uncle Patrick! Uncle Patrick!" He swung her high in the air, making her squeal with delight before he deposited her back on the ground and bowed carelessly to the others.

"Well, they haven't taught the child to bear a grudge," Lady Barnaby observed.

"About what?" Cecily asked distractedly.

"The fire, of course."

"Well, they know he had nothing to do with that."

Aunt Barny regarded her. "And how do *you* know?"

"Because Alvan believes it."

"Well, Mrs. Longstone doesn't," Lady Barnaby said bluntly. "For she's been shouting his guilt all over the country for years."

MRS. LONGSTONE WELCOMED them formally to Finmarsh House just before tea. They were summoned to the formal drawing room on the first floor, which Cecily had only glimpsed before from the passage. It had the air and scent of a room that was never used.

Walking in, Cecily was immediately aware of Lord Verne who stood by the empty fireplace, resting his shoulder against the mantelpiece. Although she did not look closely, she imagined his expression was sardonic. Certainly, it did not appear he was joining in the conversation, which broke off as she and Lady Barnaby entered.

The plump lady, dressed in a very fashionable blue day gown, rustled toward them, holding out her hand. "Lady Barnaby, Lady Cecily, I am so sorry I could not be here to greet you when you arrived," she exclaimed. "But honestly, you could have knocked me down with a feather when I received Verne's note."

"Well, it was an accident, really," Lady Barnaby said easily. "We meant to go straight to London from Audley Park, but one of our horses went lame and we ended up at the Hart Inn—where, by chance, we encountered Lord Verne! Nothing would do but that we come to Finmarsh. I hope we haven't inconvenienced you too badly."

"Not in the slightest," Mrs. Longstone assured her. "It is my pleasure to welcome you here."

Cecily wasn't convinced it was pleasure she read in Mrs. Longstone's bright eyes. Avid curiosity, yes. However, she was a perfect hostess, and at once presented the elegant gentleman who had risen on their entry.

"My son, Mr. Henry Longstone," she said proudly.

Mr. Longstone was indeed a fine figure of a man. Like his mother, he would not have looked out of place in the most fashionable of London salons. More than that, his shoulders were pleasingly broad under his perfectly-fitting coat, and his legs, encased in flattering, skin-tight pantaloons, muscled and strong. He bowed gracefully over Lady Barnaby's hand and turned to Cecily.

"Lady Cecily, I am enchanted. You'll never believe how often I have tried and failed to obtain an introduction to you."

Cecily, who had long been immune to flattery, merely raised one eyebrow. "Why?"

Mr. Longstone smiled. "Why did I try? Or why did I fail?"

"Neither. I meant why would I never believe it? I presume you do not lie as a matter of course."

Lord Verne, approaching in time to overhear the exchange, emitted a crack of laughter. A frown flickered and vanished from

Longstone's brow, so quickly she might have missed it had she not been deliberately looking at him rather than Verne. A twinkle of amusement entered Longstone's eyes instead.

"And my cousin," Mrs. Longstone continued, "Madame de Renarde."

Cecily shook hands with the cousin who was one of the most beautiful women she had ever seen. Tall and regal, her almost drooping posture and lethargic movements expressed unutterable weariness with the world. And yet, her blue eyes were piercing in her lovely face. She could have been any age between five-and-twenty and five-and-thirty, but she was the sort of woman who would always be beautiful.

"I'm the governess," she said unexpectedly.

Over her shoulder, Cecily caught Verne's sudden scowl. But he wasn't the only one who objected to such a description.

Mrs. Longstone tuttted. "My cousin is helping educate my grand-daughter, until we can engage a governess," she explained. "And this is my granddaughter, Miss Jane Verne."

At her grandmother's summons, the little girl came closer and curtseyed to Cecily, her eyes wide with curiosity.

"How do you do?" Cecily said, gravely, offering her hand.

Jane took it with something approaching awe and risked a smile, which Cecily returned. As soon as she was free, she slipped back to stand with Verne. Cecily thought another frown disturbed Mrs. Longstone's brow, but she couldn't be sure.

As everyone moved to sit, Cecily found her hand taken and placed on Verne's arm. His touch caused her skin to tingle and she made an instinctive move to withdraw.

"Remember how diverting you find me," he murmured in her ear.

Which at least made her blush, no doubt reinforcing the fairytale he had concocted. For once, she could think of nothing to say, and merely sat on the sofa he selected for her before he took his place beside her. Since no one told Jane where to go, she plonked herself down between Verne and Cecily.

"Jane, don't bother Lady Cecily," Mrs. Longstone snapped.

"She is no bother to me, ma'am," Cecily assured her. "I have just come from Audley Park where there were several children to entertain me, and I miss them."

"Ah, were you there for Miss Maybury's wedding to Lord Dunstan?" Mrs. Longstone asked. "I was surprised not to be invited, for I have known the Overtons forever."

"There was only family present," Lady Barnaby assured her.

Mrs. Longstone gave a tinkling laugh. "I suppose the new Lady Dunstan's nose was out of joint anyhow, her unmarriageable sister having snared the duke, your brother!"

"Oh, her nose looked as straight as ever to me," Cecily said mildly.

"I suppose you also attended His Grace's wedding?"

"It was another quiet, family ceremony," Cecily said evasively.

At that point, two large tea trays were carried in by Daniel and an unknown maid who unloaded everything onto the tables set up for the purpose. The teapot was placed in front of Mrs. Longstone, and something in the way she moved in the simple act of pouring tea made Cecily think of pride and triumph. Certainly, no one would have guessed from her manner that her daughter had died so terribly in this house only five years ago.

Or would they? Verne rose to take the poured cups and saucers from her and ferry them to each of the company. Only then did a stiffness enter her posture. She passed the saucers almost gingerly so their fingers did not touch for an instant. And she did not look at him.

In fact, Cecily realized that neither Mrs. Longstone nor her son had looked at Verne, let alone addressed a word to him, since she had entered the room. They were ignoring the man in his own home, and yet seemed happy enough to be here. It was… odd.

Madame de Renarde, on the other hand, regarded him quite often, and it seemed to Cecily that she made certain their fingers touched as she received her tea. This irritated Cecily, though she refused to think of why.

But all of this went on beneath the civilized conversation which was at first almost excruciating. Cecily, who hated awkwardness, set out to entertain, bringing Jane into it for lightness, and indulging in a little witty banter with her aunt. Slowly, everyone thawed and genuine smiles and laughter grew more frequent.

Only the man beside her said nothing except to Jane. When Cecily glanced at him, the question forming on her lips vanished, for he was already watching her with disturbing intensity. She felt imprisoned by his gaze.

He rose abruptly. "I feel the need of fresh air. Who would care for a turn in the garden? Such as it is." Since he held one peremptory hand down to Cecily as he spoke, she felt obliged to rise with him.

"I would like to!" Jane said at once, and Lady Barnaby, who had clearly felt obliged to make the effort as chaperone, relaxed back into her chair.

"You and Lady Cecily, Jane, may chaperone each other," Madame de Renarde drawled.

"Come with us," Cecily invited at once.

The French lady laughed. "Oh no, I have seen the garden before and shall refuse to walk there again until he restores it to its former glory."

"What does she mean?" Cecily asked as they descended the stairs, and Jane was sent scuttling to fetch her shawl.

Verne shrugged impatiently. "She prefers formal gardens, like my sister-in-law. I like it better now that it's more natural."

"Is she really Mrs. Longstone's cousin?" Cecily wondered.

"Distant cousin, I believe. The Longstones looked after her and her parents when they first fled from the revolution in France."

"And Monsieur de Renarde?"

"Another émigré. They live largely apart."

Cecily glanced back up the stairs to see Jane rushing down with her shawl. "And now she teaches your niece."

"Apparently so..." He took the shawl from Jane and placed it around Cecily's shoulders. There was nothing lover-like in the gesture, and yet, she felt ridiculously aware of the light touch of his hands. "What exactly does Madame teach you?" he asked Jane, leading the way across the hall, away from the front door.

Jane wrinkled her nose. "Deportment. Watercolor painting. Piano-forte."

Verne curled his lip. "Accomplishments," he uttered with undisguised contempt. "Wouldn't you rather learn about history and other countries, science, and literature?"

"Yes, but I don't think she knows about those," Jane said naively.

"I expect she has just forgotten," Cecily said. "And will remember shortly."

"More likely she's bored with them," Verne said cynically, pausing to open a side door. He glanced quizzically at Cecily. "I don't suppose you number governesses among your large acquaintance?"

"I can make inquiries, but Mrs. Longstone is under no obligation to follow a stranger's recommendations!"

Verne took a small cloak from the coatrack at the door and handed it to Jane. "But you are not a stranger, are you?" He ushered her out the door. "You are the Duke of Alvan's sister."

Jane, released from the restrictions of normal adult company, bolted ahead like an arrow from a bow, straight into the long grass that had clearly once been a shaped lawn.

"And about to become my betrothed," he finished.

Cecily frowned. "Or not. Surely by coming here, they have bestowed respectability upon my visit and I need fear no scandal."

"It depends what they say when they leave," Verne said wryly.

Cecily searched his averted face, learning nothing. "Your relationship with them is… ambiguous. To be frank, I can't understand why they came when you and they so clearly dislike each other."

He shrugged. "A mixture of shock and snobbery. They could not stay away. For example, I would wager you any amount of money you like they are even now at the drawing room window watching us. Don't look up. Look at me. Imagine you find me fascinating."

"Oh, but I do," she said, gazing up at him adoringly. "Is this too much?"

His breath caught, and it wasn't all laughter. Something ignited in his eyes. "Not for me. I only wish you meant it. I suspect you are a minx, Lady Cecily. How is it you are not yet married?"

"I told you. Because I have not yet accepted anyone who offered for me."

"Yes, but why *is* that?"

She shrugged. "None of them… moved me."

A smile curved his lips. "Even the gentleman favored by your aunt, whom you have been considering? Are you a romantic?"

"No," she retorted. "But if I give up my freedom, I insist upon at least not being bored."

"Just think how flattered I shall be when you accept me."

"Should I be equally flattered when you ask me?"

"Certainly. I have never offered anyone marriage before."

"I don't think we need discuss what you did offer," she said hastily. "And I think our point is made. You may stop looking at me now."

The smile still playing around his mouth broadened. "But I like looking at you."

Cecily had been fending off flirts, from the clumsy to the exquisite, since she was seventeen. And yet, even though she knew Verne was not serious, heat seeped up through her neck and into her face. His turbulent eyes had darkened impossibly. And even though he still walked beside her, very slowly, the manner in which he all but leaned over her was predatory. He took her breath away. Like the moment outside the Hart when he had kissed her, she no longer felt in control.

And so, she fought back. "Likewise. For it's quite true you do fascinate me. For instance, I'm still dying to know what you were doing in the Hart with those strange men last night."

His brows flew up, acknowledging the hit, although the appreciation in his eyes intensified. "Drinking, gambling, looking for beautiful women to abduct. I was surprisingly successful at all three."

"I doubt it," she said sweetly. "Surely none of you were looking for marriage."

"No, but I've no objection to betrothal and the opportunity to gaze at you so adoringly."

She narrowed her eyes. "Would the Longstones be very shocked if I slapped you?"

"I'm sure they expect it. But are you willing to come so close?"

She swallowed and finally dragged her gaze free. "No. And I think we have courted quite enough for one day. Where is Jane?"

CHAPTER FIVE

DINNER THAT EVENING was deliberately informal, since the baggage had not yet arrived back from London and the guests had nothing to change into. However, Cecily and her aunt went through the motions with the aid of Shilton, refreshing themselves and allowing the maid to repin their hair.

Cecily left her bedchamber almost on the heels of the maid, meaning to collect her aunt and go down to the drawing room, but a faint commotion from the far end of the passage attracted her attention. Shilton was disappearing through the door to the servants' stairs, while Mrs. Longstone glared after her.

"Why is that woman still here?"

"It is none of our business, Mama," her son said hastily from what was, presumably, the open door to his bedchamber.

"My daughter has had no need of her for five years!" Mrs. Longstone exclaimed. "And there has been no other lady here for her to serve."

"Well, we cannot say there have been no *women* here," her son said wryly. "I'm sure they enjoy the services of a good lady's maid."

Mrs. Longstone snorted. "I'm sure he does, too."

Cecily whisked herself the few paces to her aunt's door, her one desire to escape the unpleasant conversation she had not been able to help overhearing. In fact, had they *meant* her to hear it? Even making allowances for the grief of the late Lady Verne's family, it was surely not their place to question which servants he employed.

On the other hand, Shilton's retention here with nothing to do and no one to serve *was* strange. She should have been engaged by another lady long since. Least of all did Cecily like the suggestion that Verne kept her to look after his mistresses, or that the maid herself *was* his mistress. The whole conversation seemed unhealthy and left her with a sense of discomfort.

Of course, it was not her business. It wasn't as if her upcoming engagement was real. The incident only served as a warning, for she knew she had enjoyed the flirtation in the garden just a little too much. Whatever else he might be, Verne was not boring.

Neither, it seemed, was Henry Longstone, whom she sat next to at dinner. He talked amusingly on many subjects and appeared to enjoy her company. Occasionally, she glanced across the table at Verne, who watched proceedings with sardonic humor.

After the meal, as the ladies left the gentlemen to their wine, Cecily wondered what on earth they would say to each other.

"Your family and the Vernes must have known each other for a long time," she said to Mrs. Longstone.

"Indeed." Mrs. Longstone sat on the sofa, her eyes softening. "We are each other's closest neighbors. I was so glad when Verne—the late Lord Verne—offered for my Marjorie." She smiled a little mistily. "It seemed the perfect match."

"I'm sure it was," Cecily said gently.

"It would have been, had *he* not lived in the same house!"

"Cousin," Madame de Renarde admonished, patting her shoulder. "Nothing is achieved by dwelling in the past. And after all, the late Lord Verne could not have had his brother sleeping *outside* the house!"

Mrs. Longstone looked as if she had a few such outdoors locations in mind, but she lowered her lashes and gave a small laugh. "You must not mind me, Lady Cecily. I am a grieving mother still."

"The grieving need someone to blame," Madame de Renarde

observed. "It is human and natural, but it is not always fair."

Cecily regarded her with increased interest, although she could not help saying to the older lady, "If you blame the current Lord Verne, why did you come here?"

Mrs. Longstone raised her gaze to Cecily's. "To be sure he ruins no one else's life."

Stupidly, Cecily wanted to defend him. At the same time, a hundred questions rose to her lips, all clamoring to be asked.

"Don't be so melodramatic, cousin," Madame Renarde said mildly. "Lady Cecily, come sit by me and tell me the latest *on-dits* from London."

Civilly, Cecily allowed herself to be steered to a nearby sofa while Lady Barnaby sat with Mrs. Longstone.

"I'm sorry if my cousin's words make you uncomfortable," Madame de Renarde said with rather less drawl than usual.

"There is a lot that is uncomfortable about this house," Cecily allowed. "And as she says, she is a grieving mother. It was a terrible tragedy."

"It was, and leaves no one untouched. Sometimes, my cousin forgets Patrick's own pain."

"But you do not," Cecily observed. Apart from Jane, Madame de Renarde was the first person she had heard use Lord Verne's Christian name.

"Patrick and I are old friends. I understand him."

Cecily was fairly sure she understood the other woman, too, but she refused to think about a closer relationship between the Frenchwoman and Verne. Certainly, she would not talk about it. "Then *you* do not believe he was responsible for the fire?"

"He did nothing wrong and was never accused," Madame de Renarde said impatiently. But there was no irritation in her eyes. Only... pity. "Not under the law, at any rate. My dear, Lord Verne is a complicated man, a man of impulse and sudden passions that change like the weather. He may be innocent of arson but yet not of the other crimes the world attributes to him. Do you understand me?"

"No," Cecily said starkly.

Madame de Renarde sat back. "I think you do. He is charming, mercurial, just dark enough to intrigue one who is bored by the shallowness of London's social whirl. But the darkness *is* there. Make no mistake, my lady, he is a dangerous man. Never more so than when he concentrates all that unconventional attention on a young, innocent girl who imagines she is sophisticated enough to deal with him. She is not."

A flush rose into Cecily's cheek, not just because the other woman imagined her to be this smitten young innocent, but because according to Verne's plan, that was exactly who she *had* to be. She had rarely felt so frustrated, so hobbled, in her life.

"It is fortunate," she managed at last, "that if any such comes along, she has you to warn her off."

An amused twinkle pierced the boredom in Madame's bright, blue eyes. "Exactly."

Verne and Longstone strolled into the room.

"That is five minutes longer than I imagined," Madame drawled. "And look, they have not killed each other."

"Does Mr. Longstone also believe in Lord Verne's guilt?"

"Who knows what Henry believes? The enmity between them goes back much further. But I'm sure you have had enough of my gossip. Just remember I am your friend, should you need one."

As she stood and glided away to Mrs. Longstone, pausing only to exchange a few words with Verne on the way, Cecily thought Madame de Renarde was the last friend in the world she would choose.

Verne eased his long person into the space on the sofa beside her.

"I used to think *my* family was strangely disunited," Cecily said.

"Until you met mine? But I think you'll find them all pretty united against *me.*"

She searched his face. "Don't you mind?"

"No." His lips curled. "Why would I? I worked da—*very* hard—to alienate them."

"Why?"

He shrugged. "Why not? They're Marjorie's family, mere connections."

"And neighbors," she pointed out, "whom you are quite happy to make use of."

"What else is family for?"

"Connections," she corrected, and he laughed.

"Incidentally," he said, "I'm told your baggage has just arrived, along with two maids and a pack of coachmen and grooms."

"I hope you don't mind putting them all up."

"The more the merrier," he said carelessly. "I believe it was my idea. Walk with me in the moonlight."

She blinked. "That would be stretching propriety too far."

"I suppose it would, although it does have the advantage of getting us out of this benighted room."

She frowned at him. "I am quite happy to be in this room. Or at least I was."

A faint smile played around his lips. His eyes gleamed with more challenge than amusement. "Don't you know I can't be dismissed like all your other, callow suitors?"

Her heart bumped. "You are not my suitor at all," she said crossly.

"Hush," he mocked. "Someone will hear."

She was about to answer back in kind, when some strange expression in his eyes halted her. Some black, determined despair.

"Are you doing it to me now?" she blurted.

"Doing what to you?"

"Alienating me."

She thought she glimpsed confusion before his thick lashes swept down, concealing.

"Why would I trouble? I imagine you're utterly alienated already." His lip curled. "And if you weren't before, you will be after this evening. Bear up, it will all soon be over." He stood up and strolled over to Lady Barnaby.

His place was quickly taken by Mr. Longstone. "I'm told you plan to leave us for London in just a couple of days."

"We feel that is quite long enough for an impromptu visit! You have all been so kind to us."

"Not at all. But at least you will be more comfortable now you have been reunited with your servants and your baggage." He hesitated. "I shall be visiting London myself in a couple of weeks. I hope I may call upon your aunt."

"Of course, you must."

The tinkle of pianoforte keys interrupted their conversation, drawing their attention to the instrument by the windows. Verne had lifted the lid and was running one finger across the keys.

"It's still mostly in tune," he said, as though surprised. He raised his gaze. "I'm sure you play, Lady Cecily."

"With more enthusiasm than accuracy," Cecily replied.

"Oh, please play for us," Mrs. Longstone said brightly.

"Do," her son urged. "Let me help you choose the music and turn it for you."

Cecily, who played largely from memory—hence the frequent comments about her inaccuracy—agreed politely. Eventually, she found a French song she remembered from childhood, and set it on the stand. Longstone stood protectively beside her, but he had no competition for the honor of turning the pages. Verne sat back on the window seat, apparently waiting to be entertained.

She tried to ignore him as she played and sang, but all too often she felt his gaze burning into her skin. It might have added a little too much emotion to the plaintive song, so when pressed for another, she played a short comic piece from memory, and then stood up to laughter and applause.

While she gathered the music and put it away, Verne said in her ear. "You play from the heart."

"Don't be silly," Cecily said lightly. "I have no heart. Ask anyone."

"Just because the fools cannot win it, doesn't mean it is not there."

"Oh, well said, sir. So I shall tell them."

"Are you making fun of me, Lady Cecily?"

"Of course not," she said in shocked tones. "That would be rude."

Their eyes met. His lips quirked. "You *are* a minx, aren't you?"

Before she could respond, Mrs. Longstone called her to her side, and when she next saw Verne, he was strolling out of the room.

It appeared he was an erratic host, for he did not come back while tea was served. Afterward, they played cards until Lady Barnaby asked Cecily to fetch her shawl. As soon as she crossed the wide hallway to the bedchamber wing, she could hear a commotion. A woman was crying, and another woman's voice was raised until a male roar bade her hold her tongue.

Cecily hurried to see what on earth was the matter, praying that none of *her* servants were responsible for whatever contretemps was taking place. The door to Jane's chamber, where Cecily had spent last night, stood open to reveal several maidservants she did not know, and Shilton, who was doing the weeping.

They all looked petrified, staring at someone she couldn't see. She heard, though, as soon as he spoke. It was Verne, and he was furious.

"The only reason any of you are still here is because my niece is not in the room to hear you. As it is, *you* and *you* will get to your own quarters now and stay there. You'll leave first thing in the morning. I will not tolerate such behavior in my house, or to my servants. Those of you with duties, get on with them. Those without, go to bed."

"Please, sir, Miss Jane…" one of the maids all but whispered.

"You are her new nursery maid? She's asleep in the library. I'll carry her up in a moment. The rest of you, get out."

"Sorry, my lord," Shilton whispered as the maids fell over each other to get out of the room and fled toward either the servants' stairs or other bedchambers. There was a manservant among them, too—Longstone's valet, no doubt. "I like to look after Miss Jane, but they said I had no business to be there, said such—"

"I know what they said," Verne said, much more gently. "I heard them." He stepped into Cecily's view, putting a hand on Shilton's shoulder. "You know you always have a place here. No one shall make you leave against your wishes."

"Thank you, my lord." There was enough devotion in the look she cast up at Verne to shock Cecily. But Verne, perhaps sensing the other presence, frowned toward the door and saw Cecily standing there. His hand slid off the maid's shoulder. "Off you go, Shilton."

Shilton sniffed, wiped her nose on her cuff, and scuttled off, casting a quick glance at Cecily as she went, like a dog expecting to be kicked.

"Can I help?" Cecily asked mildly.

Verne wrinkled his nose. "There are times when I feel the lack of a mistress for this house. I am not the man to sort out stupid servants' squabbles."

"Should not Mrs. Longstone do it while she is here?" Cecily asked. "Especially since these other servants appear to be hers."

"She will only defend them, especially against Shilton, whom they use quite shamefully for no better reason than rumor and gossip." He dragged his hand through his already wild hair. "Has the poor girl not suffered enough?"

"I don't know," Cecily said. "I am a stranger. But... she is a trifle *odd* for a lady's maid."

"She wasn't always so," he snapped. Then, when she raised her eyebrows, he shrugged impatiently. "She was my sister-in-law's maid."

"So she told me."

He drew in his breath and spoke in a rush. "She saved Jane,

brought her out of the flames. Daniel had to stop her going back in."

"*You* didn't stop her?" She didn't know why she said it. Just that there seemed to be some bond between him and the maid.

His eyes narrowed slightly. A strange little smile flickered across his lips and vanished. "No. I didn't stop her. But she lives with guilt. I understand that." He stirred. "What brings you here so early in any case? Bored with the company already?"

"Hardly. I came for my aunt's shawl. Um… why is Jane asleep in the library?"

He shrugged. "I let her. Sometimes, she looks at the books until she falls asleep."

"That's where you vanished to!"

His eyes gleamed. "You noticed. I shall treasure the memory."

"I'd be surprised, but please do," she said cordially.

"This chamber is directly above the library. I couldn't fail to hear the racket and went to tell them off. Even before I realized they were baiting poor Shilton." He walked out of the room toward her, and she backed away instinctively.

"I'll fetch the shawl," she muttered, hurrying toward her aunt's chamber. Before she reached the door, she heard him running downstairs, presumably to the library.

He was a man of many layers and contradictions, but she could not doubt he cared deeply. For some, at least.

CHAPTER SIX

A FRENCH DOOR led from Verne's library into the gardens where he'd walked with Cecily earlier that day. He stepped outside, raising his face to the breeze and breathing in the fresh night air. Sometimes, it helped him to sleep.

"Waiting for someone?" asked a soft female voice in the darkness.

Yes, but she won't come. He turned toward the voice, and made out the figure of a woman near the side door. Isabelle de Renarde. "Izzy. Afraid to sleep in my house?"

"Why should you imagine that?" she wondered, picking her way toward him.

"I thought you were leaving," he said flippantly.

"No, you didn't. I'm merely taking the air, like you. Recalling times past. Again, like you?"

"I don't dwell on the past." *Except when it gives me no choice.* "I prefer to look to the future."

"And what does the future hold for my wild lord?" She halted close to him.

By the light spilling from the library, her beauty shone as it had always done. Perhaps it was his eyes that had grown dim. At any rate, her use of the teasing nickname she had given him as part of their love play, served to irritate rather than inflame him. Even though she gazed up at him with her offer clear in her sultry eyes.

He stepped back and looked up at the sky. It was clear tonight, the stars bright in their velvet blackness, although there was little light from the still-new moon. "I thought I might see about rebuilding the north wing. And hire a few more servants."

"If they'll come," she said contemptuously.

He inclined his head in acknowledgement. "If they'll come." He brought his gaze back down to her face. "And what of you, Izzy? Playing the governess for long?"

"God, no, but I need to be somewhere since Pierre shows no signs of saving what fortune we have left."

"Then make him, Izzy. We all know you can make any man do whatever you want."

There was a pause. "Not *any* man. What do you mean by that girl, Patrick?"

"What girl?"

"Don't be obtuse. It doesn't suit you."

He raised his brows. "It's a genuine question. I am accused of affairs with everyone from the maids to—"

"To me," she finished for him. "But I doubt you mean to ruin a duke's sister. Unless she *really* annoyed you. You don't look annoyed."

"Why should I be? Her brother is a friend."

"He'd have to be an extremely good friend to put up with her staying in your house."

"That is why the Longstones are here."

"You are a manipulative devil, aren't you, Verne? You have that girl eating out of your hand."

It's all pretense. "I wish I did," he said mildly.

"It isn't kind."

He blinked and met her gaze once more. "Since when have either of us cared for kindness?"

"You don't fool me, Patrick. You never did. Don't hurt her. It will just be one more guilt to bear."

"My shoulders are broad. Why this sudden care for a mere woman?"

"I like her," Izzy said unexpectedly. "She reminds me of me before I married Pierre de Renarde. Full of innocence and confidence in equal measure. I wouldn't like her to lose both."

"As you did?" he asked.

Her lip curled. "My confidence came back."

He touched her cheek, a gesture of old affection. One never stopped caring entirely. "Then go and whip your husband into the man he should be. He'll be grateful."

She caught his wrist. "This from you?" she whispered.

"We used each other, Izzy. I know you don't love me."

She smiled. "I came close."

"So did I."

She stepped past him into the library, just as she had many times before. He gazed up at the sky once more, knowing she would merely pass through and return to her own chamber. Part of him, the physical, desperate part, regretted refusing her unspoken offer. The slaking of lust was no small thing at this moment. But she deserved better, and so did... not he, but Cecily.

CECILY'S NEW BEDCHAMBER looked out onto the overgrown formal garden. She was in her nightrail and trying to compose a letter to her brother when she became aware of the faint hum of voices outside. Since she had bade the maid leave the curtains open, a dim glow of light touched the window from below.

Curiously, she returned the pen to its stand and stood up. At first, she saw no one, until she pressed her face to the glass and glimpsed two figures some yards to the left, close to the house. They were bathed in light spilling from the room beyond them, so it was not difficult to recognize her host and Madame de Renarde.

All at once she remembered the scene at the Hart, as Verne said farewell to his shady companion in French. This woman was French, too, which reminded her she had never solved the mystery of why he was there that night. She still had no clue about the identity or purpose of any of his companions.

On the other hand, eavesdropping at a public inn was somehow not quite the same as doing so to your host in his own home. And Madame de Renarde had already implied some knowledge, some intimacy between them that she most assuredly did not wish to witness. For an instant, a paralyzing surge of jealousy swept through her, depriving her of breath. And so she saw him touch the French-woman's cheek with tenderness, saw her catch at his wrist. He did not draw it free. Instead, after a brief, low-voiced exchange, she walked past him into the house. Cecily guessed it was his library, where he had taken her when he had first brought her here. She knew now it led to his own private apartments.

She should not care, but it seemed she could not take her eyes off the man who stood below, gazing up at the stars for several long moments. She thought he smiled as he finally turned and followed Madame de Renarde inside.

Cecily tried quite hard to laugh at herself. *My engagement has not yet happened, and when it does, it will be false. I should rejoice that he has a lover. It provides me with an excuse to cry off.*

THE NEXT DAY dawned fair and sunny, inspiring Henry Longstone to suggest an expedition to the priory ruins with an al fresco luncheon.

"It sounds a delightful scheme," Cecily approved, eager to escape Finmarsh House for a few hours. "Is it far?"

The whole party, save their host, was at breakfast, and Henry laid down his fork before he answered, "No, it's about an hour's gentle ride, still on Finmarsh land. It wasn't a terribly important monastery but it makes a most romantic ruin."

"But does Verne have enough horses to mount us all?" Mrs. Longstone asked.

"We can only ask him."

"Ask who what?" Verne said, sauntering in in riding dress.

There was mud on his boots, as though he had already ridden out this morning. He seemed to bring a gust of fresh air into the room, contrasting with the constant air of dangerous dissipation that always hung around him. His hair was wild and tangled, his eyes strangely turbulent beneath the thin veil of careless calm.

Deliberately, Cecily did not glance at Madame de Renarde, who was the one, inevitably, who answered him. "We were thinking of riding over to the priory. Can you lend us enough horses for everyone?"

"You may exclude me," Lady Barnaby said hastily. "If Mrs. Longstone is going. I do not ride for pleasure any longer."

"Cousin Isabelle can play chaperone," Henry said to his mother. "You could stay here with Lady Barnaby if you wished."

"No, I shall join you," Mrs. Longstone said bravely. "If Lady Barnaby does not object to being left alone for a few hours."

"Not at all," Lady Barnaby assured her. "I may write some letters and will almost certainly take a nap."

"There are plenty of horses," Verne said, throwing himself into the seat next to Cecily and pouring himself a cup of coffee. His elbow brushed against hers. "We should give Daniel an hour to prepare. And the kitchen if we're taking a luncheon."

"You mean to come?" Mrs. Longstone addressed one of her rare remarks to her host with undisguised dismay.

Verne's lips twitched. "Certainly. Can't have a parcel of strangers riding roughshod over my land. Besides, I need to speak to Grimshaw."

"Who is Grimshaw?" Cecily asked to break the awkward silence.

"Local builder," Verne replied.

"Verne is thinking of rebuilding the north wing," Madame de Renarde told the company.

Mrs. Longstone's eyes widened. "Why?"

"Because it's an eyesore," Verne said impatiently. He met her gaze. "Whatever you imagine, a blackened ruin is not a suitable monument to your daughter or my brother."

"You are a monster," Mrs. Longstone whispered.

"Hush, Mama," Henry said, patting her hand while he glared at his brother-in-law. "People might wonder what you're trying to hide behind your new stone and plaster," he said contemptuously.

"They've been able to see quite clearly for the last five years," Verne pointed out. "For myself, I do not care to associate the dead with crumbling, empty ruins."

"Unfeeling—" Mrs. Longstone broke off, dabbing her eyes with her napkin.

"Undoubtedly. But frankly, ma'am, it is not your business whatever I decide to do with this house."

He had a point, though no one but Cecily seemed to see it.

"Have a pleasant excursion," Lady Barnaby murmured to her as they left the breakfast room.

"You are a wretch, crying off like that," Cecily accused.

"You only wish you'd thought of it first," her aunt replied complacently.

In truth, considering the bad feeling in the family which had boiled over at breakfast, Cecily was not looking forward to her ride. However, by the time they set off, everyone seemed to have returned to normal, with the Longstones addressing nothing to the man whose horses they rode. Of the adults, only Cecily and Madame de Renarde seemed prepared to be civil to all. And Cecily, ashamed of her reasonless jealousy, made an effort to be pleasant and friendly to the

Frenchwoman.

Besides, if Madame de Renarde rode beside her, neither Henry nor Verne could.

Fortunately, Jane joined them, too, riding a pony. Already, she appeared to be a proficient rider, although all the adults kept a close eye on her. Surely, in this one common interest in Jane, lay the possibility of ending their peculiar feud.

"Why do you not tell them?" she demanded as a sudden change around of positions brought Verne to her side.

"Tell them what?"

"What they already know in their hearts. That you are innocent of this terrible crime!"

There was a pause. "If you mean the deaths of my brother and my sister-in law," he said with sudden savagery, "I cannot. I am very far from innocent."

Her shock must have stood out in her face, for he laughed, an odd, bitter sound, and then Jane urged her pony between them, and Cecily let her mount fall back behind them while she recovered.

After a few minutes, she could again appreciate the gentle beauty of the Sussex hills, for she still did not believe Verne was guilty of the tragedy of the fire. However, she had to wait until they were at the ruin before she had the chance to speak to him again.

While everyone else explored the priory remains with enthusiasm, he merely sat on a broken stone wall, one knee under his chin, and gazed out over the green landscape to the sea beyond. Henry told Cecily a little of the priory's history and destruction—which had benefitted the Verne family—and then she played tag with Jane for a little, before collapsing on the same wall as Verne to catch her breath. Jane raced off to find the luncheon basket.

Cecily felt sure Verne was watching her, but when she glanced at him, he still looked toward the sea.

"I still don't believe it," she said.

"You don't believe what?" he asked without obvious interest.

"Your guilt. You work too hard to make people believe ill of you."

He shot a quick glance at her. He might have been startled. Then he dragged his gaze back to the sea. "You of all people have no reason to think well of me. I've no idea why you do. Nor why I like it."

"Oh, I don't think *universally* well of you," she assured him. "For instance, I still want to know what you were doing at the Hart with those strange men."

A breath of laughter escaped him and he turned to face her. But whatever he would have said was lost in Madame de Renarde's demand that they join the others for luncheon on the blankets she was spreading at the center of the ruin.

Cecily found no other opportunity to speak to Verne alone during the excursion. In fact, she began to suspect the others were deliberately keeping them apart. Which was interesting in itself. She wondered if they imagined they were protecting her. However, since Isabelle de Renarde seemed to have become something of a friend, she took the opportunity of riding home beside her to ask about the fire.

"Were you with Mrs. Longstone at the time? What actually happened?"

"Don't you know?"

Cecily shrugged. "I can only have been about fifteen years old. If I overheard gossip, it passed me by."

"But you've been in London for several seasons. You must have heard what they say about Verne."

"If only half of that were true, I should already have stumbled across at least a black mass and probably several maidens being sacrificed in the woods."

Isabelle cast her a crooked smile. "He had a wild reputation even before the fire. For the most part it was deserved, but not understood. He carried a heavier burden than anyone knew."

"What burden?"

Isabelle glanced behind her, presumably to judge the likelihood of being overheard. "There is madness in the family. Arthur—the previous baron, Patrick's brother—was so afflicted. Everyone concealed it, of course, but the main burden of it fell on Patrick. And on Marjorie, though she would not leave her husband."

"Did the Longstones want her to?"

"The Longstones never knew about it. They never wanted to admit their daughter's brilliant match was to a lunatic."

"Then how…" Cecily broke off with an apologetic wave of one hand.

"How do I know about it if they did not?" Isabelle guessed. "Well, that comes back to Patrick's wildness, I'm afraid. I have no wish to shock an unmarried young lady, but I was one of his less publicized scandals. Before and after the fire. I saw Arthur at his worst, and I saw what it did to Patrick."

It should not have surprised Cecily. She had seen Isabelle go into his rooms last night, but that the relationship was of such long standing caused a fresh twist of incomprehensible pain. She had spent too much of last night trying not to think of them together, and imagining it anyway. In remembering his devastating kiss at the Hart and wondering what it would be like if only he meant it. And kisses would only be the beginning…

With an effort, she concentrated on Isabelle's somewhat harrowing words which were the true point of the conversation.

"But you don't believe he committed such a terrible crime," Cecily said. "That he actually set the house on fire."

There was silence save for the gentle thudding of the horses' hooves on the mud track. Above them, the wispy clouds had grown denser and darker.

Slowly, Isabelle turned her head toward Cecily. "I don't believe he did it for the reasons gossip gives—to inherit the title and Finmarsh. Titles never interested him and he was already more or less running the estate. He wanted for nothing and he held his poor, mad brother in deep affection. Nor did he do it by accident in a drunken stupor. But yes, I do believe he did it. To end his brother's misery."

"Why?" Cecily whispered, staring at her. "How could you possibly believe that?"

Something very like pity sprang into Isabelle's eyes. "Why? For the simple reason he told me so."

CHAPTER SEVEN

C ECILY HAD NEVER lost her enjoyment in dressing for dinner or evening entertainment. It reminded her of dressing-up games in childhood. But tonight, her maid Cranston did most of the work without a great deal of instruction, for Cecily's mind was occupied with other things.

Although she knew it was wrong, she could just about understand a man as unbound by conventional morality as Verne, putting a beloved brother out of his misery. If every waking moment was torture, not even of the body but the mind, then she could at least sympathize with what had driven him. A large dose of laudanum, perhaps. Or even a shot in the head or the heart. A quick, nearly painless death. Despite her own repugnance at such an act, it made a terrible kind of sense.

But to set someone's rooms on fire, not only killing the intended victim's wife as well, but risking his child? And Verne was fond of his niece. Anyone could see that. And what was the point of inheriting a house that could easily have burned to the ground?

No, it may have been Isabelle's belief, and Verne's own assertion, but Cecily could not accept it.

Still deep in thought, she accompanied her aunt to the drawing room where the Longstones appeared to be arguing with Verne over his dismissal of their servants. Though perhaps argument was the wrong word, since it implied Verne contributed to the process. In fact, he sat in an armchair, his long legs stretched out in front of him, crossed at the ankles, gazing at his boots while the torrent raged over him without obvious effect.

He glanced up as Cecily entered, and a smile rose spontaneously to his lips. He stood and came to her without releasing her gaze.

"How beautiful you are," he murmured. The heat in his eyes burned her. Then his quick glance took in Lady Barnaby, too. "Both of you."

"Oh, get along with you," Aunt Barny said impatiently. "We'll have no nonsense from such a practiced flirt."

"Verne, have you heard a single word I've said?" Mrs. Longstone demanded.

"I have heard every single word," Verne replied. "None of them alter the fact that you have not troubled to train your servants properly. Until you do, the two imbeciles I sent home this morning will not return."

"Imbeciles? It is Shilton who is the imbecile," Mrs. Longstone muttered.

Everyone pretended not to hear her.

"A glass of sherry, Lady B?" Verne offered casually.

"Thank you," Lady Barnaby replied, settling herself on a sofa.

"And for you, Cecily? Sherry? A little brandy, perhaps?"

Of course, he meant her to be outraged by this reference to the first night spent in his house. She ignored it and sat by her aunt. "A small sherry, if you please."

"Don't you have ratafia, Verne?" Henry asked.

"There may be some at the back of a cupboard somewhere. Didn't know it was your tipple."

Henry glared at him. "I meant it for Lady Cecily, as you very well know."

"I prefer sherry," Cecily said hastily. "Now that my aunt has relented on the subject."

"What a beautiful gown, Cecily," Isabelle said from the opposite sofa.

Cecily glanced down, faintly surprised to find she was wearing the cream silk embroidered with red and gold. "Well, since I am no longer a debutante, I see no reason to wear white all the time."

A loud, peremptory knock sounded from below.

"Is that the front door?" Mrs. Longstone said in surprise. "You're not expecting anyone, are you, Verne?"

"Lord, no. Someone will be lost. Daniel will point them in the right direction."

However, after a minute or two, Daniel came into the room with a card on a silver plate. Cecily, who hadn't known the household possessed such things, was impressed. Verne, on the other hand, cast his expressionless henchman an amused glance as he picked up the card.

"Lord Torbridge," he said blankly. "Who the devil is Lord Torbridge?"

"Oh, no," Cecily said in dismay, while her aunt frowned at her.

"He is the Marquis of Hay's son," Mrs. Longstone said.

"I'm afraid he may be here because of us," Lady Barnaby said diplomatically. "We have been on friendly terms in London and he is a particular admirer of Cecily's."

"Excellent," Verne drawled. "Shall we have him up? Or will Alvan shoot him, too?"

Henry frowned. "Why would his grace shoot him?"

"He wouldn't, of course," Cecily said hastily. "You must do as you wish, my lord."

Verne searched her face, glanced at Lady Barnaby, then shrugged. "Show his lordship up, Daniel. And you'd better get them to lay another place for dinner."

Lord Torbridge all but burst into the drawing room, wrenching the door out of Daniel's hold as though he expected it to be slammed in his face. He paused for a moment, dramatically sweeping his gaze around the room as though ready for any iniquity. It crossed Cecily's mind that he had expected to discover some kind of orgy, and instead, found himself confronting two thoroughly respectable middle-aged ladies and a fashionable young matron along with at least one unmistakable gentleman. The other, Verne, strolled toward him, one hand held out with supreme casualness.

"Lord Torbridge, is it? I'm Verne. What can I do for you?"

Torbridge's jaw dropped. He took Verne's hand mechanically and then, looking quite annoyed with himself, all but snatched it free. "I am searching," he declared, "for Lady Cecily."

"Felicitations," Verne said sardonically, bowing him in Cecily's direction. "You have found her."

"Thank God," Torbridge exclaimed. For a horrible moment, Cecily thought he was going to hurl himself at her feet, but he contented himself with clasping her hand and gazing at her like a desperately worried cat who'd mislaid her newly born kitten. "I came as soon as I heard."

"As soon as you heard what?" Cecily asked, bewildered.

"That you were here, of course. I—"

"Once you have remembered your manners," Lady Banbury interrupted sternly, "you may tell us what you heard and from whom."

Torbridge flushed to the roots of his hair. Genuinely mortified to have been found so wanting, he dropped Cecily's hand and bowed to her aunt in a slightly jerkier movement than was usual for him.

"Allow me to present your hostess, Mrs. Longstone, who was mother-in-law to his lordship's late brother. And Mr. Longstone, her son. And their cousin, Madame de Renarde."

Under their slightly bemused gazes, Torbridge bowed gracefully to each and said all that was proper, apologizing for arriving unannounced and uninvited. Verne presented him with a glass of sherry, which appeared to startle him more than anything else.

"Drink up," Verne said. "We're about to go in to dinner."

"Let us go in now," Mrs. Longstone suggested with unexpected discretion. She set down her glass and stood up. "And Lord Torbridge may discuss his business with their ladyships before joining us. They will show you the way, my lord."

"You are kindness itself, ma'am, but I could not possibly intrude," Torbridge assured her. "I can easily dine at the inn—"

"Verne won't hear of such a thing," Mrs. Longstone said firmly, while Verne regarded her with sardonic amusement. "Your place is already set. Henry, your arm."

When they had left the room, Henry sank into the chair closest to Cecily and her aunt and leaned forward anxiously. "Are you truly well? How do you come to be in this place?"

"Of course we are well," Lady Barnaby said crossly. "And though it's none of your business, we are here because one of the carriage horses went lame and Lord Verne came to our aid. And then we decided to stay a few days longer."

"Yes, but… dear Lady Barnaby, do you not see what harm accepting the hospitality of such a man, a stranger—"

"He isn't a stranger," Lady Barnaby interrupted. "He is an old friend of Alvan's. And of course, I am always careful of Cecily's safety *and* her reputation!"

"I did not mean to suggest otherwise," Torbridge said hastily.

"Oh, but I think you did."

"Cheer up, my lord," Cecily urged. "Aunt Barny had quite the same reservations as you, until she met Mrs. Longstone and her family. They are very civil people and even you, Torbridge, could find no fault with the propriety of the household. What I want to know is what you heard and from whom to send you flying down here to find us."

"I called in Grosvenor Street just as your servants were leaving to join you. I could not *believe* their destination. Of course, I knew it would look too odd if I travelled with them, so I came on my own a day later, and here I am."

"Well at least you had that much sense," Lady Banbury allowed. "Your dashing down here could easily have caused exactly the sort of talk we all wish to avoid. The world knows you're dangling after Cecily."

"Aunt!" Cecily objected.

But Torbridge did not appear to mind. He merely smiled. "Well, I am. But I fully acknowledge I have been granted no rights."

"I have a perfectly capable brother to take care of me," Cecily pointed out. "And if he has no objections to Verne's friendship, I see no reason for yours."

"Of course not," Torbridge said humbly. "I was not aware of his grace's friendship, or the fact you were at all acquainted with Lord Verne."

"They were at school together," Lady Barnaby said. "And kept up the friendship ever since. And now that we have established all the proprieties and facts, can we please go and eat? I'm famished."

"No, you aren't, Aunt," Cecily said, standing. "But we shouldn't keep the others waiting."

"One more thing," Torbridge said, offering his hand to Lady Barnaby to help her rise. "He—Verne—has not *pursued* you in any way, has he?"

"You are being ridiculous," Cecily said coldly. "What's more, it is disrespectful to me, to my aunt, and to your host." She stalked out of the room, leaving the others to follow.

Poor Torbridge, she thought ruefully. Although she had less intention than ever of marrying him, there was something about him she had always rather liked and she did not wish to hurt him. Perhaps they could get rid of him tomorrow, before her false engagement to Verne was announced. She couldn't really take him into her confidence. Besides, the betrothal might cure him of his silly infatuation for her.

INEVITABLY, LORD TORBRIDGE was persuaded to spend the night at Finmarsh House rather than put up at the Hart. His man and his luggage were sent for, he was the perfect dinner guest, and in all, Cecily spent a more pleasant evening than she had expected to since his arrival.

Lord Verne again vanished after dinner, no doubt to say goodnight to Jane, but this time, he returned to the drawing room. He seemed restless and more silent than ever, brooding into the flames of the fire lit against the evening chill or pacing up and down the room.

When she and Lady Barnaby retired, he presented her with her night candle in the hallway. His eyes were more intense than ever as they met Cecily's, glittering with some deep emotion she could not fathom. Or it may have been the trick of the candle flames.

"Good night," he said abruptly.

"Good night." She inclined her head and followed her aunt across the wide hall to the passage. Her heart was beating too fast without reason. He always had some strange effect on her.

He also seemed to have communicated his restlessness to her, for when she had left her aunt, she found she had no desire to sleep. She let her maid undress her, then sent her to bed while she herself went to the window seat and gazed out into the darkness. Last night, she had witnessed some promised intimacy between Verne and Isabelle in the garden below. But there was no sign of anyone tonight. Were they together again? She should not care, except she would look foolish when the engagement was announced. She wondered who else knew about Verne and Isabelle.

She was unsure how long she sat there, gazing into the night, watching the stars wink between scudding clouds. With her knees tucked under her chin, she rested her head against the window pane. From this position, she could make out the edge of the ruined wing, and wondered about the late Lord Verne and his wife, about Verne's declared guilt and her own belief in his innocence—of that crime, at least.

Perhaps this was her form of insanity. His wife's family, his lover, all believed in his guilt. According to Isabelle, he had admitted it to her. Cecily had no reason to hold him innocent, and yet she did. Wishful thinking, because the man had kissed her and made her laugh. He made her skin tingle when he touched her, caused her heart to gallop and her breath to vanish whenever he was near. It did not feel like fear, and yet the feeling itself both frightened and thrilled her.

Lust. Desires of the flesh, such as young ladies were not meant to know about, let alone entertain, least of all for men whose reputations were soiled beyond any level of marriageability.

Marriage! Where had that word come from? Engagement, even a false engagement, was quite bad enough.

Her train of thought was interrupted as the figure of a man appeared below. She hadn't noticed where he had come from, but he carried a lantern which cast an eerie glow over him. Visible only for an instant, he seemed to vanish into the ruined walls like a ghost.

Cecily sat up, both intrigued and alarmed. Lifting the sash as quietly as she could, she stuck out her head and peered toward where she had last seen the man. The breeze lifted her hair and cooled her cheeks, but she could see no sign of anyone... unless that was a faint glow coming from inside the ruined part of the house? The lantern?

Why would a ghost carry a lantern? Of course, it was no ghost, but a person, only why would anyone enter the ruin at night? She frowned. In fact, *how* did anyone enter the ruin from the front of the house? There was no doorway.

Thoroughly curious now, she drew her head back inside and closed the window. For a moment, she sat still, trying to talk herself out of it. This kind of impulsive investigation was what had got her abducted by Verne in the first place. But this case was different. She was not in a public inn. She no longer believed Verne would harm her, or allow harm to come to her. And he, surely, was the greatest danger in the county.

With a breathless laugh, she sprang up and swung her voluminous travel cloak around her before stuffing her hair inside the collar. She lit a larger candle from the now-tiny one, slid her feet into slippers, and crept out into the passage.

All was quiet and dark. By the pale light of her candle, she found her course to the hallway in front of the drawing room and the formal dining room. From there, she took the other passage leading toward the ruined wing. A bolted door blocked her. This must have been the door she had seen Shilton peer through that first morning.

Transferring the candle to her left hand, she used her right to slide back the bolts. They moved easily, almost silently, and she pulled open the door. At once, the draught hit her, making her shiver. She shone the candle around, trying to make out what was left of the floors and walls. To her surprise, enough remained that she could make out the layout of the rooms. There were large holes in many of the floors and some of the walls had partially tumbled, so without moving very much, she could see through this floor to the one below and the one above.

She turned to peer toward the back of the house and something moved near her feet. She gasped as it loomed suddenly upward, resolving into the figure of a man. A man with Verne's face.

"Marjorie," he whispered.

Alarmed, Cecily stumbled backward. "It's Cecily," she got out and then her foot went straight through the floor and she lost her balance. The candle fell and went out. Her stomach dived as she began helplessly to fall.

Strong hands seized her, jerking her to safety against his hard body. She could see nothing, hear nothing except the pounding beat of her own heart.

"For God's sake, what are you doing here?" he whispered into her hair.

"I saw a light."

A choked sound escaped him. It might have been laughter. "Were you looking out of the window again?"

"Yes, but I didn't know it was you."

"Who else was it likely to be?" he demanded. "Are you hurt?"

She shook her head.

"Frightened?"

She nodded.

"Don't be. I have you safe."

"We have no light," she reminded him shakily.

"I don't need one. Cecily…"

She drew back enough to look up at him, though she could see nothing except deeper darkness where his head should be. A groan escaped him and then the blackness surged and his lips slid along her jaw to claim her mouth.

He kissed her with fierce, abandoned passion. Overwhelmed to the point of fright, she reached up to make him stop, found his soft, tangled hair, and the rough, damp skin of his jaw. She gasped into his mouth, her fear lost now in the wonder of his kiss, and in distress because she understood the wetness running still down his face.

"What is it?" she whispered against his lips, stroking his cheek, his hair. "What is wrong?"

"Nothing." His mouth gentled with the movement of speech. "Absolutely nothing. Kiss me."

She couldn't help it. This was what she had wanted ever since the first time he had done it. In total surrender, she threw her arms around his neck, glorying in the hardness of his body pressed against hers. Her lips yielded and parted for his, as she kissed him back with shy yet ever-soaring passion. Her heart, her stomach, her whole being was in utter turmoil and she loved it.

In the end, it was he who ended the kiss. "This isn't a safe place to make love," he said hoarsely. "Stand still while I light the lantern."

She nodded dumbly, and he released her to crouch and feel behind him. She heard the clank of the lantern and the scrape of the tinder box, and then light flared, casting its wavery glow over the sculpted lines and hollows of his face. He rose and took her hand, leading her the few paces to the door she had entered by.

"How did you get in?" she asked, remembering.

"Through the ground-floor window."

"Did you climb up?" she demanded, watching him close and bolt the door.

He lifted his finger to his lips. "Yes."

"Is it safe?" she whispered.

"Not very, but I didn't much care at the time." He took her hand again. "Come." He urged her along the passage toward the staircase and they ran down it silently, hand-in-hand while the lantern bobbed, casting wild, ever-changing shadows up the walls and bannister.

At the foot, he led her across the hall to the room she remembered only too well—the library. As he opened the door and light spilled out, sense began to return to her and she hesitated, staring up at him.

He doused the lantern and placed it on the floor before taking her in his arms and kissing her again, this time with soft, devastating sensuality, seducing her mind, body, and soul.

He lifted her, swinging her into the room, and kicked the door shut with the heel of his boot.

"I won't hurt you," he whispered. "I couldn't. But I can't leave you alone either, not yet. You are so soft and sweet and beautiful…"

"I'm not. I'm proud and stubborn and overly-curious. Why did you go there, Patrick?"

He smiled, cupping her cheek. "That's the first time you've used my name."

In spite of everything, she flushed. "You're avoiding the question."

"Yes, I am, because I don't have an answer. I'm drawn there at high times and low times, just to remember what I've lost." Letting her go, he swung away and paced across the room. "And who I've destroyed. Why are you here with me?"

"You asked me. Without words, admittedly."

He cast her a wicked glance over his shoulder and heat surged through her whole body. It was a good question. Why *was* she here? This man, this situation, was not *safe*.

"Come here," he said softly.

He had been crouched alone in the corner of his burned-out ruin, silently weeping. He had called her Marjorie as though he'd thought her his sister-in-law's ghost. He was in pain. That was why she came. She could not leave him alone with such agony.

"You called me Marjorie. Do you see her ghost?"

He stared at her. "In my mind. Along with my brother's."

"But I was real."

"I didn't know that until you almost fell. Are you going to come to me, or shall I come back to you?"

"Why did you kiss me?"

"Because you're beautiful and I want you."

"And I was there."

"It is difficult to kiss someone who isn't."

"And last night, Isabelle de Renarde was there."

A frown flickered across his brow. "Not much escapes you, does it?" He began to walk back toward her, slow and predatory. "And if you are right, would it bother you?"

She lifted her chin. "You are free. As I am."

"And here you are," he murmured, devouring her with his hot, turbulent gaze. Lifting his hand, he cupped her cheek and softly, deliberately, kissed her mouth.

Every inch of her wanted to hurl herself into his arms and surrender, to discover the true meaning of the passion, the desire coursing through her. Resisting the temptation was the hardest thing she had ever done in her pampered life, for his kiss was sweet and thrilling and blatantly seductive.

Very gently, she detached her mouth from his and caught his wrist. "Are you trying to seduce me *now*? After we have gone through all this to convince people you didn't do so three nights ago?"

His lips curved. "I'll grant you it makes no sense, but then desire rarely does. Are you going to threaten me with Alvan again? Or Torbridge?"

"No. I want to talk to you."

"What about?"

"What devastates you still about the fire."

He stared down at her. "What do you think?"

She waved her hand dismissively. "There is more than grief and loss in you. More even than the horror. Everyone believes it is guilt."

He sighed and released her, turning away to throw himself on to the sofa. "There you are. Why won't you leave it alone?"

She followed him. "Because I don't believe you're guilty. I don't believe you would be stupid enough, even utterly drunk, to set fire to anything, let alone your own home."

His brow twitched as he searched her eyes. "I've no idea where you find such belief in me. I'm touched and appalled at the same time."

"Why appalled? Why are you so determined to take the blame?"

"Because the blame is mine," he retorted. "If this is all you wish to talk about, you should go."

"Yes, I probably should," she agreed. "And yet, as you pointed out, here I am."

"You are a very strange girl."

"So my aunt says when I won't do as she wants."

"Does she really want you to marry Torbridge?"

"She thinks I could do worse."

"Will he stand by you when you engage yourself to me and then throw me over?"

"I have no idea," she said impatiently, for he had turned the subject too easily. "I heard a rumor the late Lord Verne, your brother, was insane."

"It's in the blood."

And suddenly, several little pieces of information and opinion all came together. He had been devoted to his brother, covered for his spells of insanity. He hadn't been the one to prevent Shilton going back into the blaze to try to save the others because far from drinking merrily in his own rooms, he was in his brother's apartments trying to save him and his wife. Failing was the root of his guilt. Taking the blame was the fault of love.

"You're still covering for him," she whispered, sinking to the floor at his knees. "He started the fire and you let everyone believe it was you."

He stared at her. The shock in his eyes was almost fear. "You're wrong," he said shakily.

"And no one guesses. Not Marjorie's family, not even Isabelle. And they treat you like... Patrick, how can you stand it? *Why?*"

"Because he was defamed enough, and I had nothing to lose." His expression grew fierce. "Leave it alone, Cecily. You are not to rake this up."

His hands rested on his knees, gripping so hard his knuckles shone white in the candlelight. She pried one off, holding it between both of hers. "I won't," she promised earnestly. "But, Patrick, you do not need to punish yourself with the loathing of the world. You did nothing wrong."

"Didn't I? I left him there rather than send him to an asylum or even hire the right people to look after him. I *did* kill him, and Marjorie, as surely as if I'd set the fire myself."

"And so you invite his mother-in-law around as a sort of flagellation?"

His breath caught. It might have been laughter, hastily choked off. "Something like that, yes." His hand moved, gripping hers and dragging it to his lips. "But never think I am a good man, Cecily, for I'm not. I would still take you to bed."

Her heart thudded. She thought they were both aware how easily he could persuade her if he put his mind—and his lean, tempting body—to the task. He turned her hand over and kissed her palm and then her wrist over the galloping pulse.

"But I won't," he said. "I am too churned up and I don't think you know what you want."

He was right. Some strange feeling, a deep, powerful emotion was struggling for recognition, but became so muddled with his pain and her own pity, she shied away from it.

"You should go," he said, standing and drawing her to her feet. "Come. I'll escort you to the top of the stairs."

"I remember the way." Quite unreasonably, she felt piqued he was sending her away, even though she would not have stayed. At least, she didn't think she would. He confused her too much for sanity.

He smiled down at her, still holding her hand as he led her to the door. "Don't ever change, Cecily."

"Meaning I'm perfect as I am?"

He took up one of the candles by the door and gave it to her before collecting another. "I'll leave such superlatives to Torbridge. But I do *like* you as you are—though most young ladies would not take that as a compliment from me."

She considered him. "I don't think you like many people."

"I don't."

"Then perhaps I will accept it as a compliment."

"Be still my heart."

She glanced at him with suspicion as they began to climb the stairs. "More Shakespeare?"

"Homer," he confessed apologetically.

She couldn't help smiling. As they reached the landing, she turned. "For what it's worth, my lord, I like being your friend."

Startlement crept into his eyes. But he held onto her hand when she would have withdrawn it. "Then you might like to know that Isabelle did not stay with me last night. She merely passed through the library on her way to her own chamber."

Her foolish heart leapt with pleasure. He took advantage of the moment, swooping to kiss her mouth, to the imminent danger of both candles.

"Verne!" exclaimed a shocked voice.

Gasping, Cecily sprang away, but he held onto her hand, turning without shame or even irritation to face Mrs. Longstone who was fully dressed and bore a branch of candles in one hand.

"Well met, ma'am," he drawled. "You may be the first to congratulate me."

"Congratulate you?" she said in outrage. "On abusing a guest under your roof?"

"You misunderstand," he said gently. "I must be allowed to express just a little joy, for Lady Cecily has just agreed to be my wife."

CHAPTER EIGHT

Mrs. Longstone wobbled. She stared from Verne to Cecily. "Is this true?"

It was the whole point of being at Finmarsh. Yet, everything in Cecily revolted against the lie, against anything so unsavory touching this strange friendship she'd found with Verne. Everything was so confusing, she wanted to run to her room and hide.

Instead, she managed a tremulous smile. "Yes, I have accepted Lord Verne's offer. Of course, we need my brother's consent, but I'm sure that is a mere formality."

Mrs. Longstone walked up to them. "Good night, Verne," she said sternly. "*I* shall escort her ladyship to her chamber."

Verne bowed to her with sardonic amusement, before he turned to Cecily with the faintest wink, inviting her to share the joke. "Of course. Good night, Cecily. I look forward to seeing you in the morning."

As he descended the stairs, Cecily felt something akin to panic. The beauty of the evening was being spoilt with this lie she had to perpetuate on her own. But she merely walked toward the bedchamber passage, wondering how to apologize for her lapse in propriety.

In the end, she didn't need to, for Mrs. Longstone said intensely, "Has that man coerced you into this?"

"Of course not!" Cecily exclaimed with such genuine shock that her companion seemed mollified.

"Forgive me," she said. "But you are a young and lovely lady of the highest rank, possessed, I understand, of a considerable fortune. I know you are not short of suitors. I cannot understand why Verne of all people should have won you."

"Neither can I," Cecily replied, a little shakily. "But in truth, I have never met anyone like him."

CECILY AWOKE THE following morning with both happiness and excitement in her heart. It was not, of course, the normal emotion of a happy betrothal. The excitement came from the necessity of playing her part, of making the nonsense believable. It might be difficult and reprehensible but there was, she had to admit, a certain, childish fun in play acting.

Her happiness stemmed from something quite different. The thrill of Verne's kisses and her own awakening desires. Even more reprehensible, of course, but there seemed nothing she could do about it, except to be sure to allow no further intimacy. For deeper than the sweet physical reaction to his misbehavior was the growing trust and deeper understanding, the connection of friendship between them. That was what she truly valued.

She rang for her maid early and was fully dressed by the time she heard stirrings in the bedchamber next door. She went at once to warn her aunt of her betrothal.

"I imagine word will be all over the house by now," she said, sitting on the edge of Lady Barnaby's bed, "that I am engaged to Lord Verne."

Aunt Barny shot her a look of undisguised suspicion. "I find that odd when you weren't engaged when we last spoke!"

"Well, I couldn't sleep and I ran into Verne. Mrs. Longstone saw us together in the upstairs hall and so we brought matters forward a little."

"That was pure idiocy, Cecily," her aunt scolded with a frown. "You have left yourself open to new scandal. What if Mrs. Longstone spreads this tale?"

"I doubt she would. I believe she welcomes the connection with a duke's family."

"Though she'd prefer it closer still," Lady Barnaby said shrewdly. "You have noticed Henry Longstone has been dangling after you?"

"Only in a polite way, and possibly trying to protect me from Verne! But talking of politeness, there is the problem of Torbridge. I wish he had not come, just to be hurt by this."

"Well, if he's worth having, he will still be there when all this has blown over. And if he isn't, it's the price you pay for wandering about inns alone at night. Besides," Lady Barnaby added, relaxing her self-righteousness, "you never seemed more than half-interested in him."

"That doesn't mean I wish to hurt his feelings or his pride."

Lady Barnaby gave her a quick smile. "Did I bring you up to be so kindhearted?"

"You must have, because no one else did." Cecily gave her aunt an affectionate hug and went downstairs to breakfast.

She was somewhat alarmed to find the whole party already gathered in the breakfast room, although the unexpected presence of Verne soothed her. Everyone rose to wish her happy with a kind of hectic enthusiasm that didn't really speak for sincerity.

Torbridge pressed her hand, smiling, although his eyes searched hers rather more piercingly than she was used to. Henry Longstone bowed to her with a smile that didn't quite touch his eyes. "I wish you luck with this reprobate," he said with clearly false joviality. Everyone knew that reprobate was exactly what he thought of Verne.

Madame de Renarde regarded her with sleepy eyes. "I hope you have not bitten off more than you can chew," she murmured.

"Why, so do I," Cecily agreed amiably.

"Then I wish you happy." She laid a very slight emphasis on the wish, as though there was very little likelihood of it coming true. She was certainly right in that.

Blushing, Cecily sat by Verne's side. It was undoubtedly expected.

"So that is why you wish to rebuild the north wing," Madame de Renarde said to him.

"It is certainly one reason," Verne admitted.

"Will you live there?" Henry demanded.

"That will be up to my bride. She will order the house as she sees fit."

Everyone looked at Cecily, who laid down her half-eaten toast. "I think there will be time enough to decide such things once the building work is done and it is habitable," she said firmly.

"Quite right," Mrs. Longstone approved. "And of course, we must not preempt his grace of Alvan's permission. I trust you will write to him, Verne."

"I wrote to him two days ago," Verne replied unexpectedly.

Cecily blinked. "Did you?"

"Yes, and I should have waited for his reply before I addressed you, but there, it is done now. I shall just hope friendship will carry the day."

"Good luck with that," Henry murmured, dabbing his lips with his napkin.

"Thank you," Verne said.

Lady Barnaby made her entrance at that point, and everyone watched her with unusual avidity—no doubt to see how she took the news of her niece's engagement.

"I see you have all heard," she remarked cheerfully, though with just a hint of disapproval in her gaze as it swept over Cecily and Verne. "Young people today! In my time, we did things in the proper order, not engaging oneself *before* the parental permission."

"Sorry, Lady B," Verne drawled. He turned to Cecily. "Would you care to ride after breakfast? I'll show you some more of your new home."

"You will need to take a chaperone," Mrs. Longstone said anxiously. "Without his grace's permission, you are not truly engaged."

"Oh, I think as long as a groom is present, we may dispense with such niceties," Lady Barnaby said. "I don't believe Alvan will object. For some reason he likes Verne."

"I thought you said he'd shoot me?" Verne murmured to Cecily.

She smiled for everyone else's benefit. "He still might."

VERNE SEEMED A different man as they rode around his estate. His demeanor was lighter and more relaxed as he showed her the improvements he had made and the problems which still existed, including more marshland which he planned to drain. He introduced several of his tenants, none of whom seemed remotely frightened of the sinister baron.

On the way back, they talked of many things from politics to literature, until the subject of Lord Byron came up. Verne was not an admirer.

"I'm disappointed," Cecily said. "I find it most romantic, dramatic, and appealing. In fact, when I first saw you at the inn, I thought immediately of Childe Harold."

Verne looked thoroughly revolted, and Cecily laughed.

His eyes narrowed. "Is that because you found me dramatic or appealing? Or merely romantic?"

"Dramatic," she said, flushing slightly, and hoping the breeze would cool her cheeks before he noticed. "And engaged upon nefarious deeds."

"Such as abducting innocent maidens and riding off with them to my lair."

"At least it was maiden in the singular."

"Sadly, it was a slow night for maidens."

"You are outrageous," she said severely. "Come, I'll race you over this hill."

They returned to Finmarsh House in high, good humor, with Cecily's groom toiling after them. The others were gathering for luncheon in great excitement because several letters had arrived from Alvan. Mrs. Longstone and Lady Barnaby had read theirs while Cecily's and Verne's waited for them on the table.

"He has agreed," Lady Barnaby said at once. "In fact, he seems to desire to hold a ball in your honor."

Cecily paused with her hand on the back of her chair, staring at her aunt. "A *ball*? Alvan?"

"Well, he is obliged to do something at the hall, you know, following his own nuptials. People expect it. Besides, I'm sure Charlotte would appreciate your support."

"And I, hers," Cecily said ruefully before pulling herself together and laughing. "How like my brother to kill two birds with one stone, as it were."

"But you will not wish to leave Finmarsh just yet," Mrs. Longstone said anxiously. "I'm sure you would like to stay a few more days now that you are engaged."

Cecily threw a glance at Verne and then at her aunt, who nodded. "Of course, we would love to. But only if it does not put you out to be here longer," Lady Barnaby said. "For we can easily depart today or tomorrow as we originally planned."

While Mrs. Longstone assured her nothing was more delightful to her than being at Finmarsh House with such charming guests, Cecily broke the wafer on her own letter and read it. It didn't take long,

My dear Cecily,

What are you about now? You had better both come here and reveal all, for you must know I smell a rat. Please be good.

Yours etc.

Alvan.

PS: Charlotte sends her love.

"Typical Alvan," Cecily said indignantly, folding the unsatisfying letter and tossing it on the table. "How can he demand to know everything and yet tell nothing?"

AFTER LUNCHEON, SINCE it was a fine afternoon, the party took a walk in the woods, and almost immediately felt the less comfortable side to her pretend engagement, for Jane accompanied them and skipped along beside Cecily, smiling.

"Are you going to marry Uncle Patrick?"

The direct question offered little opportunity for evasion. "If he's good," Cecily managed, in what she hoped was a joking kind of way. There was little chance of him being good, after all. However, sticking to the letter of truth while completely ignoring its spirit did not sit well with her and she remembered why she had opposed this scheme in the first place.

Jane laughed and slid her hand into Cecily's. "I'm glad. I think he'll be less sad now."

Since Verne had chosen not to accompany them but gone about whatever business was normal for him, Cecily asked blatantly, "Has he been sad?"

Jane nodded. "He hides it and always makes me laugh, but I know he isn't happy. Or wasn't."

"Why do you suppose that is?"

"Because of my parents, I suppose," Jane said. There was an acceptance of tragedy in her voice, something she had long come to terms with. After all, she had been three years old when it happened and had lived more than half her life since. "But I think he is lonely, too. He and Grandmama quarrel, and no one else will speak to him. Apart from the Finmarsh people, of course, but they cannot really be his friends."

"I suppose not."

Jane bestowed a dazzling smile upon her. "But now that *you* are friends, everything will be better."

"I hope so," Cecily said, trusting her voice didn't sound too hollow.

Henry stepped forward to help her over a stream. Jane leapt over it unaided and ran ahead to catch her grandmother.

"He told us he would marry you," Henry said conversationally. "Having met you, I seriously doubted it, but it seems he was right. Or at least come that all important step closer."

Cecily, having nothing to add to that, merely smiled.

"Forgive me," Henry said abruptly. "But have you considered what marriage to such a man will mean? No one receives him and there is good reason for that."

"I don't believe there is good reason," she said at once. "You should know, I don't believe most of the accusations rumor throws at him." She met his gaze. "Including his responsibility for the fire."

Henry looked away, swallowing hard. "He cannot be exonerated. It may or may not have been deliberate, but by God, he bears the blame. Don't you know he was dead drunk when it happened? That he was in there with them? And yet, only he got out."

"And Jane," Cecily reminded him, although she was shaken.

"And Jane," Henry allowed, clearly reining in his passion. "You want to think well of him, believe him to be a changed man, and I hope you are right, but please, my lady, remember me if you need a friend."

This offer both touched and irritated her. She managed to mumble a few words of thanks.

Mrs. Longstone, thankfully, seemed to have been distracted from

Verne's iniquities by Alvan's invitation to Mooreton Hall and asked Cecily a lot of questions about the house and land, and how many people would attend the ball, and how many would stay at the hall. Cecily was almost relieved when Isabelle de Renarde stepped up on her other side, and Lord Torbridge guided Mrs. Longstone around a muddy puddle in the path.

"I suppose everyone is telling you what a bad idea your engagement is," Isabelle said with a slightly cynical if sympathetic smile.

"Apart from Jane."

"Don't look at me like that," Isabelle said, apparently amused. "I've said my piece already and have no intention of adding to it. Just remember engagements can be broken. Marriages are for life. I should know."

Cecily regarded her with curiosity. "You are referring to your own marriage?"

"I should have known what was in the wind," Isabelle mused, not answering directly. "That marriage was on Verne's mind. He has been urging me to go back to my husband."

"You live apart?"

"Informally, by mutual choice. It is wiser to make such decisions *before* one makes the mistake of marrying."

"You are cynical."

"I have cause to be. Verne, however, is not Renarde. Nor is he the bad man many people will claim. But neither is he an easy man. My only advice to you—which I know you will not heed, because no one ever heeds well-meaning, unwanted advice—is to understand what and who you are getting in such a husband. And now, I shall say no more."

Thank goodness, Cecily thought. At least her aunt was doing a good job of keeping Lord Torbridge away from her. She suspected he had dashed down here in the hope of avoiding just this event, which made her even more uncomfortable. But Torbridge made no effort to buttonhole her during the walk, and when they returned to the house, Cecily took herself to the bright morning room on the first floor, where she set about writing a few letters to make sure everyone knew about her engagement. To keep it quiet would be to cause the sort of talk she was trying to avoid.

Half an hour later, Torbridge eventually found her. He strolled into the room remarking how pleasant it was and how fine the light.

Cecily set her pen it its stand and turned to regard him.

He smiled faintly. "Don't worry. I haven't come to question your decision or try to talk you out of it. I imagine you have had enough of that. I can understand why you like him."

"But with everyone else, you believe he will make me a terrible husband?"

Torbridge dragged a chair closer to her and sat down. "What do you think?"

Cecily's eyes widened. "About Lord Verne?"

"Yes. What sort of a man is he? In your opinion."

It was an odd question, but then Torbridge was an odd man, for all his conventional propriety. "In my opinion, he is a troubled man but a good one," she said defiantly. "He has been charged with no crime and yet the world has convicted him with no right and less cause."

"Then you believe in his honor?"

He had abducted her under a misapprehension, but however reprehensible that act, he now put himself through this social torture in order to make things right again. She lifted her chin. "Yes, I do."

But even as she said it, she realized she had never fully established exactly who or what he had imagined her to be when he'd thrown her into the saddle and ridden off with her. A "hussy" was somewhat vague. Surely one had no need to abduct such women to obtain their favors? The true mystery of that night had got lost somehow in her own difficulties.

Torbridge was gazing at her with that unexpectedly sharp perception she occasionally found in him. "Is that what your engagement is about? Honor? Or love?"

Cecily raised one eyebrow. "Are the two mutually exclusive? I hope not." She turned back to her letter, reaching for the pen. After a few moments of silence, she heard him rise and imagined him bowing to her back before he walked away with a murmured "Excuse me."

"My lord." She twisted around to face him once more, and he halted politely. She said, "I hope we are still friends."

"I shall always be your friend. I think you know that."

The idea of marriage with him had occasionally crossed her mind. For some reason, meeting Verne had clarified the impossibility of such a union from her point of view. She did not love Torbridge. And yet somewhere, she was sorry she did not.

SINCE VERNE DID not appear for tea, Cecily sought him out in his library. She invited Jane to go with her, but to her surprise, the child hung back.

"Oh no," she said earnestly. "He does not like to be disturbed if the door is closed."

"Oh. Well, I'll risk it on my own," Cecily said with a quick smile.

"You're very brave," Jane blurted, and bolted back to her grand-mother.

Cecily thought it an odd thing to say about merely knocking on a door. After all, although he appeared to use the library as an extension to his own rooms, Verne had often said anyone who wished was welcome to use it.

The door was indeed closed. Cecily knocked and, receiving no answer, walked in. But the room was not empty as she had assumed.

Lord Verne sat at the desk with his back to her. "The door was closed," he snapped irritably.

"And now it is open," Cecily observed.

He sprang up, knocking the chair over in his haste. He had not been reading or writing as she had assumed. Instead, the brandy decanter and a glass stood there, as though he had been systematically drinking himself into a stupor.

He groaned. "Not you! Why are you here?"

"You told me I should laugh at your jokes and show a preference for your company. I assumed this was to work both ways, so I've come to keep you company and be laughed at."

"I'm not sure you know the right kind of jokes."

At least his speech was not slurred. "I probably don't," she agreed. "How much have you had?"

He regarded her with more curiosity than irritability. "Not enough for my purposes. Too much for yours. You should go."

"I shall, in just a little." She walked further into the room and began to look around the bookshelves.

He watched her, frowning. "Why are you not more alarmed? Or appalled?"

She shrugged, plucking a book off the shelf at random. "I've seen you drunker than this," she said frankly.

"And look what that led to!"

"Well, yes, but you didn't actually touch me."

He moved toward her. "We were not engaged, then."

"We're not engaged now."

"The world believes we are." He halted so close beside her she could smell the brandy on his breath. "I'm almost expected to ravish you."

"Because of your reputation?"

"That and the fact you're so damned alluring." He raised one hand, pushing a stray strand of hair off her neck.

"I don't believe you're drinking because I'm alluring," she argued.

He laughed. "That's exactly why I'm drinking." His fingertips strayed across her cheek and lingered on her lower lip. Her breath caught. She seemed incapable of moving away. She remembered last night's deep, sensual kisses and was shocked by how much she wanted him to repeat them.

His hand fell away. "You should go," he said abruptly. "Cry off before Alvan's wretched ball. You don't want to find yourself leg-shackled for life to me."

"I expect I will. Cry off, I mean," she added hastily. "But I came to ask you another question. You abducted me because you thought I was merely some hussy. What hussy? Who did you think I was?"

The last vestiges of softness vanished from his eyes, leaving them like flint. Worse, a glint of cruelty took her by surprise.

"To be honest," he said deliberately, "I didn't much care."

She held his gaze, just to prove she could. Then she walked away from him to the desk and picked up the decanter before marching to the door.

His mocking laughter followed her. "I'll only fetch another."

"And who knows?" she replied sweetly. "In the time it takes you to do so, you might have realized what a stupid idea it is."

She shut the door behind her with a decided click. It was quite satisfying, only now she was left carrying a decanter of brandy and had no idea what to do with it. It wasn't something she particularly wanted the Longstones or anyone else to see.

She turned toward the kitchen, and by chance encountered the ubiquitous Daniel emerging through the baize door.

"Ah, Daniel," she said briskly. "Take this away, if you please, until a more suitable occasion."

Daniel's mouth fell open. "How did you manage that, my lady?"

"I took him by surprise," she said honestly.

Daniel took the decanter and cast her a quick, crooked smile. "You know he'll only fetch up another."

"So he told me. But it's a start."

"Thank you, my lady." He turned and vanished back through the door to the servants' domain.

Since she still carried the book, she decided to take it up to her bedchamber and read until it was time to change for dinner.

CHAPTER NINE

VERNE STARED AT the closed library door with some astonishment. After a moment, he let out a breath of wry laughter. While he admired her style and her courage, the removal of one decanter could make no possible difference to his intentions.

His intentions. He wasn't even sure what they were, except to stop himself from thinking. From feeling. But he hadn't truly meant to be bosky before dinner. Nor could he refuse to attend and make a nonsense of his own scheme to persuade the world that he was at Cecily Moore's impetuous little feet. The trouble was, he'd begun to suspect it was true and he didn't like it. He didn't like it at all.

Touching her last night had been a mistake. It had been giving in to impulse... and desires that had haunted him since he'd first seen her. It had been sweetness itself. And unforgivable weakness. It was no use telling himself he had been vulnerable when she had found him. He had simply taken advantage of her nearness because rightly or wrongly, desire was one of the ways he blotted out the pain. But she was no whore, nor even a sophisticated lady who understood the rules of illicit liaisons. She was an innocent and his friend's sister whom he had already wronged. But for a moment—*be honest, Patrick, for many moments!*—her unique combination of compassion, purity, fun, and latent passion had been irresistible.

He had almost ruined everything. What if someone other than Elvira Longstone had seen them and initiated the gossip he had begun this masquerade to avoid? He had to draw back from the intimacy he had initiated, and never, ever repeat it. Because the truth was, he could never have her in reality. Even if he could win her—and God, her response made him dream of possibilities—he was too soiled, too mired in lies and madness and sheer bad behavior. He could not visit that upon her.

His plan, for her to appear to be taken in by him, engaged to him, and then, discovering his true nature, jilting him, still seemed the only available solution. He should not be making that harder for either of them.

Still, he kicked the side of the bookcase, because she'd taken away his damned brandy. And then he laughed and walked out through the garden door.

THEY WERE ALL gathered in the drawing room—a motley group of people, all of whom he had wronged in some way and yet who, for various reasons, were happily accepting his hospitality. Cecily's gaze flew to him at once, as though she wasn't quite sure what to expect. He smiled at her, and she smiled back with relief. He bowed to the company in general and exerted himself to be at least a pleasant host.

Lord Torbridge came up to him. "I hope you don't mind that I'm still here! Mrs. Longstone invited me to stay longer."

I'm sure she did. She would be hoping that if Henry couldn't cut Verne out with Cecily, then perhaps Torbridge could at least make her think twice.

"Very glad of your company," Verne said civilly.

"Did I offer my congratulations on your betrothal?"

"I believe you did."

"We are old friends, Lady Cecily and I."

"So I've been told."

"I suppose you've also been told that I wish I stood in your shoes as far as she is concerned."

"You never asked her."

"I didn't think she would say yes. A more decisive man has stepped in and won her."

Verne regarded him. "Don't hold back on my account. We both know I am not the better man. But before you appeal to my honor, no, I shall not give her up."

He would, of course, but it did his heart good to pronounce the denial.

"Why not?" Torbridge asked unexpectedly. "No one ever imagined you were hanging out for a wife."

"I wasn't until I met Cecily."

"But I thought you were a family friend who had known her since childhood."

Verne shrugged. "It was not until we met again more recently that I noticed her as more than Alvan's little sister." He met Torbridge's gaze. "It makes no difference, you know. She won't marry you."

"I know," Torbridge said ruefully. "The trouble is, I'm not sure she should marry you either."

"Meaning if I had any honor left, I would release her? Sadly, I don't."

This appeared to flummox Torbridge, until Cecily rescued him with more polite conversation.

AFTER DINNER, SINCE there was a precedent, Verne again invited Cecily and anyone else who cared to accompany them for an evening stroll.

"Don't worry," he murmured so only she could hear. "I will be good."

Her lustrous eyes betrayed a rare hint of uncertainty. Either she did not wish to be reminded of last night, or he had aroused desires he should not. The latter idea set his pulses racing. But tonight, he would not give in to temptation.

"Just ten minutes, Cecily," Lady Barnaby instructed. "The evening feels damp and chilly and I don't want you catching cold."

Clearly no one wished to play gooseberry to a newly engaged pair, and since most of the garden was visible from the drawing room window, there was little to object to in the way of propriety.

"So," Cecily said, wrapping her shawl tighter around her as he opened the side door for her, "you did not fetch more brandy."

"No, you were right. I resorted to a brisk walk and a pint of cold water instead."

She waited until the door was closed behind them, then took a deep breath and looked him in the eyes. "I'm sorry you are in this intolerable position. I think my aunt and I should leave the day after tomorrow for Mooreton Hall. Then you may return to your peace."

"Thank you," he replied without enthusiasm. "Such peace is over-rated. Do you plan to give me my congé by letter? Or shall we quarrel publicly at Alvan's party?"

She shuddered. "I could not do that to Charlotte at her first ball as duchess. I shall write to you first, then to all the friends I have just informed of our engagement."

"I shall cry into my brandy. Very publicly."

"Then I shall take the brandy with me!"

He laughed. "I wouldn't put it past you. My advice would be to wait a week after you reach Mooreton Hall. That way it looks as if Alvan and the rest of your family talked you out of it."

"What an excellent notion," she approved. She appeared to brighten. "And then when you come to the ball, we may gaze at each other broken-heartedly across the room. Without ever speaking, of course."

"Couldn't we speak in stilted, tragic tones?"

"I think I might spoil everything by laughing."

"Hysteria, poor girl," he told an imaginary person beside him. "She'll never get over me, never."

"Not before supper, at any rate," Cecily interpolated.

"It is a pleasant prospect," he observed. "But sadly, I won't really be there."

Flatteringly, Cecily frowned. "You won't? Why not?"

"No point," he said brutally. He should have averted his eyes so he didn't see the sudden hurt in her face. "Cecily—"

He broke off, for a rustling sound in the darkness ahead distracted him. He halted, grasping her arm as she tried to hurry ahead. She glanced up at him in outrage, and he put a finger to his lips, moving softly in front of her.

They were almost at the corner of the house, at the edge of the formal garden where the lights did not reach. Panting breath, the quiet thud of feet in the earth, the rustling of leaves, all shrieked sudden, unexpected danger, for this was no small animal. At least one man lurked ahead.

"Go back to the house," Verne ordered urgently. "Now." He lunged forward just as a grunt and a heavier thud reached him, as though someone had fallen, and then more sudden rustling and a black figure darted away at the edge of the dark. Verne broke into a run to catch him, but his foot caught on something soft, eliciting a groan from the man on the ground.

Verne dropped down beside the fallen man, one fist poised as his other found the man's shoulder. There was wetness.

The man was lying on his front, his head turned to the side. Verne moved, allowing the distant light to penetrate. Two large, pain-wracked eyes stared back at him. *Jerome.*

"Sir, it's me," the wounded man uttered. "Get him."

Every instinct urged him to do just that, to race after the fugitive, and find out what on earth was going on, for there was something very, very wrong here. But he could not leave Jerome.

"Get who?" he asked grimly, gathering the injured man into his arms. "Who did this, and why are you here?"

Jerome let out a sound that was half-groan, half-whimper. His eyes rolled. "Betrayed," he whispered, and his head lolled.

Verne staggered to his feet, carrying Jerome's not inconsiderable weight, and swung toward the house. Which was when he realized Cecily had not obeyed him after all.

She stood exactly where he had left her, staring at Jerome's unconscious face. Verne had no time to waste on feminine vapors. But before he could tell her sternly to go back inside and say nothing to anyone, she spun on her heel and silently led the way back toward the side door, which she held open for him to carry in his burden.

Before he could step inside, another breathless figure trotted into the light from the front of the house. Lord Torbridge. Verne almost groaned.

"Lady Cecily!" Torbridge exclaimed in surprise. "Verne? What's going on?"

"Nothing," Verne said grimly. "This man has had an accident and I don't want my family or Lady Barnaby upset."

He followed Cecily inside, hoping Torbridge would go back the way he'd come.

Without being told, Cecily marched in the direction of the library and went in, holding the door wide. Verne nodded toward the connecting door to his private apartments, which she also opened.

He walked through into the cramped hall and kicked open the door to the small bedchamber. Suddenly, Torbridge was there, too, helping him lower Jerome to the bed. There was nothing he could do about it now. In fact, he was glad of the help to lay down the injured man as gently as possible.

"On his side," Verne ordered. "Cecily, will you bring some light in here?" He hurled the last over his shoulder as he strode out toward his own bedchamber to fetch the water bowl.

When he returned, Cecily had lit a lamp and several candles, and by their glow, Torbridge was easing off Jerome's coat. Which meant he was in danger of discovering exactly what sort of accident had befallen him.

Verne set down the bowl. "Thank you, Torbridge. Much appreciated. Would you and Lady Cecily be so good as to return to the drawing room? Mrs. Longstone is morbidly nervous of every accident at Finmarsh and I would rather she suspects nothing is amiss."

Torbridge straightened. "As you wish. My lady?"

But Cecily sat down on the bed. "I imagine I'm more capable than either of you dealing with injury. I am not afraid of a little blood and I have been brought up to care for the sick and hurt. At the very least, I shall know if he needs a physician."

Verne shrugged, and after an instant's hesitation, Torbridge left the room. The echo of his footsteps in the hall drifted back to them. Cecily tore open the shirt, and in spite of her words, could not hide a gasp of horror at the gory wound.

"We must stop the bleeding," she said shakily. "But I think I can safely say he needs a physician."

"Well, he can't have one tonight," Verne said. "He'll have to make do with us." Opening the cupboard under the window, he took out a box with piles of bandages, a needle, and silk thread.

Cecily cleaned the wound as best she could, while he held the needle in the candle flame.

"Is your stitching neater than mine?" he asked.

Without a word, she cut a length of silk and took the needle from him. While she worked, he raised his eyes from Jerome's wound to her face. It was paler than usual, a frown of concentration and perhaps pity on her brow. He couldn't help admiring her calm efficiency, the steadiness of her hands. She was a woman in a thousand. Unique.

She said, "Someone stabbed him and ran away."

"I know."

Her eyes flickered to him as she reached for the bandages. She made a clean pad and pressed it to the stitched wound. "Who was he? The man who did this?"

"I don't know." He lifted Jerome so that she could wind the bandages around his body. "But I will find out."

She tied the ends of the bandage and stood up. Together, they covered him. Only then did she look at Verne fully. She touched Jerome's hair. "I've seen *him* before. He's the Frenchman you said goodbye to at the Hart the night I met you."

Damnation. He managed to smile. "Perhaps. But he is not French." He emptied the bloody water from the bowl and poured in some clean, indicating she should wash her hands first. "You should return to the drawing room. I need to change."

Her gaze strayed back to Jerome. "Will he live?"

"I hope so. If he does, it will be because of you."

"You don't need to flatter me to keep me quiet," she snapped. "You just need to tell me the truth."

"Later," he said steadily.

She curled her lip, dried her hands, and walked out.

Verne followed her moments later, shrugging off his coat as he went. In his own chamber, he rang for Daniel, then hastily changed his shirt and donned a fresh coat.

Daniel entered, just as he was about to leave.

"There's an injured man in the small chamber," Verne told him. "Keep an eye on him and give him water if he wakes. Keep the other servants away."

"Yes, my lord."

"Oh, and lock all the doors behind me. Stay awake."

"Of course, my lord."

Verne clapped him on the shoulder. "Good man. I'll be back in an hour or so."

He left once more by the side door, hurrying round to the stables, where he saddled Jupiter himself and then rode off at a gallop in the direction of the Hart.

THE INN SEEMED fairly quiet as he handed Jupiter into the sleepy ostler's care and strode in by the front door. From the taproom, Villin caught sight of him and immediately came to meet him, wiping his hands on his apron.

"Evening, my lord. Pleasant surprise. Do you want the private parlor or will you take a mug of ale in the taproom?"

Verne pretended to consider. "Who's in?" he asked, nodding at the taproom door.

"No one you know," Villin replied. "Except the French gent."

Verne frowned. "What French gent?"

"Mr. Renarde," Villin replied in surprise. "Enjoying a mug of ale. Just like an Englishman."

Verne's eyebrows flew up. "Is he, by God? When did he get back?"

"He never left. Not since the night you were all in the parlor."

Thoughtfully, Verne drew his lower lip between his teeth, then strode toward the taproom. "Thanks, Villin. I'll go in and drink some ale with him."

Looking at him, no one would have guessed that Pierre de Renarde had been born a Frenchman. He had none of the slightly desperate elegance, or the appearance of downtrodden bad luck that haunted many of his fellow émigrés. Instead, he looked more like a bank clerk with pretensions above his station. Verne had never quite understood how he had won Isabelle, unless it was his air of elusiveness that almost amounted to mystery. He was a knowledgeable and well-read man, of course, but if he had a sense of humor, he kept it well hidden. There were times when Verne thought unkindly that he had all the character of a not very busy snail.

On the other hand, he had proved helpful in certain endeavors.

He lounged alone in the corner with his ale, obviously deep in thought, though he straightened in apparent surprise when he saw Verne approaching.

"An unexpected pleasure, my lord."

"Likewise," Verne said amiably, dragging over a chair from the next table and sitting opposite him. "What are you still doing here?"

Renarde shrugged, but did not look away. "Why, since my engagement diary is not full, I decided to stay on in the hope of seeing my wife. Who is, I hear, a guest at your house."

"Along with her cousins and other guests. It is all mind-numbingly proper."

"Ah, she has tired of you, too."

Verne regarded him sardonically. "Don't play the wronged husband, Renarde, it doesn't suit you. If you had remained faithful to her a week, things might have been different. But what is sauce for the goose, my friend, is also sauce for the gander. And vice versa. Meanwhile, if you wish to see your wife, call at the house, write her a letter. Don't just sit here watching and listening to passing gossip."

"Yes, my lord," Renarde mocked him.

Verne accepted his ale from Lily Villin with a smile, and turned back to Renarde. "I didn't come to discuss affairs of the heart. Or the pocket."

Renarde lifted his mug. "I didn't think you had."

"Jerome is back," Verne said.

Renarde lowered the mug more slowly. A frown formed between his brows. "Back? But he's only just left."

"He was betrayed, either on the way or when he landed. And he seems to have been pursued, for someone tried to kill him tonight."

"*Mon Dieu*... is he still alive? Where is he?"

"Safe, and alive for now. But the others need to know."

Renarde nodded. "I'll leave at first light. In which case, I should sleep now." He drained his ale and rose to his feet. "I'll bid you good night."

"Good night." Verne watched him walk to the door. In particular, he watched his boots, which were muddy. It could have been old dirt—or new mud from riding full tilt back to the Hart from Finmarsh.

Thoughtfully, Verne finished his ale. He contemplated another, but the urge to return to Finmarsh House was too strong. Jerome could die. If Renarde was not responsible, the culprit could still be waiting and watching.

In fact, as he thought about recent changes in the neighborhood, the arrival of Lord Torbridge was a little too timely. He couldn't quite imagine the mild, proper lord involved in such nefarious doings, but people had surprised him before. And chasing down here uninvited just to see Cecily was not really part of the character he portrayed to the world.

He rose abruptly, throwing a coin on the table before he strode from the taproom. He should never have left her or Jerome.

CHAPTER TEN

I N THE DRAWING room at Finmarsh House, Cecily played around the keys of the pianoforte. She had already sung twice for the company, but she and Torbridge lingered at the piano while the others began a game of whist.

"How is our wounded friend?" Torbridge murmured.

Cecily picked out a key that was very slightly out of tune and pressed it twice. "Alive."

"And our host?"

"I have no idea." She spread both her hands across the keyboard and struck a couple of chords.

"Forgive me," Torbridge said, low. "But did you see what happened?"

Cecily shrugged. "There was some kind of movement. He pushed me behind him, told me to go back to the house. I didn't, of course. He dashed forward. I heard a sort of groan and then he was crouching over the poor man."

"Forgive me, Cecily," Torbridge said again. "But could Verne have done it?"

She stared at him. "Done what?"

"Stabbed our victim."

"No! Someone else ran away into the darkness."

"Did you actually *see* that? Or was it just an impression you had?"

"Both. You're being silly, Torbridge, influenced by foolish gossip and an undeserved reputation. Of course Verne did not stab that man! If he had, why would he carry him into his own home and do his best to save him?"

"Because you were there?"

"Then why try to kill him in the first place?" she demanded.

"Because he might say something no one should hear? Least of all you. I don't know. I'm thinking aloud."

"He is not as black as he is painted, my lord," Cecily said with dignity. "Far from it."

"I know, but he is painted *very* black." Torbridge hesitated. "You don't know him, Cecily. You don't know what he's capable of."

That much was true. When she thought about the sudden flurry of events in the darkness before the wounded man lay at her feet, everything was blurry. She could have conjured up the indistinct figure she'd imagined running away... but she didn't think so. Nor did she see Verne attack the victim. and she didn't believe he had.

"Neither do you," she told Torbridge. "You are accepting his hospitality and yet saying such dreadful things about him."

"Dreadful possibilities," Torbridge corrected. "No more."

She ran her fingers down the keys in an angry swirl. "What do you want me to do? Cry off my engagement already?"

Torbridge sighed. "All I ask is that you are careful, that you do not marry him this week or next."

"There will be no marriage until after we have seen Alvan," she said impatiently. "But that is my decision and Verne's. You have no say in the matter."

"Of course I do not," he said humbly. "I care only for your happiness."

AFTER SHE AND her aunt had retired, Cecily sat on the edge of her bed, deliberately not ringing for Cranston. She counted to one hundred and then slipped out of her chamber and downstairs toward the library.

Her heart thundering, she raised one hand to knock at the library door. Before she could touch it, it flew open, and Daniel appeared, halting his precipitous exit in surprise.

"Daniel," she said, trying to sound as if she had every right to be asking, "how is our injured friend?"

"He's quiet, my lady, but seems peaceful enough."

"Is there anything I can do?"

"No, my lady, not tonight. Maybe speak to his lordship in the morning."

"Very well. Good night, Daniel."

"Good night, my lady."

Well, that was awkward! But at least their patient had not died.

Returning to her chamber, she gazed out of the window for some time, wondering where Verne was and what he was doing. If the attempted murderer still lurked in the vicinity. If Verne was in danger.

But the night was still, and she could make out no one skulking in the darkness. Eventually, she sighed and rang for her maid. While she waited, she began to pull pins from her hair.

A scratch sounded at the door. "Come in," she said impatiently. Cranston didn't usually trouble to knock, but staying at Finmarsh House seemed to have set her on edge. Obviously, the maid did not hear her, for she did not enter. Half-amused, half-annoyed, Cecily went to the door and threw it open.

"Cranston, will you just—oh!"

Verne stood there, looking very much as she had first seen him, with his coat open and his cravat loosened. His lips quirked upward in a spontaneous smile.

"Forgive the interruption," he murmured. "I wanted to be sure you are well."

"I'm quite well," she said, catching nervously at the unpinned sections of her hair.

His gaze followed her movement, drifting back to her face, her lips. She couldn't help licking them, for his scrutiny made them dry. He stood very still, though his gaze drifted lower, and then, determinedly, back to her eyes. His own glittered with heat. Suddenly, she could not breathe.

"Good," he said abruptly. "Then I'll bid you goodnight."

He swung away and strode down the passage. Bemused, Cecily stared after him until she saw Cranston come through the door from the servants' stairs. She went back inside and sat down at her dressing table. She found she was smiling at herself in the glass as she removed the rest of her hair pins.

CECILY WOKE BEFORE it was light. If servants stirred, they were deep in the bowels of the kitchen and she couldn't hear them. And yet, something had woken her. She lay very still, listening. A very faint sob reached her, followed by silence, and then another chilling wail, so muffled it might have been the wind. But she knew it wasn't.

She sat up and lit the bedside candle. It was not in her nature to leave anyone suffering if she could help. On the other hand, she had been caught often enough wandering this house in little more than her nightrail. She really didn't want to run into Verne again. Truly, she didn't.

She rose and donned her dressing gown, with the cloak over everything, then picked up her candle and opened the bedchamber door. She could hear nothing now, but just to be sure, she crept as far as the servants' stairs, then back again. As she made her way toward the upper hall, she thought she heard another cry, but she could not easily tell which direction the sound came from. She carried on to the dining room and drawing room—both empty—and then she saw the door to the other passage stood open. The one that led to the ruined north wing.

The ruin was like a magnet for nighttime grief. With her heart hammering, she made her way toward it. She did not think the sobs were Verne's. His grief had been silent and all the more shocking for it. How could anyone imagine him unfeeling? Of course, they would say it was guilt… and he would probably agree. But Cecily did not believe in his guilt.

The draught reached her through the open door, long before she got to it. As she stepped through the door, her candle blew out and she halted in dismay. But there was another light, a bobbing lantern coming from the front of the ruin. It showed her a hooded figure walking around the edges of the damaged floor, sometimes from beam to beam.

"Shilton?"

The figure stopped, held the lantern higher with hands that trembled. "My lady? I've never told! I'll never tell!"

"Never tell what?" Cecily asked, startled.

There was silence. The wind whipped at Shilton's cap, blowing her skirts against her legs.

"Lady Cecily," the maid said, only just audibly.

Cecily held out one hand. "Come back here, Shilton, where it's safe. Mind your footing."

As the maid obeyed, Cecily saw she was shivering with cold. How long had she been out there?

Cecily took the lantern from her icy hand and led her back into the passage, closing and bolting the door.

"You shouldn't have been in there, my lady," Shilton blurted as Cecily urged her across the landing to the bedchamber passage.

"Neither should you," Cecily scolded. "Why do you keep going?" Detaching her cloak, she swung it around the trembling maid's shoulders.

Wild eyed and astonished, Shilton stared at her. "Her ghost is there."

Cecily didn't need to ask whose ghost she meant. It had to be Marjorie's. She urged the maid into her bedchamber and closed the door before lighting another candle. "Does she speak to you?" Cecily asked, pushing Shilton into the armchair. She knew instinctively that denouncing the existence of ghosts would not work.

Shilton nodded. "Which is why I know *you* shouldn't go there at all."

"Neither of us should," Cecily said tartly. "It's dangerous."

"Not for me. But he likes you. Anyone can see that, and she's noticed. She knows. She won't let that pass."

Presumably, Shilton was talking about Verne and their engagement, which Cecily could hardly explain was false.

"Why would the late Lady Verne be concerned about such things? Not to blow my own trumpet but in most circles, I am considered quite a catch."

"Of course you are, my lady."

Cecily sat on the edge of the bed and regarded her. "You think Lady Verne would not want the current lord to be happy?"

Shilton shook her head. "Not in that way."

Cecily drew in her breath. "Do you imagine she means him ill because he started the fire? But he didn't, Shilton."

"Of course he didn't," Shilton said. "She knows perfectly well he didn't."

"Then what do you imagine she holds against him?" Cecily demanded.

Shilton's brows flew up. "Nothing. Nothing at all. That is why she does not like your presence."

Cecily gazed at her. "She is *jealous* of me?"

A look of fright leapt into Shilton's face. She jumped to her feet. "Don't go thinking ill of him. There's no need." She tugged off the cloak. "Thank you for the warmth, my lady. Promise me you won't go into the north wing again."

"Promise me *you* won't."

"Not unless she calls," Shilton said vaguely and wandered out of the chamber, leaving Cecily to gaze after her in frustration and unease.

EVEN CECILY BAULKED at asking Verne if he had been conducting an illicit love affair with his brother's wife, and she was not prepared to gossip with anyone else. *Besides,* she told herself repeatedly, *it does not matter. Your engagement is false and he has no intention of seeing you again. He will not come to Mooreton Hall.*

Then why did he kiss me?

Because he could. Because men like him kiss easily.

But he cares a little, she pleaded. *Why would he have knocked on my door last night, looked at me in that particular way, if he does not care?*

Because you are his friend's sister. He does not want harm to befall you... or for further attention to be drawn to him, his house, his family, and whatever he gets up to at the inn. This is all about the Hart, not the heart.

Accordingly, at breakfast, she suggested an expedition. "It's such a beautiful morning, why don't we ride to the shore? We can have luncheon at the Hart—or tea if you would rather ride a little later."

The younger people exclaimed with pleasure over this idea, while Verne merely watched Cecily in silence, his expression sardonic.

"Wouldn't you prefer Finsborough?" he said at last, "It's a pretty town, with shops and a beautiful old church. And many more salubrious places to eat. Besides," he added, as though this fact was bound to tip the scales in his favor, "I have business in Finsborough."

"Then you should see to your business while we ride on the beach," Cecily replied at once. She met his gaze with a hint of defiance. "And you may still meet us at the Hart."

His eyes narrowed, but there was amusement as well as irritation there. "Is that a command, my lady?"

"Of course it is!" she said, smiling. "Let us start as we mean to go on."

Henry let out a crack of laughter. "Why, I believe you have met your match, Verne!"

"Indubitably," Verne agreed. "I am, of course, at my lady's disposal. Let us by all means go to the beach. There are some pretty views, for those who care to sketch."

Only as they all left the breakfast room to prepare for the expedition, did he murmur in her ear, "What are you up to, minx? Why are you so determined to go the Hart?"

"To discover what happened to your patient, of course," she replied, low, smiling and nodding to Mrs. Longstone's advice about their departure. "How is he?"

"Alive. Daniel will fetch the doctor from Finsborough. But he was not attacked at the Hart. What is it you hope to discover there?"

The others were heading upstairs to change for riding. Cecily lingered beside him until everyone was gone. "What you were all doing there the night I met you," she said steadily, "and who tried to kill your patient."

Verne raised his black eyebrows. "Those are big questions no one at the Hart will be able to answer. You could try simply asking me."

"I have," she retorted. "You never answer."

He shrugged. "They are not all my secrets to tell, but you may ask me what you wish, and I'll answer what I can."

Cecily inclined her head in a mocking kind of way, for she wasn't sure she believed him and hurried on the staircase while Verne turned right toward his library. After a few steps, she couldn't help turning to watch him over her shoulder. There was no sign of Verne, but at the door of the breakfast room stood Lord Torbridge. She had not noticed he hadn't left with the others. Now, she wondered guiltily what he had overheard and how it might color his opinion of their host.

ALTHOUGH THE EVER-PRESENT Daniel was left behind, a surprising number of male servants accompanied the expedition. Both Lady Barnaby's and Mrs. Longstone's grooms rode with them, as did a couple of large stable lads who, presumably, served Lord Verne.

"Why do we have all these fellows?" Torbridge murmured to Cecily. "It's not as if they're carrying luncheon hampers."

Cecily wondered the same thing, for her aunt had only ordered the presence of one of their grooms. The other said Lord Verne had instructed him to be there, too. Did he expect another attack?

"I almost feel we have a military escort," she told Verne as they walked their horses along the forest path.

"Better safe than sorry," he murmured.

"But what if he returns to the house to finish off your patient?" she asked anxiously. "My aunt and Mrs. Longstone are there alone."

"They are protected, too."

She glanced at him. "I did not know you had so many servants."

"Oh, there are a few I can press into service when the need arises."

"Like those two?" She indicated the burly stable lads whom she couldn't recall ever seeing before.

"Indeed." He met her gaze. "Ask your questions before you burst."

A breath of laughter escaped her. "Why am I never offended by your quite improper remarks?"

"Obviously because I've never been quite improper enough."

"Well, I shan't encourage you," she said hastily. She paused, trying to get her thoughts in order. "Was last night's attack anything to do with your meeting at the Hart when I first met you?"

"I suspect it was."

"Why was he attacked?"

"To silence him, I imagine."

"About what?" she pounced.

"I won't know until he tells me."

"Hmm. What were you all doing at the Hart that night?"

"Talking. Planning."

"Planning what?"

He smiled faintly. "I can't tell you that. The secret is not mine alone."

"You are infuriating." She drew in her breath. "Does it involve France and the war?"

He nodded once.

Her heart sank. "You thought I was a spy," she said, low. "That is why you abducted me."

"The timing misled me. I'm sorry. I thought I needed to keep you away, both from Jerome and whoever you were meant to report to, until he was well away. It was not the finest hour, even of *my* life."

She waved that aside. Somehow, it had become unimportant. "Why were you speaking French? *Is* he French?"

Verne shook his head. "Why do you think that?" he challenged.

She sighed. "I thought at the time you were French spies in England. Now, I think…" She met his gaze. "I think your Jerome is a British spy who was sent to France by you and those other sinister gentlemen at the Hart."

He smiled, a quick spontaneous burst, like sunshine. "I am not at liberty to say and you must not speak of this to anyone."

"Oh, I won't," she assured him. "But what is your role in all of this?"

He wrinkled his nose. "Mainly, I know the smuggler captains who can cross safely between France and England."

"I won't ask how."

"My youth has been misspent. Sailing on smuggling vessels is great fun when you're fifteen and ripe for trouble."

She could imagine him as that wild, reckless youth. In fact, she could quite easily imagine him committing similar follies today. "Why do you think they attacked Jerome?" she asked.

"I don't know," he said with a hint of grimness. "Nor do I know why he came to Finmarsh. He shouldn't have done that."

She understood at once. "He should have gone to the Hart. That is why you don't want us there. You think something is wrong at the inn."

"It's one possibility," he agreed. "The other is that something is wrong at Finmarsh."

Emerging from the wood, he urged his horse into a gallop. As she followed, instinctively racing, euphoria flooded her, not just from the speed of the gallop, but because he was trusting her.

Only later did she wonder what could be wrong at Finmarsh.

WHEN VERNE HAD fallen into his role of passage arranger for the shady, if undeniably brave, spies going into France and French territories, he had never imagined it would touch his family or guests. For one thing, he never had guests. For another, what was left of his family had as little to do with him as possible. Yet here he was, escorting all of them—along with the beautiful heiress masquerading as his betrothed—on an expedition of pleasure when he had no idea of the risks or who presented them. It was not comfortable.

He itched to ride on alone to the Hart to ask some more questions about Pierre de Renarde's stay—and to make sure he had gone. But his other equally unlikely suspect was Lord Torbridge, and despite the guards he'd arranged for the expedition, he could not bring himself to leave Torbridge alone with the others.

Or was he just jealous of the man's older friendship with Cecily?

He brushed that aside with irritation and gritted his teeth, trying not to watch too obviously for signs of attack from within or without their little group. It made him nostalgic for the days of loneliness and nights of solitary drinking when he could hurt no one but himself.

Led by Cecily, they walked on the beach, built castles in the sand, and admired the view which was duly sketched and described. Verne and his men acted as sheepdogs, unobtrusively—he hoped—keeping their little herd together until it was time to ride on to the Hart.

"You're very silent," Cecily observed as they neared the inn. Verne had been leading the way, watching the path ahead, and she had urged her mount alongside his.

"I am a man of few words."

"Pithy and occasionally scathing words," she agreed, "which have been quite absent this last hour. One would almost think you had something else on your mind."

He cast her a lascivious look. "You know I have."

To his delight, she flushed, although her determined little chin came up and she retorted, "You needn't bother with that fustian. No one is close enough to hear or see."

"You are." Even as he said the words, he wondered what the devil he was doing.

It was second nature to flirt with a beautiful woman who understood the rules of the game. But Cecily did not. Misjudging her in the first place is what had led to this mess, and yet some unkind or simply lustful part of him seemed to be still trying to win her. He had kissed her, not once but several times, each sweeter than the last. His courtship was becoming dangerously real, which was neither fair on her, nor good for either of them.

Witty, amusing, and light-hearted, she was also well-read for a lady, thoughtful and intelligent, kind and vital, with rich layers he longed to explore. She was a breath of fresh air of *life* in his bleak existence. Her laughter was pure music, her eyes so deep and so brilliant a man could happily drown in them.

She saw the best in people, in *him*, but he must not allow her to imagine the bad was not still there. Overwhelmingly there. The truly worrying thing about their relationship was not that he had kissed her, but that she had kissed him back.

Not only was she unafraid of him, she *liked* him. And as Alvan's sister, she was bound to be loyal by nature. He had to draw back from this, from her, before it was too late for either of them.

He glanced back over his shoulder. Quite a gap had developed between them and the main party, so he pulled Jupiter to an abrupt halt. Cecily was more right than she knew. For all sorts of reasons, their flirtation should be solely for public consumption.

A sharp crack rent the air, and Jupiter reared, whinnying with fright. At the same time, something whizzed past Verne's ear. He acted on pure instinct. As soon as Jupiter's front hooves landed on the ground, he pushed him forward and seized Cecily's reins, dragging her with him at a gallop.

Her mount, as startled as Jupiter, was happy to bolt.

"To the inn!" Verne yelled for the benefit of those behind as well as Cecily.

Fortunately, there were no hysterics. She seemed to understand the need for speed, to reach shelter before whoever had fired the shot had time to reload.

Verne spared one glance over his shoulder. His men were protecting Jane, one holding the leading rein while they all galloped after him and Cecily. As satisfied as he could be, he searched the surrounding countryside for movement, for any sign of the shooter.

He thought it had come from the trees to the left, and he was sure there was movement there now. Someone running, which was good. Perhaps he no longer had to worry about stray shots hitting Cecily, Jane, or his other guests. But he had to squash ruthlessly the urge to pursue, for there could still be others out there, and he still needed to protect.

They galloped into the inn yard under the slightly bemused stare of Jem the ostler. Verne threw himself out of the saddle and reached up for Cecily.

Wide-eyed but surprisingly calm, she demanded, "Was someone *shooting* at us?"

"At me," Verne said carelessly, swinging her to the ground. "But I've no idea how good his aim is."

"Whose aim?"

Verne resisted the compulsion to hug her close. "That is what I would like to know."

Releasing her, he cast an anxious eye over the others now entering the inn yard. No one was missing. Which meant nothing, of course. Torbridge could have henchmen. So could Henry. Or even Isabelle.

He turned to Jem, inquiring as to the inn's current patrons, but apparently there were no overnight guests—Renarde had indeed gone—and only a few locals lurked in the taproom.

"Let's go in," Verne said, with one last glance toward the trees. It was a hard decision to make—to stay with the rest of the party or to ride out in the hope of catching the shooter...and risk him doubling back. He suspected they would all be safer away from him. And yet, he could not draw attention to the fact someone was trying to kill him. Too many questions would be asked, and the smuggling of spies in and out of France could only work in secrecy.

Chafing at the bit, he entered the inn, joining the others in the private parlor from which he had sent Jerome to France only a week ago.

"What the devil is going on?" Henry demanded. "Why the sudden bolt?"

"There was a shot," Verne said vaguely. "It frightened the horses."

Henry curled his lip. "We all heard it. The horses all started but only you bolted for cover."

Cecily opened her mouth, clearly about to take issue with this contemptuous interpretation, until Verne sat down beside her at the table and warningly pressed his knee into hers. Her eyes flew to his face instead, but he could see no offense or fear in her eyes, only a sweet, startled desire.

Dear God, how do I give her up? Her warmth, her softness made him ache.

To Henry, he said only, "Well, it was fun in the end, making a race of it. Ah, Mrs. Villin," he added as the innkeeper's wife appeared. "A luncheon, if you please, and I expect the ladies would like a room to refresh themselves."

A little later, when the ladies and Jane had gone upstairs, Verne left Henry and Torbridge to traduce him in peace and strolled off to the taproom in search of Villin. But he learned little more than he already knew. Renarde had indeed packed up and left early this morning. He had even payed his bill. No other strangers, let alone foreigners, had stayed at the inn recently, or asked questions about him.

"And Renarde," Verne pursued, accepting a mug of ale from the innkeeper. "Did he write any letters, receive any messages?"

"Not using any of our people," Villin replied. He hesitated. "He did go out late, though, every evening."

"Including last night?"

Villin nodded once. "I don't gossip about my patrons, my lord," he said sternly, "and I wouldn't have mentioned it to anyone but you."

"Did he walk or ride?" Verne demanded impatiently.

"Walked, usually. Last night, he rode."

So, he could have ridden over to Finmarsh, tried to kill Jerome, and returned to the inn before Verne came looking. Only there was little motive. The man hated Bonaparte more than the British did. Verne could swear that was genuine. Was it possible he had only been pursuing, or even spying on, his wife? But if he had been around the grounds of Finmarsh House, wouldn't he have seen or heard something? A man was entitled to walk or ride where he chose. Avoiding the marshes, of course.

In any case, if he'd left for London, he couldn't be responsible for the shot aimed at him just now. Unless he had a henchman. Anyone could have a henchman.

Verne sipped his ale, then gave Villin a curt nod and left the taproom. Cecily was just descending the stairs, alone, reminding him of their first encounter. He halted civilly to wait for her, but to his surprise, she beckoned him away from the taproom and the kitchen. Half-amused, half-wary of his own lust, he sauntered toward her.

"It just struck me," she confided, her voice low. "Everyone always says how respectable the Hart is, and the Villins are indeed most obliging and pleasant people. But it isn't really respectable at all, is it? Alvan and Charlotte found it deserted and someone shot at them, too. All sorts of nefarious meetings must go on here—including yours. Everyone agrees their brandy is smuggled. What if the inn, the Villins themselves, are somehow involved in this?"

Verne stared at her. "You mean they are traitors? Would-be murderers?"

"Is it less likely than what you believe?" she retorted. "What Henry and Torbridge believe?"

"Henry's and Torbridge's beliefs do not weigh with me in the slightest," he snapped. He frowned at her, mulling it over only because it was she who had said it. "No," he said at last.

"Only think about it," she urged, drawing closer. "Do you not feel something…sinister about the house?"

He searched her face. "No. It is I who am sinister, remember?" He offered her his arm, which she took. He liked that simple gesture of trust too much, hated the surge of intense protectiveness that came with her lightest touch. Who would protect her from him?

"Poppycock," she said roundly.

He paused just outside the parlor door, frowning ferociously down at her. "Cecily, I am not a good man," he warned. "Never think it."

"I have never let anyone tell me what to think," she said, "and I am not about to start."

He longed to seize her, show her just how bad he was. He wanted to shield her from all the harms in the world. Before he could discover which yearning was strongest, he reached past her. The fresh yet exotic scent of her hair, her skin, filled him. Her eyes widened, entrancing him. She drew a sharp breath at his looming nearness but did not move away. Dear God, had she any idea… was she *tempting* him?

Deliberately, he lifted the latch and opened the parlor door. She smiled and sailed past him.

For many reasons, it was time to end this.

CHAPTER ELEVEN

"VERNE AND I have decided we should leave the day after tomorrow," Lady Barnaby told Cecily in her bedchamber that evening.

"So soon?" Cecily blurted before she could help it. "That is, I thought we were to increase credibility by staying longer."

"We both believe we have achieved enough. As it is, we give the impression of a sudden but shallow passion which quickly dies when you are apart. Verne may return to his own debauchery, and you may break the engagement with barely a ripple of gossip. We shall go straight to Mooreton Hall and explain all to Alvan."

"Should we do that?" Cecily asked. "I don't want to spoil his friendship with Lord Verne."

"I don't believe you *could* lie to your brother, whether or not you should."

Cecily walked restlessly to the window. "You are probably right," she allowed, though she seemed to have difficulty telling the lies from the truth. Perhaps Aunt Barny was right and it was time to leave. Only it piqued her that Lady Barnaby and Verne had decided on this between them without consulting her. It refuted the closeness she had imagined forming between herself and Verne.

SHE DID NOT see him at breakfast the following morning, and so made the bold move of knocking on the library door. It opened almost immediately and Verne stood there dressed for riding. He didn't look particularly pleased. Something twisted inside her.

"You're going out," she said stupidly.

"Yes, I have estate matters to attend to. If you need anything, speak to Mrs. Longstone or Daniel."

"I merely wished to inquire after Mr. Jerome," she managed.

He stepped out, closing the door behind him. "Walk with me," he said abruptly.

They left the house by the side door and he turned immediately toward the stables. Clearly it was not to be a lovers' stroll for anyone's benefit.

"I've sent Jerome out of harm's way," he told her when they were clear of the house.

"Are you sending us away for the same reason?" she asked, keeping her voice light.

"Yes. Partly. And partly it's time to end our charade. Our lives are complicated enough."

"But surely it's you who are in danger?" she objected. "Not us."

"Yes, but I can't do anything about it while you are here. I want rid of Jane and the Longstones, too."

Rid. However fine the motive, it was brutally said and she felt her face whiten.

"I almost feel I should apologize for putting myself in the way of your abduction," she drawled.

He glanced at her then, frowning.

"Enjoy your day," she said carelessly and walked away toward the garden.

It was luck that she caught sight of Lord Torbridge there, but she seized on the opportunity, her pride forcing her to show Verne she cared nothing for his company above any other's.

Still, she strained to hear his voice to call her back, for his footsteps to hurry after her. Instead, they faded, and before she even reached Torbridge, Verne and Jupiter galloped out of the stable yard and away.

CECILY FOUND IT hard to leave Finmarsh House—which was odd considering how hard she had tried to escape it when she had first arrived. Part of her longed to fly from Verne's coldness, to show him she cared nothing for it or for him, but mostly, she longed to find out the cause, to make things as they were before. She wanted to solve the mysteries of the house and his past, to see him happy.

But however amorous he had been on occasion, she was forced to acknowledge it meant nothing to him. He had told her as much. He and everyone else had warned her, and still she had imagined she must be different, that he cared just a little. She didn't even know why she wanted his affection, and she refused to dwell on her feelings when he so clearly did not. But as she prepared for departure, something hurt within her, some desperate misery threatened to overwhelm her.

And as they stepped outside and everyone else followed to wave them farewell from the steps, she was suddenly terrified that she would never see him again, that whatever assassin had tried to kill Jerome and Verne, would finally succeed.

A smile fixed to her face, she said all that was proper, gaily thanking everyone for a most delightful visit and looking forward to seeing them all at Mooreton Hall next month. Finally, she hugged Jane, whom she doubted she would see again either, before adulthood at least, and turned brightly to Verne himself, offering her hand.

"Goodbye, sir. I hope you will write to me."

"Depend upon it." Bowing over her hand, he kissed it and, still clasping her fingers, walked down the steps with her to hand her into the carriage. Her aunt was already climbing inside with the aid of a footman. "Don't forget to send me my congé," Verne murmured.

"Depend upon it," she said sweetly.

A breath of laughter shook him. "Well, my first and last, perhaps you will break my heart after all."

"If only you had one," she said lightly.

They had arrived at the open carriage door and she began to draw her hand free. Unexpectedly, his fingers tightened, and with no further warning, he pulled her roughly against him and kissed her thoroughly on the mouth.

Everything in her leapt and melted… and yet seethed, for although it was so much what she wanted, she knew he did not mean it. He was playacting the eager lover. And yet, she recognized his own desire as well as her own in that kiss. If she only had time… for what, she could not think.

Bemused as he released her, she let him hand her into the carriage under the disapproving scowl of her aunt. Verne closed the door and blew a sardonic kiss to them both before he stepped back, allowing the horses to move forward.

Cecily waved out of the window, but the figures on the steps and the terrace were merely blurs. Perhaps it was raining. Certainly, her cheeks felt damp.

UNTIL MOORETON HALL loomed into distant view, Cecily didn't realize how much she wanted to be there. It hadn't been her home since she was very young. She couldn't remember living there on a permanent basis, and yet in her only half-understood misery she longed for her ancestral halls, her brothers, and Charlotte, her new sister-in-law, who made everyone happy.

Fortunately, Charlotte's pet terrier, aptly named Spring, was the first to greet her, enabling her to hide her unwanted emotion in laughter. Taking advantage of the open front door as the footmen hurried down to the carriages, Spring bolted outside with his usual enthusiasm and then, with astonished joy, swerved course and hurled himself straight into Cecily's arms.

"Do you know, I would be sorry if you ever taught him to behave?" Cecily said to Charlotte, fending the animal off her face.

Laughing, Charlotte plucked Spring off her. "I'm sorry, Cecily, but at least it wasn't Lady B. he chose to savage. How are you both? Was your journey bearable?"

There was no artifice to Charlotte. No one could doubt the genuineness of her open welcome. Or her happiness. She still glowed with it. Alvan, of course, was more reserved in his greeting, strolling down the steps to kiss their aunt's hand and cheek before embracing Cecily.

"I'm glad you're home," he said simply. "Spring, *sit* or I'll eat your supper."

Cecily laughed. "Now that I would like to see!"

"Well, the threat seems to work," Charlotte observed, watching her dog sit on the step with his tail wagging furiously. "Though he still won't do it for me. Come inside quickly and tell me what you think of the hall."

Cecily walked into what had been the medieval great hall, now the massive, imposing entrance to the current house. There was something new about the familiar place, though she couldn't at first think what it was. Then she saw the old, dark sofas had been recovered in bright fabrics, and the whole space was scattered with mirrors and flowers, giving an overall impression of light and space.

"Why it's beautiful!" Cecily exclaimed, "What a difference you have made with a just a few little changes!"

Someone unwound himself from the sofa at the far end of the room and sauntered toward them.

"Good God, Julius!" Cecily exclaimed. "Have you been sent down from Oxford again?"

"No, no, just left for summer a little early," her brother assured her with a grin. "Couldn't wait to hear how you had snared the sinister baron."

"Odious boy," Lady Barnaby said. "Alvan, can I still send him to his room?"

"As you wish, of course," Alvan replied generously. "But he'll only come out again."

Julius grinned and kissed his aunt's cheek before offering his arm, knowing he could always twist her around his finger.

Having refreshed herself and changed out of her traveling clothes into a more suitable day gown, Cecily hastened to join the others in the drawing room, which had also received the Charlotte-brightening touch without losing its character.

"Aunt B. is resting," she told the others. "Traveling takes it out of her, poor thing, though she will never stay put for long. Oh good, tea already!"

"Don't keep us in suspense, Cecily," Julius urged as Charlotte began to pour the tea. "How did you snare the sinister baron?"

Cecily sighed. "Actually, it was he who snared me," she admitted. "Mistaking me for a hussy, he abducted me from the Hart Inn and then came up with this idea of engagement to save my name."

Charlotte set the teapot down with a bump. Alvan and Julius stared at her.

"Please tell me you're jesting," Alvan uttered.

"No, I'm not," Charlotte said ruefully, "but there's no need to get yourselves in a miff over it, for we have already sorted it out."

"A *miff*!" Alvan exclaimed, jumping to his feet and striding toward the window as if he couldn't be still. "What the devil did he mean by—" He broke off and swung around to face Cecily again. "What were you about that he mistook you for a hussy?"

"What was *I* about?" she demanded, outraged. "Why must the woman always be blamed for a man's iniquity?"

"Oh, trust me, Cecily, the iniquity will not go unpunished," Alvan said chillingly. "I am searching desperately for any small mitigation to the behavior of a man I called my friend."

"Well, he's still your friend," Cecily said crossly. "It was a misunderstanding brought about by... well, by things he was involved in at the Hart. Which are not bad in themselves," she added, "only it all contributed to the general confusion. And as soon as he discovered his mistake—which was as soon as we reached Finmarsh House, I assure you—he sent for a maid and Aunt B. and Mrs. Longstone to be hostess. I own I didn't like the scheme at the time, but it is probably the best we can do. And apart from the act of abduction, he never behaved other than as a perfect gentleman."

Memory of his kisses rose up to confound this assertion, but she successfully ignored it. "I told him you would most likely shoot him, which seemed to intrigue him," she offered.

Alvan, scowling still, sat back down and stared at her. "Is he coming here for the ball?"

"Oh, no," Cecily said carelessly, accepting her tea from the anxious-looking Charlotte. "I'll break it off before then, of course. It will look as though you've talked me out of it."

Alvan's face relaxed into a sardonic smile. "Casting me as the heavy-handed guardian again, Cecy?"

"And myself as a silly, fickle girl," Cecily agreed. "But apparently, both those things are better than being the entirely innocent victim of a man's silly mistake."

"Wicked mistake!" Charlotte corrected, incensed. "Whoever or whatever he imagined you to be, he had no business taking you anywhere against your will!"

"Granted," Cecily agreed, trying to resist the urge to defend him. In the end, she said only, "There were reasons why he was disposed to think as he did, but he would be the first to admit he was entirely in the wrong. You won't cut him, will you, Alex?"

"I will certainly have a word with him first," Alvan replied grimly. His frowning gaze focused on her once more. "His is undoubtedly the blame, but you were up to something, weren't you? He didn't abduct you from your bed."

"Of course not," Cecily said with dignity. "I have already said there were reasons for his mistake and a few of those—though not all!—may be my fault. However, there is nothing you can say that I don't know, or that Aunt B. has not already blasted me with. I beg you will not lecture me or harass me, for it has been a difficult week and I don't wish to talk about it anymore."

Sympathetically, Charlotte passed her a scone. But her brothers were less impressionable.

"Good line of defense, Cecy," Julius remarked, "though I doubt I'd get away with it."

"There's more than one way to skin a cat," Alvan said obscurely. Meaning, Cecily suspected, that he had more subtle means of investigation. Or punishment.

IN FACT, CHARLOTTE was his secret weapon. Since the sun came out during tea, she and Cecily put Spring on his leash and took him for a stroll in the gardens.

"So you have actually met the sinister baron," Charlotte said, with awe.

Cecily cast her a humorous glance. "There was no cleverness on my part to bring it about. You sound envious."

"Oh, I am," Charlotte confessed. "Up to a point. For although you take it so much in your stride, I'm not sure I care to be abducted. Is he very terrifying?"

"Not in the least!" Cecily exclaimed. "In fact, you would like him, Charlie, for he is quite droll. I believe the world has demonized him quite unjustly."

"People do love to spread rumor and gossip," Charlotte agreed. "Probably because their imaginings are so much more fun than reality. Certainly, in our occasional visits home to Audley Park, we avidly swallowed all the rumors we could overhear and made up our own stories about him to boot. I'm almost disappointed to discover he is dull."

Cecily regarded her. "I said droll, not dull."

"Then at least he made you laugh while he abducted you?"

"Not then, though I suppose I should have been more frightened than I actually was. But later, yes, he did make me laugh. He is... not just in the common way."

"Then you will miss him when you break your engagement?"

I miss him now. "In a strange way, I will. You know me, Charlotte. I hate to be bored."

"And are you bored with Lord Torbridge?" Charlotte inquired, pausing to allow Spring to sniff among the shrubs.

"I am never bored with friends."

"Will his affection withstand your engagement, do you think?"

"I hope not," Cecily said. "I shall not marry Torbridge."

Spring lunged at the hedge, dragging Charlotte several steps before she managed to haul him back to the path. "How can something so small be so strong?" she demanded.

"Determination," Cecily replied, amused. "And the element of surprise."

"I shouldn't be surprised by anything he does. Does our sinister baron have anything to do with your decision not to marry Torbridge?"

"Why should you imagine so? Torbridge has never offered for me."

"And Lord Verne... what is he like?"

"You mean you have never even seen him?"

"I may have glimpsed the back of his head once in Finsborough, but I can't be sure. Is he tall and dark?"

"Yes, And somewhat careless in his dress."

"Handsome?"

Cecily thought about it. "Not really. Though one doesn't really notice… he has a distinctive countenance, dramatic, dark…" She smiled. "The first time I saw him, he reminded me of Childe Harold, which thoroughly disgusts him!"

Charlotte smiled. "You like him," she observed.

Cecily watched Spring zig-zag across the path, following his excited little nose. "Is that so surprising? Alvan likes him, too."

"He never abducted Alvan. To my knowledge."

"They have some things in common," Cecily offered. "Loyalty. Adventurous spirit. And they both have very different faces they show the world."

"Fascinating, isn't it?" Charlotte said softly.

Cecily slid a sidelong glance at her. "Did Alvan fascinate you?"

"From the beginning."

Cecily opened her mouth to ask more. But there was no point. She suspected she already knew the truth of her own feelings. It seemed to be falling on her, crushing her, filling her with terrifying power and even more terrifying helplessness.

"I thought so," Charlotte murmured.

Cecily closed her eyes. "What am I to do, Charlotte?"

Charlotte gave her a friendly nudge. "Cheer up. You are engaged to him after all!"

Cecily laughed.

DESPITE HER LAUGHTER, it was true she *was* engaged, in the eyes of the world, at least, until she said otherwise. The knowledge kept coming back to her throughout that day and those which followed. Excitement built with the growing certainty of her love. To have him, to marry him, all she had to do was *not* break the engagement, for he would not be so ungallant as to do the breaking.

Marriage to a reluctant husband was not, of course, appealing. But there had been moments at Finmarsh... she could not pretend he loved her, but he did desire her. It was up to her, surely, to turn that desire into love. If she could.

Oh, I could. Behind the mask he longs for love and trust, and I can give him those things. If only he wants them from me.

Toward the end of her fourth day at Mooreton Hall, she wrote to him.

VERNE DID NOT rejoice in the return of peace to Finmarsh. Torbridge departed for London the same day Cecily left, and the Longstones were gone by luncheon, taking Jane with them. Although glad to see the back of the latter, Verne found the house intrusively quiet. He missed Jane's engaging, childish chatter. But more than that, he had grown too used to walking into a room and seeing Cecily there, to hearing her ready laughter and bright conversation.

Moodily, he stared into the brandy decanter, then pushed it across the desk and sprang to his feet.

Rebuilding the north wing became an urgent project and was under way the day after his guests left. Which took care of the unbearable silence, at least in the hours of daylight, and kept him busy, as did his fruitless inquiries into the traitor who had tried to kill Jerome and himself. But at least there were, so far, no further attempts, and Jerome was still alive.

One day, he visited the isolated farm where he had installed Jerome. When he discovered the spy awake and eating gruel fed to him by the farmer's pretty daughter, he was finally hopeful of discovering the truth.

"Good to see you looking better," he observed. He glanced at the suddenly nervous daughter. "And so comfortable."

"A man must eat," Jerome observed, his voice just a little weak. "But I believe I've had enough for now. Let me speak to his lordship, Jenny."

Relieved, the girl fled, taking her bowl of gruel with her.

Verne pulled a stool up to the bed and sat. "What happened?"

"They were waiting for me. I barely got ashore."

"Not a regular patrol?"

"Oh, no. They knew exactly where and when to expect me. I was on the run for days before I found a friend of Captain Cromarty's to take me back. Only I don't know who to trust back home. Someone at the Hart betrayed us even before I left, so I couldn't go there. I was trying to reach you when someone got me from behind."

"Who was it?" Verne demanded, sitting forward. "Did you see?"

Disappointingly, Jerome shook his head. "No. I head your voice and moved toward it, for I knew by then someone was following me. They knew I was back."

"Then if they tried to kill you, they must fear you know something that threatens them."

Jerome curled his lip ferociously. "I know one of them is a traitor and sent me to be slaughtered."

Verne scowled at his feet for a moment, then raised his eyes to Jerome. "How do you know it wasn't me? Or my men who attacked you on my instruction?"

Jerome gave a grim, crooked smile. "I didn't. My plan was to spy on you and try and find out because my instinct said you were the least likely traitor. But I never got that far. The fact that you looked after me exonerates you."

"Which doesn't bring us much farther forward," Verne said in frustration. "We need to know which vessels sailed to France just before yours… and which came in after. I'll make inquiries, while you get well again." He stood. "Take care, get well, and leave Jenny alone!"

DESPITE THE DISTRACTIONS of his building work and his inconclusive inquiries among the local seamen, he found his thoughts haunted by Cecily. He even dreamed of her. They weren't only lustful dreams. Sometimes, it was just her laughter in the distance. Sometimes, she was merely beside him doing everyday things like reading, eating, or playing the piano.

Every morning when Daniel brought him his post, he waited for his letter of dismissal from her. He thought it would be witty and good natured, nothing he could not leave lying around to be read by the curious and the gossips. He would even enjoy it in a perverse kind of way.

But when the letter did come, he spent a long time merely staring at it. Daniel had brought it with his first morning coffee which he preferred to consume in bed, and it sat by the saucer, seeming somehow larger than the newspaper and the tray beneath.

He curled his lip. *Come, Patrick, take your congé like a man.*

Sighing, he picked up the letter and broke the wafer.

He read it twice to make sure he hadn't missed anything the first time, for it was mostly amusing anecdotes about her journey and reunion with her brothers at Mooreton Hall. She mentioned the havoc caused by the duchess's pet dog in the rose garden and on the dining table, which made his lips twitch. And she asked after him, Jane, and the Longstones, and Shilton, to all of whom she asked to be remembered. She inquired about "the Hart matter" which he took to mean Jerome and the shot which had so nearly hit him. But nowhere did she call off their engagement.

Well, she had barely been gone a week. Another week with her family before being convinced of his total unsuitability would no doubt appear more convincing. Oddly, it seemed like a weight off his shoulders, almost like a stay of execution.

He laughed at himself, raised the coffee cup to his lips, and read her letter for a third time. She did indeed write as she spoke. Her vital character shone out of it with enough force for him to imagine her saying the words. Sitting on the edge of his bed, perhaps... or *in* the bed, beside him, curled into his shoulder after making love with him for hours...

And then her final sentence broke into his dull brain like a hammer.

I shall close now and in case you change your mind, I shall not write again until I hear from you.

For several seconds, he did not breathe.

Was he wrong?

In case he changed his mind about what? Going to the Alvans' ball? No, that made no sense. The only way it made sense was if he were to change his mind about their engagement. She would not write again to break it until she heard from him that he still wished her to.

He exhaled in a rush. Was he an utter coxcomb to even imagine she truly wished to marry him? Why the devil would she? He had insulted her, abducted her, inconvenienced her in the extreme, and come close to ruining her reputation. And truly, in the eyes of the world, being engaged to him was only one step better than being abducted and ravished. He had done her no favors.

Letting the letter slip from his fingers onto the tray, he threw back his head, pressing it into the pillows. Just for an instant, he returned to his earlier vision of her waking in this bed with him. Every morning. Married to him. His companion, his friend, his wife. His lover. He could have that. He could have *her*.

One of Shilton's wails broke into his sweet, impossible dream. This was a house of insanity, of fire and damage. He had taken on a burden he could not lay down whenever it suited him. Dear God, even without that, his character was very little better than his reputation. He could not inflict himself upon any gently bred girl, let alone Cecily, and expect her to share his very well-deserved disgrace.

Oh yes, it was a delightful dream, but not one he could ever indulge in reality. He closed his eyes and let the pain and longing wash through him.

Then he rose and yelled for Daniel to see to Shilton.

He would not write back.

CHAPTER TWELVE

WHILE SHE WAITED anxiously for Verne's reply, Cecily helped Charlotte prepare for the upcoming ball and mulled over the many mysteries surrounding Finmarsh and its master. Most urgent from her point of view, was who had tried to kill him.

One morning, over breakfast, it struck her that the shooting at the Hart was not necessarily related to the attack on Jerome or his involvement in the smuggling of spies into France.

She paused, with her fork half in her mouth, then slowly lowered it back to her plate. What if, like her, Verne was blinded by the French matter? What if the motive for the attempt on his life was far more mundane?

"Alvan," she said abruptly, "who is Lord Verne's heir?"

Alvan didn't lift his gaze from his newspaper. "His cousin, while he has no sons. Why?"

"I'm just curious. Who is his cousin?"

Alvan glanced up at her. "Henry Longstone, of course."

"Henry?" She stared at him. "But surely he is merely the late Lady Verne's brother?"

"Half-brother. He took Longstone's name when his mother married again, but his own father was a Verne, a distant cousin of Arthur and Patrick."

She put her hand to her head. "Why did I not know this?"

"Because it doesn't matter?" Julius suggested. "After all, your engagement is entirely fake."

"Talking of which, have you written yet to tell him so?" Alvan asked with a frown.

Cecily shook her head. "Not yet. Do you know Henry Longstone? What sort of man is he?"

"No idea," Alvan said. "Never met the man to my knowledge. Don't think Verne likes him much, though."

"I know the Longstones," Charlotte interjected. "Mrs. Longstone is a friend of my mother's."

"And Henry?"

"I never had much to do with him. I suspect I was beneath his notice."

"More fool him," Cecily said cynically. "I'm sure you won't be now."

"What, will they come to the ball, even though Verne doesn't?" Charlotte asked in surprise.

"I expect they would prefer it that way."

Lady Barnaby spread butter on her toast, "With Verne out of the way, they probably think Henry has a chance with you. Even with Verne *there*, they were throwing him at you."

"Why?" Cecily wondered. "For my fortune? Or to prevent Verne marrying and producing an heir that would cut Henry out of the title?"

"It needn't be either of those reasons," Charlotte pointed out. "You are ridiculously beautiful and charming."

Cecily blinked. "Thank you. I think."

Julius chortled through his bacon until Lady Barnaby scowled at him. Cecily rose from the table with a murmured excuse and hurried from the breakfast room. She needed to talk to Verne about this discovery... and yet, it was no discovery to him. He must always have been aware of Henry's interest in his life and death, though of course, he would never mention it. None of it made Henry a murderer, or even an attempted murderer. But the anxiety caused Cecily to feel sick.

She wished he would write and tell her all was now well and all perpetrators in the hands of the authorities. She wished he would write and tell her they might as well continue their engagement, that he would come to Mooreton Hall after all.

But he did not write at all. She waited anxiously for every delivery, but nothing came. Her slightly hectic spirits began to droop. She should have known. Lust was not love. He could satisfy it anywhere without the constriction of marriage. She cringed when she thought of what she had written so blatantly. Then she worried she had not been clear enough. She almost wrote again, but pride prevented her. In any case, she knew in her heart he would have understood perfectly. He simply wanted the episode over with. As she should.

Only she didn't. She ached and worried for him. She missed his moody, black brow and his unexpectedly dazzling smile. As hope faded into loss and something very like grief, she waited until the last possible moment.

Only then, five days before the ball, did she write him a cool letter of dismissal.

THE MOON WAS new and the weather stormy when Verne saw Jerome's replacement aboard Captain Cromarty's intrepid smuggling vessel and watched it battle the waves and the wind to avoid the rocks, those both above and below the sea. This time, it was done quietly, with no one but his government contact "S." and himself involved in the planning. Even so, every one of Verne's nerves was on high alert until the ship had safely sailed and he had arrived back at Finmarsh House soaked to the skin.

The house looked much eerier through the driving rain. The swinging lanterns at the front threw flickering light and shadows everywhere, and without the north wing, most of which had been carefully dismantled before rebuilding could take place, the place was lopsided and unfamiliar.

On nights like this, it was easy to believe in damnation and ill-omens. He only hoped it didn't affect the poor devils he'd just waved out to sea.

Daniel materialized at the front door as he always did, and took Jupiter's reins from him, ploughing against the wind toward the stables. Verne ran up the steps and inside. Closing the door behind him, he peeled off his soaked cloak, hurled it over the coat stand, and stomped off to his rooms to change.

He saw the letter at once, propped up on his library desk, and he recognized the writing. He didn't pause, but strode past it, threw open the door to his apartments, and hastened to his bedchamber.

Dried and changed into a comfortable old shirt and breeches and soft shoes, he walked back into the library and warmed his hands before the fire, lit despite the warmer summer weather. Daniel had known he would come back soaked to the skin.

He straightened slowly and went to the cabinet to pour himself a brandy. He'd been a little more abstemious of late, but tonight, he felt he deserved it. Only then did he lift the letter from the desk and sink into the armchair by the fire to read it.

He knew what it would say—more or less exactly what he had expected her last letter to say. He was wrong again.

There was nothing of Cecily in these cold, formal few lines, which ended their engagement because she had realized they did not suit and would be happier apart.

Verne knocked back his brandy in an effort to feel *something*, even the familiar burning of spirits down his throat. But it seemed he was completely numb.

THE FOLLOWING DAY, he remembered the last of his duties in the matter, and sat down to write a letter to the Longstones. At least they would be pleased, and they still had their invitations to the Mooreton House ball, so they had a double win to celebrate.

I am sorry to inform you that Lady Cecily has put an end to our engagement to marry, and that therefore I will not be attending the Duchess of Alvan's ball. Please, therefore, make your own arrangements to travel, although you are still welcome to borrow my coach if you need it.

Yours etc.

Verne

That covered everything. "Daniel!" he yelled, folding and sealing the short missive. "Have this taken over to the Longstones, will you? Tomorrow will do."

"Certainly, sir," Daniel said, picking up the empty decanter with a sniff of disapproval before he accepted the letter from Verne.

"And take your Friday face out of my sight," Verne said irritably.

"Certainly, sir," Daniel said again with the shade of insolence that had first drawn Verne to his odd, all-purpose servant.

Verne watched his retreating back as far as the library door before he said, "By the way, Daniel, you might like to know that I am no longer engaged."

Daniel turned. "I never supposed you were, sir."

Verne smiled sourly. "You're sharp enough to cut yourself."

Daniel ignored that. "Which isn't to say as you shouldn't be," he remarked.

"Shouldn't be what?" Verne asked, frowning.

"Engaged," Daniel said mildly, and left the room.

THE RAIN HAD gone off and the wind dropped by the time Verne left the house the next day to ride to Finsborough, so the men were working away on the north wing, painstakingly placing each usable stone, and replacing those too damaged to be any use. He left them to it.

It was market day in the town, so it was busier than usual. Verne pushed through the crowd, too inured to the stares to pay much attention to anyone. Only as he emerged from the bank with his business completed, did he catch sight of a face he knew. Isabelle de Renarde, fingering a piece of cloth while she looked directly at him.

He nodded curtly and went on his way, but to the dismay of the stall holder, she abandoned her fabric and hurried to intercept him.

"Patrick. What brings you out on a market day?"

"Business," he replied shortly.

"Setting your affairs in order in case you feel the urge to abandon this life?"

He curled his lip. "You have read my letter, but I assure you I am not remotely suicidal."

She searched his face, then took his arm without invitation and walked on. "I believe you are not. However, you are somewhat less happy than you expected to be when you regained your freedom."

"You give Lady Cecily little credit," he observed.

"On the contrary, I give her a great deal."

"For having the sense to dismiss me?"

"For having courage and a sense of fun. However, I doubt she could dismiss you, for I don't believe for a moment you were ever truly engaged."

Verne stared down at her in fascination. "You don't?"

"No, I think she got into a scrape and you discovered the remains of your nobility and helped her out."

She was alarmingly close to the truth, and his eyes must have told her so, for she let out a breath of laughter. "Have no fear, I am the soul of discretion. Nor do I like to see you unhappy."

"I am not remotely unhappy."

"You didn't mean to be, but you are. She crept into your black heart when you weren't looking, and now you can't forget her."

"You have been reading novels again. My heart is the same color as everyone else's, though my memory is less reliable than you imagine."

"Then you have forgotten her?"

"Don't be silly. What do you want, Isabelle?"

"I don't know." She cast him a quick glance. "I think I want you to be happy."

"And you imagine being leg-shackled will do that for me?"

"Maybe," Isabelle said vaguely. She drew in a breath. "I'm going back to Pierre."

He frowned. "Why?"

"There's no pleasing you, is there? Only a few weeks ago, you were advising me to do so."

Before he suspected Pierre's loyalties and motives. "You never listen to me."

"You never listen to me either." Her fingers gripped his arm too hard. "We almost loved each other once, Patrick, and I will always care for you. So, accept my advice. Don't pass up the chance of happiness if it comes your way."

He could have verbally annihilated her. His lips even parted to do so, but the words caught in his throat. He cared for her, too.

"You cannot believe Cecily is my chance of happiness," he got out instead.

"Isn't she? Don't you love her?"

"Of course, I don't," he spat. "I barely know her. And even if she proved to be my happiness, I am most certainly not hers!"

"How do you know?"

He blinked. They had come to the inn where he had tied up Jupiter, and he halted, frowning down at her. "How do I know what?"

"That you are not her happiness? She seemed pretty struck with you to me."

"Did she?" The words came out too quickly, too wistfully, giving him away.

There was hurt in Isabelle's eyes, hurt for the past, but mostly, they smiled. "You know she was. If you want her, Patrick, fight for her."

"Don't be naive, Izzy. What do I have to give her but a soiled name and a sordid past? She deserves better."

"Blah, blah," Isabelle said rudely. "Perhaps she deserves who and what she wants. But who am I to give anyone marital advice? You will do as you wish, of course. I suppose you know my cousin and Henry are rejoicing?"

"I like to spread happiness where I can."

"Keep trying." She withdrew her arm. "Goodbye, my lord. I hope I may see you at Mooreton House."

"Not unless you take your own portrait of me. Goodbye, Izzy. Good luck." He tipped his hat and walked into the inn. He knew he would not go, because the best thing he could do for Cecily—whether or not he loved her, which, of course, he didn't—was to stay away from her.

At the inn, he ordered some pie and sat down in a quiet corner with a mug of ale. After a moment, he took Cecily's dog-eared first letter from his pocket and read it yet again. She had been happy when she'd written this. Hopeful even. Hopeful of *him*, God help her. The contrast with her second note couldn't have been greater. Crushing the letter, he stuffed it back into his coat.

His silence had hurt her. He could only begin to guess at the courage it had taken her to suggest they could keep their engagement. And he hadn't troubled to reply one way or the other. Because he thought it would be easier for her? Or for himself. The second stiff note, sticking to the requirements of their agreement, surely spoke of an unhappy woman holding her pride together because the happiness, the hope of the first letter had gone. Did he not owe her an explanation?

No, he owed her the decency, the courtesy of staying out of her way.

If you want her, Patrick, fight for her. His fingers tightened around the handle of his mug. Fight to ruin her life by tying it irrevocably to his? That was a cruelty even he could not inflict.

CHARLOTTE, DUCHESS OF Alvan, entered her bedchamber to discover her husband, coatless, sprawled across the bed and reading the book she had left there.

He glanced up as she entered and closed the book. "You look worried."

"Our first guests arrive tomorrow, with more the following day in time for the ball."

"I know. You are a wonderful hostess, Charlie. You will cope as you have before."

"I have coped on a much smaller scale!"

"It's just the same, and now we have Cecily and Julius to help."

"What if they only come to discover what a figure of fun you have married?"

He caught her hand and drew her onto the bed beside him. "The world already knows I have married a positive *whirlwind* of fun and beauty and kindness."

She smiled, resting her forehead on his for a moment. "You are biased, I am glad to say."

"No one is looking for faults in you, Charlotte. In fact, the wonder of our marriage will have faded beside the breaking of Cecily's thoroughly inappropriate engagement." A frown tugged at his brow.

"Talking of whom, what ails Cecily? She says she is fine, but she seems quite uncharacteristically listless. Is she ill?"

Charlotte rested her head on her husband's shoulder and sighed. "I think she is unhappy. About the broken engagement."

"Such a challenge would normally make her shine."

"I think," Charlotte said carefully, "that it might be the breaking of it that has made her unhappy."

The duke stared at her, frowning. "You mean she *wanted* to marry him?"

"Oh, not at first. But I daresay the pretense threw them together. She didn't mean to love him, but I'm fairly sure that is what has happened. I think we might have to throw them together again somehow."

Alvan sat up. "No."

Charlotte blinked. "No? Why ever not?"

Alvan dragged his hand through his hair. "Look, I like Verne. He is my oldest friend. You may discount some of the wilder rumors about him, but the truth is, he has earned a good deal of the reputation the world gave him. I will always stand by him, but he is not the man I would choose for my sister."

"Because of his *reputation*?" Charlotte said, surprised and not quite pleased.

"No," Alvan snapped. "Because of the wretched life he would lead her into."

Charlotte searched his face. "You cannot know that. No one is truly unmarriageable, Alex."

His face softened in the way she loved, and she knew he was mulling over what she said. After the ball, she suspected, he would go down to Sussex and visit his old friend.

CHAPTER THIRTEEN

As Cecily had expected, the broken engagement did not keep the Longstones from keeping to their plans. Mother and son arrived at Mooreton Hall the day before the ball, with not only Isabelle de Renarde in their entourage, but also another gentleman who looked vaguely familiar.

"Lady Cecily!" Mrs. Longstone exclaimed after she had been presented to the duke and duchess. "How delightful to see you again. Allow me to introduce Monsieur de Renarde, Isabelle's husband."

Cecily found she was rather pathetically pleased to see these people, most of whom she did not like above half, simply because they were connected to Lord Verne. But she knew a genuine spark of interest in Renarde who seemed an odd husband for the dazzling Isabelle.

Where she would always stand out in a crowd, Renarde seemed almost bland as he smiled and bowed over her hand. Several years older than his wife, he wore little round spectacles and his hair receded slightly at the temples, although in a distinguished kind of way. Although he reminded her a little of a banker or some other city man—which perhaps explained her sense of familiarity—his manners were pleasant and unexceptionable.

As they walked to the blue salon where the first guests were gathered, Henry said quietly, "We were sorry to hear your engagement was ended, although perhaps it is for the best."

"Assuredly it is," Cecily agreed fervently. "I don't know what either of us was thinking!"

"Verne is a difficult man," Henry said, just a little tight-lipped as though he could never sully his lips with the ways in which his lordship was difficult. "To be frank, I would not wish him on any gentle lady, least of all on you."

"Well, we are all in agreement!" Cecily said hastily. "I am glad to see you all here and looking so well. How is Jane?"

After three London seasons, Cecily could sail through social events almost mechanically, which seemed to be what she did for the next two days as more and more people arrived to stay for the ball. If her smile was too bright and her conversation too brittle, it seemed only she was aware of it.

The day after the Longstone's arrival, the day of the ball itself, Lord Torbridge appeared.

"Very glad to see you," he beamed, pressing her hand in a way he meant to be comforting. "Very glad."

He meant it. He really was a most agreeable man, kind and understanding and supportive. What a pity she could never marry him now.

The same day, Charlotte's parents, Lord and Lady Overton, arrived with their lovely younger daughter, Henrietta. They were accompanied by Charlotte's older sister, Lady Dunstan and her husband, who had just returned from their wedding trip. Cecily was particularly glad to see Dunstan at Mooreton Hall, for he and Alvan had not been on speaking terms for a long time.

Lord Dunstan had been Cecily's first love, when she was a mere fifteen summers, but it had been many years since he had stirred her heart. Perhaps there was hope in her fickleness. She would forget Verne soon, too.

Fortunately, for her rather desperate need of distraction, she had offered her "dressing" services to Charlotte. The new duchess had a beautiful new silk ball gown in the shade of dark blue that suited her best. Cecily's art lay in matching the correct jewels and hairstyle, and even the dressers, her own and Charlotte's, were forced to admit she was right to remove all but the family sapphires and diamonds. She looked regal, but with the light touch so suited to her personality, and undeniably beautiful.

Even Alvan seemed dumbstruck when he saw her, taking her hand with pride and love in his eyes. With her new perspective, Cecily realized how lucky they were to have found each other.

For once, she had taken little interest in her own dress for the occasion, doing little more than allowing Cranston and Lady Barnaby to dictate the rose lace gown and the necklace of tiny garnets.

Funnily enough, it was as she descended the staircase to the ball-room—the entrance hall, hung with masses of fresh flowers and extra chandeliers for the occasion—that she finally remembered where she had seen Monsieur de Renarde before.

He was just accepting a glass of wine from the waiter's tray and the gear of her memory clicked into place. The private parlor of the Hart Inn, with Verne and Jerome and others.

"So that's it!" she exclaimed.

"That's what?" demanded Julius, who was with her.

"Nothing," she said hastily. "I've just remembered something I should have realized days ago."

"Well, you've been a bit distracted," Julius observed. "I hope that is over," he added when she glanced at him uncertainly.

She laughed. "Of course, it is. You know I love to dance."

All the same, when she flitted away from Julius, it was to join Isabelle.

"You look ravishing as always," Isabelle told her.

"No more than you, Madame. I am very glad you came, and it is good to meet your husband at last."

"My elusive Pierre," she drawled. "He is not a great man for parties and dancing, but who can resist an invitation from the Alvans?"

"You would be surprised," Cecily said lightly.

"If you mean Verne, he is not entirely devoid of delicacy, you know."

Cecily raised her brows. "Oh no, I wasn't thinking of him at all. Though I trust you left him well."

"I left him last stomping into an inn at Finsborough with a scowl as black as paint."

"Was your husband with you?" Cecily asked, then, wished she had bitten her tongue.

Isabelle's eyes narrowed as they gazed at her. "No. Why do you ask?"

Cecily smiled. "No reason. I just thought I had seen them together once and assumed they were friends."

"Hardly," Isabelle said coolly.

"Excuse me," Cecily said, for the hall was filling up with guests from the house as well as with the arrival of neighbors, and she wanted to make sure Charlotte was coping.

She needn't have worried. Vivacious and gracious, the duchess might have been born to the position. If she was playing a part, she did it very well. So, Cecily allowed herself to be swept off to dance.

Dancing—and the mystery of Monsieur de Renarde—proved to be the perfect antidote to her blues. While she wondered if Renarde was Verne's friend or enemy, and if he was here to pursue Henry or Torbridge or mistakenly assumed Verne would be here, she threw herself into somewhat hectic gaiety, dancing three times in succession before pausing for breath.

It was then, as Lord Torbridge presented her with a glass of champagne, that she realized a sudden surge of low voices filled the void of the silent orchestra. And as she looked up, it seemed even the whispers died away. Everyone was looking at her, or toward the entrance, though she couldn't see over the heads between to discover what or who was causing such a stir.

Then the crowd parted, turning away as though they wished no part of them to touch the man who sauntered along the path they made.

Blood rushed into Cecily's head so fast the world swayed dizzily. But when her eyes refocused, he was still there, coming straight for her. Lord Verne in perfect evening attire, although his cravat, inevitably, was carelessly tied and his hair, while neatly brushed, was still too long to be fashionable. His harsh, yet handsome face bore an expression of sardonic disdain for those around him. But he looked neither right nor left as he approached, seeking only her.

Cecily glanced around wildly, seeking only escape. She was too hemmed in and no one was going to move to spoil this fantastically gossip-worthy encounter. Her champagne shuddered in the glass as she trembled, and just to have something to do, she took a desperate sip.

And then he was there, looming, large, dark and overwhelming, just as she remembered him. A flood of fierce joy hit her like a wave. He had come. *He had come.* She didn't know what it meant, only that he was here and the world suddenly possessed color once more.

Peremptorily, he held out his hand, as though commanding her. Or claiming her. But she wasn't having that, not after the weeks of silence.

Defiantly, she smiled. "Lord Verne. Just in time." And as the orchestra struck up, she placed her glass in his outstretched hand.

Startled, he blinked, and then his eyes filled with laughter, holding hers once more. Her breath caught. Deliberately, he turned the stem in his fingers until the faint moisture left by her own lips faced him, and then he drank from the same place.

Heat flooded her. Carelessly, he thrust the glass into Torbridge's hold and took Cecily's hand in a firm grip. She stared up at him, stiff and still inclined to outrage, still prepared to behave badly.

"Please," he said hoarsely. And at last, she saw the uncertainty, the desperation behind the confidence he portrayed.

Of their own volition, her fingers gripped his and she swallowed hard. She wanted to cry and laugh, hit him and hug him. Instead, she walked with him onto the dance floor and discovered, as if he had planned it, that this was the waltz.

As his arm closed around her, she felt as if she melted into his embrace. She could not breathe, her stomach was in turmoil, and yet it felt like pure happiness.

"Why are you here?" she whispered as he swept her into the dance.

"You invited me. Alvan and the duchess both invited me."

"You never wrote to me, not once."

"I didn't know what to say."

"And now you do?"

He shook his head. "No. But I might know what to *do*."

"What?" she asked, frowning.

"I'll show you later when there are less people watching."

She flushed. "I'm afraid your entrance has ensured *everyone* is watching."

"I know, but Alvan introduced me to his duchess just as the last dance ended and the gossip spread in waves. For myself, I don't actually care, but I'm sorry for your discomfort."

Cecily thought about it. "I don't believe I'm uncomfortable in the slightest."

His eyes devoured her, depriving her of breath. "That's my girl."

From nowhere, laughter bubbled up. "But you are wicked, my lord. That foolishness with my glass will have all the tabbies mewing for weeks."

His smile answered hers. "You shouldn't have given it to me."

"You shouldn't have stared at me so, as though I had no choice but to obey your commands."

His eyebrows flew up. "It wasn't a command. It was a plea. If you had rejected me, if you had sounded remotely like your letter…"

For the first time since he'd stood before her, confusion invaded her happiness. "Why *are* you here, Patrick? What are we *doing*?" There was a catch in her voice that she could not hide and she thought he swore beneath his breath.

"At this moment, we're dancing," he murmured, "and nothing and no one else need concern us. Afterward, we'll talk in private. Only tell me where."

He knew the house. He had been here with Alvan many times when she and Julius were children living with Lady Barnaby.

"The library," she said.

He nodded once and turned her in the dance. His thumb stroked her hand. His arm tightened almost imperceptibly. It was useless to deny this. He made her heart, her whole body, sing. And it was undeniably sweet to dance with him like this, as though isolated from everything but the music, their bodies moving in perfect, synchronized rhythm.

All too soon, it was over. And now, at last, Verne behaved well, bowing to her and placing her hand lightly in his arm. Somehow, he had located Lady Barnaby in the throng, seated beside her matronly friends, and he conducted Cecily there directly.

"Twenty minutes," he breathed, and she nodded once, smiling for the benefit of watchers, as though he had said something amusing.

"How do you do, Lady B?" he said amiably.

Whatever she thought of his presence, Aunt Barny had had time to get over her surprise and realize the best approach. She greeted him with cheerful good nature, allowing him to bow over her hand. "Good evening, Verne. I see we have dragged you away from your building project after all. How does it go?"

"Well, if slowly," he replied. "Though it's wretchedly noisy."

Cecily turned to greet an old friend, and after conversing civilly for a few moments, Verne strolled away. She caught sight of him a few minutes later, bowing to Mrs. Longstone and then chatting with Isabelle de Renarde. From across the room, Monsieur de Renarde regarded them from sleepy, expressionless eyes.

Almost surprised by her own deception, Cecily managed to catch the lace of her gown on a roughened chair leg and tear it. Since this was her own home, it was perfectly natural to run upstairs to have it mended. Only, she did not go to her own chamber but to the library, where she knew she could find a needle and thread. A couple of quick stitches in the lamplight repaired the tiny tear and she was already cutting the thread by the time the door opened.

Hastily, she pushed her skirt back down, just as Verne walked in and kicked the door shut behind him.

"How did you come up?" she asked nervously. "Did anyone see you?"

"I used the door at the back of the hall, and the smaller staircase beyond."

"Oh, good." Laying aside the needle, she rose to meet him, saying in a rush, "I have so many things to tell you. I did not know that Henry is your heir, and although it is a horrid idea, I wondered if you think he might conceivably do you harm for the inheritance? And then, Monsieur de Renarde is here, and I am not quite sure why. I know he was in the Hart that night and so is your friend as well as Isabelle's husband, but I own I cannot warm to him. Do you think—"

"At this moment," Verne interrupted, coming to a halt in front of her, "I find I don't care about any of these people, or even the fate of nations. I want to know about you."

"About me?" She frowned in confusion. "What about me?"

"Can you bear me?" he demanded intensely. "Can you stand my moods and my past? Do you even want to, now that you are free of me?"

"What... I don't know what you mean."

"Your letter. Your first letter, when you said you'd wait to hear from me before delivering my expected congé. What did you want me to say?"

This was unfair, throwing this at her now, making her say, admit what could not be taken back. There would be no pride left. Panic rose up.

"The truth," she got out. "I wanted to know if you still wished to end our engagement."

"We were never engaged," he said brutally. "So, you could not end it."

The blood drained from her face. The world seemed to be shaking again. "I know," she whispered.

He seized her by the shoulders, almost angrily. "It was a lie, a nothing that neither of us meant."

She tried to push him off. "I know that! Patrick, let me—"

He swooped, seizing her mouth in a fierce, hard kiss that left her gasping. "If we do it now, it's different. It means you're mine and I'll never let you go. But you have to want it. You have to want *me*."

She stared up at him, dazed, afraid to hope. "What are you saying?" she whispered. "Are you asking me to marry you? To *really* marry you?"

"You know it all. You know the worst. Will you do it? Will you marry me?"

She licked her dry lips, almost frightened by the emotion burning in his dark, unfathomable eyes. "Do you want me to?"

"God, yes, I want you, but you have to know I'll walk away and leave you alone if I've misunderstood, if it's not what you want. I—"

She swayed against him, stopping his words with her lips. "Then marry me, for I love you," she whispered brokenly into his mouth. "I've always loved you."

He groaned, his arms tightening around her. "No, you haven't, but I'll take it. I'll take you." And then he was kissing her as if he would never stop, bending her backward with the force of his ardor.

She flung her arms around his neck and surrendered, kissing him back with all the pent-up passion of the last weeks, of her whole life which all seemed to have been leading to this one moment of perfect joy.

Chapter Fourteen

O NE OF THE most difficult things Verne had ever attempted was to tear himself away from Cecily Moore when she was trembling and eager in his arms. Her heady scent, her sweet softness winding around him, and most of all, the unexpected force of her awakening passion, almost undid him.

With fierce triumph, he understood that she was his in any way that mattered. He could take her now, on the sofa or the inviting rug before the hearth. He could teach her a few of the sensual delights he longed for, achieve the pleasure he craved, the joyous release of his clamoring lust. *Oh, God, yes.*

But he could not do that to her. She must not be tainted by the habits of his past, however little resemblance there was between his feelings for her and those for the previous women in his life. He was not a good man, but he had promised himself that if she only accepted him, he would treat her only with goodness.

With a deep groan, he wrenched his mouth free of hers, detaching himself from the warm body that seemed to be glued to him. Somehow, he held her by the shoulders at arm's length while he tried to recover his composure, to regain control of the rampant desire that would still take her…

He stared down at her warm, clouded eyes, her swollen, passionate lips curved into a tremulous smile. A siren's smile.

He swallowed. "We will do this properly," he said hoarsely. "With no possibility that anyone can force us to it. It has to be our choice."

"It is," she whispered.

He closed his eyes. "I mean our marriage. You are not yet twenty-one. We need Alvan's permission, and I am sure you would prefer his blessing. Both will be hard enough to come by, even if I refrain from ravishing you."

"Have you not ravished me already?" she asked huskily.

A breath of laughter shook him. "I haven't even begun." Deliberately, he dropped his hands from her shoulders and took another step back. "I had many things to say to you, apologies and explanations, but I think they must wait. For if I stay any longer, I still won't say them. I'm going to find Alvan, while you... should call your maid to re-pin your hair."

"And then?"

"I shall see you downstairs at the ball. If Alvan doesn't throw me out. Or shoot me as you foretold so long ago."

She started toward him and he grasped her hand to prevent himself seizing the rest of her. He pressed a quick, fervent kiss into her palm before he released her and strode from the room.

He returned by the same dimly lit staircase he had climbed so recently, meaning to slip back into the ballroom. However, the side door at the foot of the stairs caught his attention, for the bolts had been drawn back. Someone was taking the air—an attractive proposition to Verne in his current state—and knowing his host as he did, he suspected the duke himself.

Verne opened the door and slipped out into the wide courtyard. Closing the door behind him, he raised his face to the breeze and breathed deeply.

She wanted him. She *loved* him, God help her. No wonder he was smiling up at the starry sky. He had a chance of happiness, of making her happy. *Please God, if you still have anything to do with me, don't let me make a mess of this...*

He began to walk, striding around the courtyard toward the archway that led to the front of the huge house. Music and the jollity of laughter and chatter drifted from within.

The silhouette of a man stood out in the darkness, to the right of the main drive where he was untouched by the lights blazing on the terrace and at the main door. He appeared to stand quite still, gazing outward over the flat, glistening fens in the distance. He was tall and lean, the right shape to be Alvan himself, so Verne walked toward him.

"Alvan?" he said into the darkness.

The figure turned. "Verne. I thought it would be you."

"I was *sure* it was you, escaping your own party."

"Only for a few minutes."

Verne stood beside him. "You gave permission for Cecily's engagement to me, but you didn't believe it, did you?"

"Not for a moment. She is far too wise to fall in love in a day, and I am well aware you couldn't have known each other any longer."

"Did she tell you what really happened?"

"Some of it."

"Then you know I deserve to be shot."

Alvan appeared to consider. "Punched," he corrected. "Quite hard. I know she is no angel and was clearly where she shouldn't have been. Beyond that... I suppose I expected you to have more sense if not more decency."

"You know what I am. What I've done."

"And haven't done." Alvan's head turned toward him. "You've come for her, haven't you?"

"She wants to marry me."

"I know."

At last, Verne turned to stare at him. He could make out his features now, if not his expression. "You don't like it."

"You're not who I would have chosen for her," Alvan said frankly. "You have too much... *baggage*."

Verne drew in his breath. "I can't undo the past. But I can make the future better. Besides, with her, the baggage is somehow lighter."

Alvan looked downward, as though peering at his feet. "Charlotte reminded me I have baggage of my own."

"I know."

"It is lighter now," Alvan murmured. "Much lighter."

"I would know her better, your duchess."

"I hope you will." Alvan drew a deep breath. "If I refused, what would you do?"

"Wait until her birthday and marry her anyway. It's what she wants. For some reason. *I'm* who she wants."

"And if you marry too quickly and she changes her mind? Or you do? The deed is done."

"As yours is," Verne pointed out.

A twitch of Alvan's head acknowledged it. His had not been a long courtship either. "Damn it, Verne, you're my friend," the duke burst out. "I want you both to be happy."

"Then give us this chance."

ALVAN MADE THE announcement toward the end of supper, proposing a toast to the happy couple who sat next to him. There was little the duke's guests could do except stand and drink the toast—which compelled them, Verne thought sardonically, to future civility if nothing else.

There was pleasure in her smiling presence at his side, in the world knowing she was his after all. His triumph somehow gave him hope, where there had been none for so long. And then his gaze fell on Henry, staring across the room at him as he retook his seat. His lips were tight with disappointment or anger, or both.

On one side of him, Mrs. Longstone smiled as she always did. On the other, Isabelle dashed the back of one hand over her outwardly happy face. And yet Pierre sat beside her. He hoped she could find happiness with him, with whatever had drawn her to him in the first place. He hoped Pierre was worthy of her, but as usual, there was nothing in his expression to give away his true thoughts. Pierre had no reason to care about Verne's marriage.

For Cecily's sake, Verne minded his manners, even set out to entertain the lady on his other side at supper and, afterward, to make friends with the duchess whom he found rather delightful. He could easily see why Alvan had fallen for her. What baffled him was how anyone had ever come to describe her as ill-favored.

To Verne, the whole evening had taken on a strange sense of unreality. Every inch of him was aware of Cecily, whether at his side or across the room, and yet they barely had the chance to say anything meaningful to each other. Although he intercepted many looks of awe, curiosity, disapproval, and plain fear—which amused him most of all— no one cut him. Mind you, he did not make the mistake of asking their daughters to dance with him. Apart from Cecily, he danced only with the duchess.

"Oh!" her grace exclaimed suddenly. "We do not have a room made up for you. I'm afraid it will not be one of the better—"

"There's no call to worry," Verne interrupted. "I'm putting up at the Alvan Arms in the village."

She blinked. "But why?"

He gave her a crooked smile. "I wasn't quite sure I would be welcome."

"By Cecily? Or my husband?"

"Both," he said frankly.

"Well, we could still send for your belongings."

"Thank you, but I'll be better at the inn." Well away from temptation. "But if you permit, I'll join you tomorrow, not too early in the day!"

"Most of our guests will be gone by early afternoon, but you are welcome at any time. We—" She broke off, a frown twitching on her brow. "Why do you look at me like that?"

"No reason. I did not expect such a gracious welcome."

"Well, you have one. So long as you treat Cecily as you should."

"You are a fierce friend," he said with approval.

The duchess smiled. "So is she."

The gentleness of the Alvans' warnings might have surprised him, though their anxieties did not. After all, if he'd had a sister, he would not have given her to the likes of him. It was interesting seeing himself through other eyes for a change, rather than alternatively railing against and cultivating the shocking reputation that surrounded him.

His dance with the duchess was the last of the ball. The orchestra began to pack up. Carriages were summoned to take guests back to their own homes or that of friends with whom they were staying. House guests began to yawn and drift away to bed, or join in a nightcap with the duke.

There was to be no private parting for Verne and Cecily. Instead, under many pairs of watchful eyes, he bowed over her hand and kissed it. "I shall see you tomorrow," he promised.

And she smiled with such open pleasure that his heart seemed to burst.

Had he ever felt like this before? Even at fifteen when he'd fallen in love with his Latin teacher's flirtatious daughter? No, this was unique. And terrifying, but he would not change it for the world.

Since the stable staff were all bound to be run off their feet, he simply walked round there, squeezed in among the chaos, and saddled Jupiter himself.

It was not a long ride by road back to the Alvan Arms, and the moon supplied a decent light without him having to resort to the lantern. Nor was he in a great hurry. A coach passed him at full tilt, almost running him off the road, but he only waved at it.

"I'm happy," he said aloud and laughed. "Happy and imbecilic."

It was true, as proved only minutes later when someone suddenly leapt out of the trees, screaming and waving his arms. It happened so quickly, there was no time to properly see the man. In the dark, he only had an impression of a bulky scarf shape muffling half his face and a large hat hiding the rest.

Jupiter reared, whinnying in fright. Verne, less than half as aware as he should have been, considering the company at Mooreton Hall, was taken by surprise and fell from the saddle, landing heavily in the road. Before he could recover his breath, something—someone— landed on top of him. Metal glinted in the moonlight, rousing him at last to the true danger.

He bucked, which at least upset the balance of his attacker, enabling Verne to protect himself with one hand and seize his assailant's wrist with the other. The man wrenched his wrist free, but Verne dealt him a mighty buffet that knocked him aside, and leapt to his feet.

While his attacker scrambled to his, the hat still clinging to his head, Verne glanced around for the vanished Jupiter. Putting two fingers in his mouth, he gave a piercing whistle and closed with his enemy.

Dodging a slightly wild punch, he got in one of his own that connected before his attacker fell back. Jupiter's whinny and galloping hooves had distracted him, or, rather, frightened him, for he suddenly turned tail and ran, as though he imagined it was Verne's reinforcements.

Instinctively, Verne threw himself on the returning Jupiter's back and charged after his assailant, but almost immediately pulled the horse to a halt. In the darkness of the forest he would not risk Jupiter on terrain he didn't know. Besides, he could hear the muffled neighing of horses in the distance. He could ride straight into a trap.

Turning Jupiter's head, he rode on toward the inn, his senses rather more alert than they had been before the attack. Which could have been a local robber or a lunatic, though he doubted it.

Frustratingly, he'd had no real glimpse of his assailant's face. He just hoped he had left a mark on him that would be visible when he visited the hall tomorrow. Perhaps, he would go earlier than planned.

CECILY SAT BY her bedchamber window, smiling up at the stars, when a scratch at the door heralded the arrival of her sister-in-law.

"Cecily? I saw the light under your door. Are you still...? There you are." Charlotte blew out her candle and came toward her. "What are you doing?"

"Nothing," Cecily said. "I'm too excited to sleep. Besides, I'm afraid if I do, I'll wake in the morning to discover tonight was a dream."

Charlotte sat on the window seat beside her. "He obsesses you."

Cecily nodded without shame. "Was it like that for you, too? With Alex?"

Charlotte flushed slightly. "It still is, if you want the truth. If you love him, if he loves you, everything intensifies with marriage."

"It's a little bit frightening, isn't it?"

Charlotte gazed at her. "You don't look frightened. You look like the cat with the cream."

Cecily laughed and hugged her. "I am. I never thought he would come. I never thought he loved me."

Charlotte returned the embrace and released her. "He is a troubled man," she warned lightly.

"I know. But I think I understand him... partially, at least. I can help him banish his ghosts. Finmarsh is full of them."

Charlotte hesitated until Cecily said bluntly, "You want to ask me about the fire and if that does not trouble me."

"Doesn't it?"

Cecily shook her head. "Not in the way you mean. I don't believe the truth of the tragedy has ever been told, or even fully known. But I know Verne was not responsible. He tried to save them." She gave herself a little shake. "I don't want to think about that. I want to think about the future. And remember dancing..." And kissing. God help her, she had never imagined kisses like those, intimate caresses like those. Her body flushed at the intensifying memory and she could not help touching her lips. They still seemed to tingle. She smiled again.

"I see you are a hopeless case," Charlotte observed, rising to her feet. "I shall leave you to your dreams, but please don't forget to go to bed or you will sleep through his visit tomorrow."

Cecily laughed. "Worse, I shall have huge bags under my eyes and look like death and he will try to wriggle out of it."

"I doubt that," Charlotte said, smiling back. "It took a lot for him to come here."

"I know." Cecily's eyes strayed back to the window but at last another thought penetrated her fog of selfish happiness and she turned back to her sister-in-law. "Charlotte? You were the perfect hostess tonight. You managed it all wonderfully."

Charlotte cast her a fleeting smile. "Thank you," she said fervently, and went out.

ALTHOUGH VERNE WASN'T expected until the afternoon, he took everyone by surprise by sauntering into the breakfast room before midday. As usual, he looked dark and windswept and inherently disreputable, and Cecily's heart gave a delicious leap that deprived her of breath.

His gaze swept around the room, alighting first on her with a quick smile that managed to be somehow both tender and predatory. But she was sure he had taken everyone in before he bowed over Charlotte's hand and apologized for interrupting breakfast.

"Not at all," Charlotte insisted. "Please join us. We are having a long and lazy breakfast as you see, after our night of dissipation! Do help yourself from the sideboard."

"No, no, I thank you. I breakfasted at the inn. Though I'll happily accept a cup of coffee."

Lord Dunstan, who was seated beside Cecily, stood up. "Sit here, Verne. I have eaten my fill and must be on my way."

"Dunstan," Verne said with apparently surprised pleasure. He even thrust out his hand, which Dunstan shook with unexpected cordiality. They were both friends of Alvan, so it was not surprising they should know each other. "How come I didn't see you last night?"

"I saw *you*. But I believe your eyes, like your mind, were elsewhere!"

To Cecily, it seemed bizarrely symbolic to have her first suitor giving his place to her new betrothed. Perhaps it was all part of Dunstan's apology for his youthful folly which had led to years of estrangement from Alvan and herself. At any rate, Verne's large figure settling beside her seemed to bring a blast of fresh air from outdoors, and a powerful physical awareness. She could barely smile and wish him a civil good morning.

But then, Verne also seemed quite distracted. He said little after his arrival, merely drank coffee and gazed at his fellow guests.

"I do not see Henry," he murmured at last.

"The Longstones left early for Sussex. I could only wave to them from my bedchamber window."

He spared her a quick, wicked smile. "Another bedchamber window," he observed. "Did the Renardees go with them?"

"No, but they have not yet come down. Why?"

"No reason." His gaze now was on the apparently oblivious Torbridge.

Alvan's hand dropped on Verne's shoulder. "I have to bid farewell to my guests," he murmured. "But we can talk afterward, in the library."

ENJOYING A GENTLE stroll with his betrothed had its own powerful charms. But Verne made a point of hanging around either the entrance hall, which was being denuded of its now drooping flowers and greenery, or the front terrace so he could observe the departing guests.

He was irritated to have missed Henry, but in truth, his distant cousin was unlikely to have attacked him in person anyway. He would have hired some bully to do it for him. Of course, the same could be said of Torbridge, whose pristine hands and face he had already observed at breakfast, or Pierre de Renarde.

With Cecily, he walked across the terrace to bid the Renardees farewell before they climbed into their slightly shabby carriage.

"We're going to London," Isabelle said gaily. "The ball has given us a taste for dancing!"

"It has given my wife a taste for dancing," Renarde said dryly. "As you may have observed, I still possess two left feet. Goodbye, Lady Cecily. My lord."

Verne casually thrust out his hand, but Renarde did not remove his glove to shake it. Nor was there any visible mark on his face.

Isabelle was embracing Cecily. "You did not heed my warnings," she murmured.

"No," Cecily agreed with a faint smile. "I did not."

"I wish you both very happy."

"Thank you," Cecily said, her smile more genuine now, and then Verne took Isabelle's hand to help her into the carriage before her husband.

They stepped back to join the duke and duchess, and let the horses spring forward. Then he and Cecily walked back into the house.

In the hallway, they met the Overtons, Charlotte's parents, and one of their beautiful daughters, who were about to depart. Cecily appeared to have a fondness for them, so Verne stood civilly aside, However, Lord Overton followed him.

"Sorry we haven't met since I came home from abroad," Overton said pleasantly. "Had a few things on my mind, you know! But if you don't object, I'll call on you very soon about a few local matters."

"I look forward to it," Verne said. Betrothal to Cecily Moore seemed to have bestowed some respectability upon him, although not so much that he was invited to Audley Park where there was still at least one unmarried daughter.

As Overton collected his wife and daughter, urging them toward the door, Verne found himself face to face with Lord Torbridge.

This close, he looked no more damaged by fists or falls than he had at breakfast.

"So, your engagement resumes," Torbridge observed.

"As you say. I shall take better care of it this time." Casually, he offered his hand.

Torbridge looked at it for so long it seemed he meant to offend, and then he took it, raising his eyes to Verne's. And suddenly, they weren't remotely prim or amiable, but hard and distinctly menacing.

"You had better be kind to her," Torbridge said softly. "Because if you break her heart, I will most assuredly break you." He dropped Verne's hand and strode away.

Verne blinked after him. *Well. Is that a glimpse of the real Torbridge? Or a momentary aberration caused by thwarted love?*

WITH THE LAST of the guests gone, Verne followed Alvan into his magnificent library.

"Tell me," he said, as Alvan seized the decanter and poured two glasses of brandy, "do you have any violent madmen in these parts who might be willing to attack your guests?"

Startled, Alvan met his gaze. "Do you wish to engage someone for the position?"

"Of course not, idiot. I'm just trying to get to the bottom of an incident last night. It is probably related to my own doings, but I need to rule out random attacks if I can."

A frown tugged at Alvan's brow as he gave him one of the glasses. "I can't imagine any of my people behaving in such a way, and certainly not to my guests. What happened?"

Verne told him succinctly.

"It sounds like someone with a grudge against you," Alvan said. "Which may not narrow down your list! Longstone? Torbridge? The husband of some woman you have debauched?"

"I don't recall debauching any women in Lincolnshire," Verne retorted. "And ladies of quality have been rather above my touch recently."

"Apart from my sister."

"I have not debauched your sister. And I trust your accusation does not mean that it was you who flew at me screaming last night."

"You would not have got off so lightly," Alvan retorted. He waved one hand at Verne's skinned knuckles. "All the same, I don't like this. Are you in trouble, Verne?"

Verne shrugged. "I'm not sure." But he'd been glad to get Cecily away from him at Finmarsh, in case whatever threatened him touched her instead. The same applied here. He should go... only, if it was a family grudge, if someone—Henry or his half-insane mother—wanted to be sure he never produced an heir, might they not attack Cecily now as an easier target than himself?

His blood ran cold. His being here, which had brought about such a wonderful result, could trigger a greater tragedy. The engagement was confirmed before her family and was now much more of a threat to Henry's position.

The door opened and Cecily came in with her aunt and Charlotte.

"If you're discussing weddings," Cecily said firmly, "then I should be here."

"I planned to leave the contracts largely to our respective men of business," Alvan said. "But if you wish to be involved in such dull stuff, then by all means, let us begin."

"You know perfectly well she meant the wedding, not the marriage contracts," Charlotte scolded. "How soon do you wish to be married?"

"Tomorrow," Verne said promptly, and Cecily blushed adorably.

"It can't be tomorrow," Lady Barnaby said. "We'll need a month to have the banns read and Cecily's trousseau ordered."

"Actually, we only need a day," Charlotte argued. And as everyone gazed at her in surprise, she added hastily, "Not that I'm suggesting you marry quite so quickly! But the banns have been read twice already, remember? To reinforce the truth of your engagement. We cancelled them for tomorrow, but a message to the vicar will have them read a third time, and then you *could* be married on Monday."

Verne stared at her. The day after tomorrow, he would have her safe where he could protect her. Leaving her here, with Alvan only half-understanding, surely would not be right.

"No," Alvan said firmly.

"No," Charlotte agreed.

"No, indeed," Verne said regretfully. "It smacks of unnecessary speed and will only cause scandal."

"Around you, my lord?" Cecily mocked. "Surely not."

Verne cast her a quick grin. "I have no objections to a week on Monday. Have you?"

"So soon…" She met his gaze, searching his eyes with a hint of wildness in her own. Then her expression calmed, and she smiled. "So soon," she repeated. "A week on Monday sounds perfect to me."

CHAPTER FIFTEEN

T HEY WERE MARRIED quietly in the tiny chapel that was part of Mooreton House. Mr. Norris, the local vicar, officiated. Alvan gave the bride away while Julius stood as groomsman, and Charlotte as Cecily's matron of honor. Mrs. Neville and the other servants cheered as she walked down the short aisle on her husband's arm and threw handfuls of grain over them.

Laughing, Cecily threw some back and passed on, leading the way to the dining room where the wedding breakfast was set out.

"Whatever am I to do with myself now that both my birds have flown their nest?" Lady Barnaby mourned. She had wept copiously throughout the short marriage service, although she denied it.

"Relax," Julius advised, "and enjoy your freedom. Besides, I'll need somewhere to go whenever they send me down from Oxford in disgrace."

"I shall be glad to accommodate you," Lady Barnaby retorted. "I hope you will be just as glad to listen to my homilies on the benefits of study and moderate behavior."

Julius grinned. "Perhaps I'll go to Verne's instead."

"You'll be welcome," Verne said, "We could use extra help re-building the north wing of the house."

"I'm your man," Julius declared.

"He was joking," Cecily pointed out "But I hope you will all come and stay—after we're home, of course!"

They were going to Scotland for their wedding trip, staying at one of Alvan's lesser houses.

"Are you sure you want to do this?" Cecily had asked when Verne had accepted the offer. "I know you have things to attend to at Finmarsh—the building, and this other business…"

"No, I would not miss this. Three weeks alone with you away from all the troubles of real life…"

They set off in the afternoon in the traveling coach which Verne had had sent up from Finmarsh along with other things he needed for his long stay, and Daniel, of course. Cranston and Daniel travelled in the coach behind, with the baggage.

They expected to make good time, since Alvan had made his horses available for changes on the road north, but in truth, such things did not matter to Cecily. She sat close beside the man she loved beyond all reason, his warmth seeping into her shoulder and thigh, their joined hands resting half on his leg, half on hers. The intimacy was unimaginably sweet and they talked of many things from the changing scenery to politics and the war—Bonaparte had finally led his troops into Russia—to music and books and people they both knew or wished to know.

They refreshed themselves at the various inns where the horses were changed and moved happily on. In York, they paused so that Cecily could show him the beauties of the minster which Verne had never troubled to visit before, and then travelled through the town to the posting inn just beyond, where they were to spend the night.

The delicious little tingle of excitement which had been present in Cecily all day, deepened as they entered the busy establishment. The innkeeper welcomed them and had his maid show Cecily to the bedchamber she would share with her husband. The heavily-curtained bed seemed to loom much too large, and she hastily averted her eyes while her baggage was brought in.

Cranston helped her wash and change into her favorite evening gown of the season, a turquoise muslin with embroidered silk ribbons banding the high waist and hem, which was lifted at the front to reveal the paler blue petticoat beneath. With it, she wore the turquoise earrings which were Verne's wedding gift. After a brief hesitation, she decided to wear no other jewels, save the gold and diamond wedding ring that felt new and unfamiliar on her finger.

With her hair appropriately dressed, she followed Cranston across the room to the inner door, which opened into their private parlor, where dinner was already set out.

Cranston stepped back and closed the door behind her.

Verne rose from the table, where he had been lounging with a glass of wine. "I thought we could serve ourselves, so I sent the servants away."

"What a good idea," she said in relief. It would have been too uncomfortable to have other people in the room, knowing this was her wedding night.

Verne poured her a glass of wine and brought it to her. As if he couldn't help it, he bent and kissed her lips before he released the glass. The deepening tingle in her belly spread lower.

"To us," he said softly, touching his glass to hers.

She inclined her head and raised the glass to her lips. As he turned back to the table, she took another, sizeable mouthful of wine to steady her nerves.

Verne served them soup from the terrine on the table, and they settled down to eat. At some point before the meat course, she relaxed back into his company. This was no different to the time she had spent with him at Mooreton Hall, or in the carriage this afternoon. This was Verne, her fascinating friend.

Her friend whose gaze grew increasingly heated and predatory and left her less and less. A strange glow, almost like a flame, burned in his darkened eyes, at once thrilling and frightening her. As night drew in and he rose to light the candles, his movements seemed deliberate and controlled. And yet, as he paused behind her, his breath came too fast. His lips closed on the soft, sensitive skin of her nape and she gasped. Suddenly, she ached to be in his arms, to take this excitement as far as it would go.

But he moved away, returning to his seat. "A little more wine?" he offered.

She shook her head and he half-filled his own glass. He was being very moderate by the standards she had witnessed at Finmarsh. She raised her gaze to his face, so full of shadowy hollows in the candle light. Darkness and brilliance, she mused, like the man himself. Some of that darkness would always be there, but she longed to banish the worst of it, to let him shine.

But she was growing fanciful, when there was nothing remotely fanciful about the man now holding her gaze. She forgot to breathe.

"Do you want to spend the night with me, Cecily?" he asked softly. "In my arms?"

Her whole body flushed. "Of course," she managed. "I am your wife."

His mouth curved into a rueful little smile. "Is there no other reason? Beyond what law and custom dictate, you must want to please me."

"That is the reason I became your wife in the first place." She lifted her chin. "I love you."

Something leapt in his eyes. His fingers slid away from the stem of his glass, but otherwise, he did not move. "I am not an easy man to love. Certainly not for very long. I suppose that is why I rushed you into this before you could change your mind! But I can give you this time, if you wish it. I can wait for you, until you are comfortable."

"I don't want to be comfortable," she blurted. "I want to be with you."

Laughter sprang into his eyes, along with a massive surge of lust. "I shall try to deserve your trust," he murmured. He raised the glass to his lips once more, and she wondered if his hand was quite steady. Then he set the remains of the wine down and rose with quiet deliberation.

Her heart leapt and seemed to dive into her stomach as he walked around the table and held out his hand. It didn't shake after all. She placed her own into it, felt his fingers curl around hers. She stood and walked with him to the door of the bedchamber.

Cranston had gone, leaving a lamp burning on the table. The bed-covers had been turned back welcomingly. Verne left her, lighting the other candles scattered about the room.

"More light?" she asked hesitantly. "I thought you would put them out."

"Oh no." He dropped the spent spill in the hearth and came toward her, lithe, *hungry*. "I want to see all of you."

She trembled as he took her in his arms, yet welcomed his hot, deep kisses with abandon. Somewhere, she was vaguely aware of his fingers busy at her back, and yet she was astonished when he stepped away and all her clothing slipped to her feet. She gasped, but his hands, warm on her bare shoulders held her still while his gaze devoured her from head to toe and very slowly back up again.

"My God, you are lovely," he said hoarsely. "I am almost afraid to touch you."

"Don't be," she whispered.

"I said *almost*," he growled, pulling her hard against him while he ravished her lips once more.

She loved the roughness of his clothing against her tender skin. His buttons dug into her. The exciting hardness between his legs ground against her abdomen as he dragged his open mouth across her jaw to her ear, her neck and lower to her breast. He bent her backward with the force of his passion and she grasped onto him, dizzy with delight.

With a muttered oath, he swept her up in his arms and carried her to the bed. The sheets felt cold on her naked back, startling her into new awareness. She scuttled under the covers while Verne tore off his clothes. She had one shocking, glorious glimpse of his fully naked body, all muscle and so wondrously different from hers. And then he pulled back the bed covers and lowered himself into her waiting arms.

She could not help the way her hips arched into him. He smiled breathlessly, sweeping his hand down the length of her before he shifted his weight to let him kiss and caress her tingling breasts. New pleasure soared, building deep in her belly. In wonder, she ran her hands over the warm, smooth skin of his back, feeling the muscles undulate to her touch.

His hands roamed at will over her body, as though claiming it. And yet, he was not rough, or even demanding, merely coaxing, persuading, until she relaxed and her knees fell apart. His fingers slid up her inner thigh in intricate patterns while he kissed her mouth more deeply than ever before. She gasped at the play of his caresses between her thighs, her hips lifting and swaying without permission. And then he covered her, and it was not his fingers that invaded and stroked, but something much larger and more serious.

There was an instant of resistance, of pain, but he did not stop, and she did not ask or want him to. She clung to him, her fingers lost in his hair, her head thrown back against the pillows as he moved within her, tender yet relentless. His eyes held hers the whole time, even when he kissed her, even when the sweetest, most intense pleasure she had ever imagined began to build and consume her. She cried out in wonder, and at last, smiling, he closed his eyes, pushing, until he fell on her, groaning with joy.

CECILY'S FIRST NIGHT of love changed everything. Or perhaps just confirmed everything she had longed to believe. She had known she was in love with Verne. Now she was in thrall to him.

She woke the following morning so full of emotion that she wanted to laugh or weep or just run for miles. Surely it was impossible to be still when her heart felt it would burst with love and joy. Perhaps she could rise and dress and at least take a long, brisk walk before he awoke. Only one heavy arm pinned her to the bed.

She turned her head on the pillow. Her heart missed a beat, for there was new, sweet intimacy in watching him sleep. In the beam of morning sunlight filtering through the half-closed bed curtain, his jaw had darkened with stubble, and his hair fell boyishly across his forehead. In sleep, he lost the harsh, sardonic expression that kept the world at bay. Like this, he was innocent, contented. Her husband.

She smiled tenderly, and discovered that after all, she did not want to be anywhere else but there. She turned, resting her cheek against his shoulder and waited for him to wake.

IT WAS NOT unusual for Verne to wake in the throes of lust. It was rarer to feel the softness of a female form in his arms, ready for loving. With a little growl, he rolled her under him and opened his eyes to a new wonder.

He smiled in delight. "Cecily."

"You needn't sound so surprised."

"But I am. I still cannot believe you married me." Nor, as his memory flooded back, could he believe his luck in finding her so sweet and responsive a lover, her passion eager and almost as urgent as his own. This was *Cecily*. His wife... he lowered his mouth to hers and kissed her. "Would you mind very much if I made love to you again?" he whispered.

She swallowed. "I think I might insist upon it."

He smiled. "As you command, my lady."

THERE FOLLOWED THREE weeks of blissful fun for Cecily. Lost in her husband's companionship, and the ever-changing pleasure of his physical intimacy, she fell deeper in love with every passing day. They laughed a lot and talked interminably, learning each other in increasing detail. They spent a couple of days in Edinburgh, where they attended the theatre and danced at the elegant Assembly Rooms in George Street, before traveling on to Alvan's secluded estate further north. There they enjoyed an idyllic fortnight, riding and walking and simply sitting quietly together admiring the spectacular scenery.

It was there that Cecily first discovered her husband suffered from nightmares.

Although two bedchambers had been prepared for them, Verne slept every night in hers. She had wondered if he would prefer merely to visit her when he desired—which was the custom, Lady Barnaby had explained to her, in most upper-class households. When Verne showed no interest in his own bed, Cecily was relieved and delighted.

"I wondered if you might prefer to sleep in your own chamber," she murmured, stroking his hair as he lay in her arms after making love to her. "Now that we have the space."

He lifted his head from her breast, "Do you want me to?"

She shook her head. "It's unexpectedly wonderful sharing a bed with someone. With you."

"I'm glad you added that," he said with a wry smile. He lowered his head once more, kissing her damp skin. "This is all new to you. When the novelty wears off, when you want your chamber to yourself, you must tell me."

Cecily frowned over the inevitability he implied. Her arms tightened in protest. For actually, it was more likely to be he would tire of her constant company and seek his own solitude. *But not yet. Not yet.*

She drifted into sleep, her limbs entwined with his.

She had no idea how long had passed when she was jerked awake by his anguished groan. At some point, they had fallen apart in sleep, or he'd pulled away from her, for he now lay on his back, his head thrashing from side to side on the pillow, his whole body making small but somehow desperate motions. He muttered incoherently, clearly in the throes of some thoroughly unpleasant experience. Frightened that he was ill, she reached for the flint and hastily lit the bedside candle.

She leaned over him, searching his desperate face, but he was still asleep, his eyes darting feverishly behind the closed lids.

She clasped his naked shoulder. "Patrick. Patrick, you're dreaming."

"Arthur," he uttered, clearly distressed. "Arthur, no. No, don't, *don't…*"

Oh, God, was he dreaming of the fire? Reliving the terrible death of his brother who had caused it and perished by it. She shook him more urgently. "Patrick, wake up. It's Cecily." Somehow, she detached his clinging hand and carried it to her lips.

His eyes flew open. Haunted, agonized, they took a moment to focus.

"You were dreaming," she said gently.

He swallowed convulsively. "I'm sorry I woke you."

"It doesn't matter," she said impatiently.

He lifted his hand to her face. "You are my talisman, to frighten away the terrible nightmares."

"Are they so terrible?" she whispered.

He moved suddenly, rolling over her, his hands urgent. "I don't know. I never remember."

Before the passion took over, she knew he was lying. It didn't seem to matter at the time. She was more than happy to be his distraction.

ALTHOUGH SORRY TO leave their isolated idyll in Scotland, Cecily looked eagerly forward to beginning her new life as mistress of Finmarsh.

"Would you object to more servants in the house?" Cecily asked diplomatically as the carriage rattled southward.

"You must engage whom you like," Verne said. He cast her a rueful glance. "I *expect* servants will be more eager to come now that there is a mistress at the house."

"We should probably have a housekeeper, and a butler, too. If Daniel is meant to be your valet, he cannot run the house and the stables, too."

"You are quite right." He stirred, stretching out one leg which had no doubt grown stiff from prolonged sitting in the coach. "And then there is Shilton. I know you have no use for another lady's maid, but I would not like her turned off."

"Oh, I wouldn't do that," Cecily assured him. "But I feel she would be better with suitable employment. As it is, she seems merely to drift around the house talking to ghosts."

"Ah, you've heard her, have you? She isn't mad, you know. Just… distressed."

Cecily nodded, although she wasn't convinced the woman was entirely sane, whatever the tragic causes. "I'll have her help me with household inventories and things, just at first, and talk to her about her future, whether that should be with us or with some other lady."

"Thank you," he said with a quick smile. "It isn't every wife who would be so accommodating. I know what they say of her and me but it isn't true and never was."

"I never thought it was." Except very briefly in the first couple of days she had stayed there. She hesitated for a moment, then said, "What about our other problem? We cannot live comfortably with people trying to kill you."

"I wish I hadn't told you about the incident at Mooreton."

"You didn't. Alvan told me."

"Well, the thing about it is, these attacks—whether on Jerome or me—only seem to occur where certain people are gathered in the same place."

"Namely you, Henry, Torbridge, and Renarde."

He smiled. "I should have known you would have noticed. Except, of course, that Renarde had left the Hart several hours before that shot was fired at me."

"Isabelle had not," Cecily blurted.

Verne blinked. "She was right behind us, in the company of the Longstones, Torbridge and several of my men!"

"Yes, but women are just as capable as men of hiring people to do their dirty work."

A frown tugged at his brow. "Isabelle would not hurt me," he said with finality. As if his words made it irrefutable fact.

"Because you are her lover?"

He stared at her. "Because it is not in her nature."

It was almost a quarrel, because she was stepping where he did not wish her to go. Where unresolved jealousy had compelled her to go. She didn't know if Isabelle was truly in his past. She did know that by all the rules of good breeding, she should neither inquire nor appear to notice. But she could not be that good a wife, not to Verne.

And so, she folded her arms and drew back from the quarrel she was not yet ready to make and hoped she would never have to.

CHAPTER SIXTEEN

THE CONTRAST BETWEEN her first sighting of Finmarsh House in the forced company of her abductor, and arriving now as its mistress, couldn't have been greater. In the summer sunshine, the house stood proud and beautiful, with none of the menacing quality she had once associated with it. Plus, it appeared to be a hive of activity. Men swarmed across the roof, presumably laying slates.

"They must have finished rebuilding the north wing," she observed, peering out of the window.

Verne didn't look. His gaze seemed to be on her. "I'm glad."

She slipped her hand into his. "You need this. To let go of the past and the guilt that was never truly yours."

He squeezed her fingers, but did not speak. Only when the carriage had halted at the familiar front door, he ignored the step and lifted her down, swinging her around before letting her slip to the ground.

"I'm glad you're with me," he said softly and, careless of the workmen, the coachman, and the stable lad who wandered toward them, he kissed her.

SHILTON AND THE cook and a couple of the men Cecily recognized from their expedition to the seaside, came out to welcome them home. Discounting the men, whom she thought of more as body-guards, that left two house servants, one of whom was superfluous. Plus, Daniel and Cranston, of course, who arrived with the baggage only a few minutes later.

It struck her, however, that while the house might not gleam to the standards of an exacting housekeeper, neither did it look neglected or dusty.

"Do you do the housework here, Shilton?" she asked curiously.

"I got a girl from the village to help me," Shilton said nervously. "I thought you wouldn't mind, my lady," she added with a quick glance at Verne. "Only there was so much dust from the building..."

"Excellent idea," Cecily approved. "Well done! Um... is this girl a good worker? Is she looking for a position? Because we certainly need more staff here."

Once inside, Cecily spoke to the cook about dinner, and then followed Verne around to the archway that led to the north wing. It had been boarded up before and painted to look like the rest of the walls. Now it gave an impression of light and much greater space. And beyond it, were walls, passages, rooms, and a staircase.

Verne stood in the archway, gazing in. When Cecily went and stood beside him, he took her hand and led her through the rooms. They were all well-proportioned and mostly spacious, but with bare, unadorned plaster walls, they had little character, and certainly none of the eerie atmosphere that had seemed to haunt the ruin she had last seen in this place.

"What was here before?" she asked.

"Reception rooms. Marjorie's morning room. And upstairs," he added, leading the way, "their bedchambers and a sitting room. Still room," he added, pointing to spaces that did not yet have doors, "and a linen cupboard. And the nursery."

"What would you like to have here now?"

He paused, looking around. "I don't know. Guest bedchambers, perhaps? It would give us more privacy in the south wing. I'm presuming we'll have guests now that you've married me with Alvan's approval."

He didn't want to think about it. She suspected he'd have simply demolished the wing if it wouldn't have made the house look so peculiarly lopsided. It warmed her heart that he'd rebuilt it largely for her, but he didn't like it. He wasn't remotely comfortable here.

He needed good memories to drown out the old.

"We could make a games room downstairs, if you liked?" she suggested. "Set up a billiard table, perhaps?"

He regarded her with surprise. "That might be fun."

She took his arm. "Then we should look into it. Now, show me where I shall sleep."

They walked along the passage, through the door that had once blocked the ruin from the rest of the house.

Verne waved one arm toward the bedchambers. "We can make any arrangement you like with these rooms. Have your own back, if you wish. Or come with me to my lair downstairs." He stroked an imaginary moustache, making her laugh.

"I might risk that for now," she said primly. "But perhaps we could think of moving up here in the future? There is space enough for us to have connecting rooms, if you wish."

"So that I can get drunk without disgusting you?"

"I'm sure there will be times," she said tolerantly. "But I was thinking more of a dressing room. I'm not sure I shall want Daniel floating in and out of my bedchamber!"

"Good point," he allowed, guiding her down the main staircase and across to the library, which had been kept neater and cleaner than Cecily remembered it.

Beyond the connecting door was the tiny room where Jerome had slept and on the other side, a spacious bedchamber with a small dressing room.

Verne waved his hand to the latter. "There's another door to the dressing room from the passage. I'll tell Daniel to use that. Can you be comfortable here for a little? Or do you wish to sleep upstairs?"

Cecily examined her surroundings. Like the library, it was alarmingly neat today, though she suspected it was normally cluttered and chaotic like its master. However, it had a pleasant feel, and was bright and airy.

"All your things are here," she said. "Besides, if we stay here, we can change things around upstairs and redecorate without being disturbed. Why did you choose these rooms in the first place? Were they always yours?"

"No, Arthur and I had the north wing. The nursery was there, too, and then the schoolroom. I had to move somewhere when he married, and this seemed as far away as possible. I could come in and out in the middle of the night, in any state I chose without disturbing anyone."

And bring in anyone he chose, she thought with a twinge of jealousy. He had brought Isabelle here, among others. No doubt he had made love to her in this room. Which was another reason for sleeping elsewhere.

Verne looked about him. "What would we do with this room, then?"

"It would make rather a lovely sitting room," Cecily said. "But we don't need to decide everything tonight! Ah, here is Daniel with our bags…"

HER FIRST EVENING as mistress of Finmarsh House was spent in fun and laughter. With barely any servants, it was Daniel who served them dinner. Cecily actually wondered if it would be wrong to bring the chaotic household into line with convention, and said as much as they settled in the library after dinner over a glass of port.

Verne's eyebrows flew up in surprise. "It was never really choice. Most of the servants left after the fire, and I never felt their lack until you arrived."

"You make it sound as though I inconvenienced you," she said, amused. "Have you forgotten you abducted me?"

"I never forget a successful abduction."

"I refuse to ask how you define success."

"My definition has changed recently." His arm slipped around her, and she rested her cheek against his shoulder, smiling.

"So has mine," she admitted.

In the morning, after yet another night of spectacular love, she left Verne sleeping and went in search of Shilton to obtain her help in taking an inventory of the house. With some unease, she eventually discovered the maid in the north wing, wandering the rooms like a wraith, murmuring to herself.

Eventually, Cecily thought she made out the words, "Where are you? Are you gone, now? Are you gone?" Was she searching for Marjorie's ghost? Perhaps it was a good sign that she thought her old mistress's spirit had vanished in the rebuilding.

"Shilton?" she called as the maid walked into the largest room without seeing her. "I need your help."

"Yes, my lady," Shilton said at once, hurrying out of the room to join her. At least it didn't seem to enter her head that it might be Marjorie calling her.

Shilton caught on quickly to what was expected of her, inspecting and noting each piece of household linen and removing those that needed mending or were beyond repair. More than that, she knew where more or less everything was kept, from household keys to glass and china.

"Do you know of other local domestic servants in the area looking for work?" Cecily asked her. "I would rather employ local people than go to a London agency. But I don't yet feel we're in a position to train maids and footmen from scratch."

"There may be one or two," Shilton said doubtfully. "I could ask in the village and send those interested up to you?"

"Tomorrow morning," Cecily decided. "By then, we should have more idea what and whom we need!"

She joined Verne for breakfast, and then, leaving Shilton to continue the inventory, rode with him around the estate to greet his people as their new lady. Returning to the house for luncheon, she then wrote to several London firms for samples of wallpaper and curtains, then took over Shilton's place with the inventory while the maid went to Finsborough with Daniel.

She was sorting through some rather beautiful porcelain from the last century when James, one of Verne's "grooms," came to tell her a "woman" had called to see her about a position in the house.

"Drat, they weren't supposed to come until tomorrow!" Cecily said a little crossly.

"I'll send her away, if you like," James offered. "Though she did say she had a letter from Mrs. Longstone."

"Oh." Cecily rose to her feet. "I'd better see her then. Where is she?"

"In the hall, my lady."

Only feet away from the front door, the young woman stood patiently waiting. She was neat and modest looking, her hair pinned severely under her cap—which did nothing to hide her beauty.

"Good afternoon," Cecily said. "I hear you have a letter for me."

The girl curtseyed and held out a folded paper. Cecily took it, broke the wafer, and read it quickly. Mrs. Longstone welcomed her warmly back to Sussex. *As the new mistress of Finmarsh, you will already be inconvenienced by the lack of servants. I take the liberty of recommending to you Anne Wilson, who was our chambermaid here and gave excellent service. I am sorry to let her go, but we are economizing. It will make me feel much better if I know she has a place with you, and that you have at least one good servant at hand until you have the chance to choose your own, of course.*

I know she will give satisfaction.

Mrs. Longstone didn't seem to doubt she would take the girl on, which set Cecily's back up somewhat. However, she raised her eyes to Anne Wilson's as pleasantly as she could.

"You will be sad to leave Mrs. Longstone."

"Oh yes, my lady. It was a good position."

"How long were you there?"

"Two years, my lady."

"Where are you from, Anne?"

"London, my lady. Mrs. Longstone took me on when she was visiting there."

"And are you happy in the country?"

"I much prefer it, my lady. It's one reason I would love a position with you."

"You would have a lot to do. We are very short-staffed at the moment and have building work besides."

A tiny smile flickered in the maid's eyes. "That just makes it more interesting, my lady."

The girl had character and experience, and the recommendation of a high stickler. Cecily could see no disadvantages. "When can you start?"

THAT NIGHT, CECILY was again woken by Verne's nightmare as his whole body thrashed from side to side.

"Patrick," she murmured, putting her arms around him in comfort and pity, but he seemed inconsolable, for once unaware of his presence. Faint sounds came from his lips. She couldn't tell if they were words or groans, just that he suffered.

In desperation, remembering the comfort he had sought on the previous occasion, she pressed her body to his in the darkness and kissed him, willing him to wake and find joy instead of the pain that so clearly gripped him in sleep.

He stilled at last. Then his mouth opened under hers. Without opening his eyes, he began to move against her, his hands roaming over her body. With a low growl, he lifted her hips and she took him inside her. Gladly, she moved to his rhythm, her passion no longer merely comfort. He held her, loving her with deep sensuality.

"Marjorie," he uttered, with shocking clarity.

She stilled, all pleasure draining away from her. His eyes were still closed, as though he had never wakened, was merely loving her in his sleep. And imagining she was his dead sister-in-law. Shilton had once hinted at Marjorie's feelings for Patrick, but had denied he had ever taken advantage, yet alone returned her affection.

"Marjorie." That one word in such circumstances raised all sorts of doubts and questions. And if he had not told her about such a major part of his life, how could she trust him now?

As he found his pleasure in her, tears ran down Cecily's cheeks. He rolled onto his side, gathering her close against him and with a grunt of contentment, appeared to go back to sleep. If he'd ever been awake.

It was Cecily who lay awake for a long time, staring into the darkness, until she fell into an exhausted sleep with the break of dawn.

She woke with rather more perspective. Saying Marjorie's name meant nothing more than that she was associated with his nightmares, and that was not surprising. Surely, it meant little that he had spoken it while making love to her. He had still been at least half-asleep, his brain confused, no doubt, between his dream and reality. She would be a fool to read too much into it. Did she not have his companionship, his frequent tender loving?

He has never said he loves me...

She thrust that aside. Words did not matter more than deeds. He showed his love all the time. Such as now, when he sank onto the bed beside her, offering her a cup of coffee from his tray. He kissed her as she took it, dispelling the fringes of unease that still clung.

"So, what are your plans for today?"

"I have a few people to interview for household positions—which reminds me, do you want James and George to be footmen or grooms? Or are they merely temporary?"

Clearly not used to regularizing his staff, Verne looked endearingly flustered. "I have no idea. I'll speak to them. Or you could. I'll be riding over to the Hart this morning, so I'll leave them with you."

She frowned. She had almost forgotten about the attacks. "It is you who need them with you," she pointed out. "No one has ever attacked me."

"I intend to make sure no one shall," he said firmly. "But I assure you, I'll be careful."

She set down her finished coffee cup and took his hand. "You had another nightmare last night. Do you remember?"

"No," he said apologetically. "Did I wake you?"

She shrugged to show that didn't bother her in the slightest. It was not in her nature to hide things, and although something caused her to hesitate, she said, "You spoke Marjorie's name."

"She's part of my guilt." He didn't sound impatient, precisely, but his brisk tone left her in no doubt that he wanted the subject changed.

She could not oblige him. "Patrick? Were you ever Marjorie's lover?"

He bolted off the bed as if she'd stung him. "Of course, I was not," he snapped. "Why would you even imagine such a thing?" And he stalked into the dressing room, yelling for Daniel.

In the end, they happened to leave the bedchamber together, Cecily to go to breakfast and Verne to the stables. Cheerful and full of energy, he seemed to have forgotten his irritation with her and tucked her hand in his arm as they walked through the library and into the entrance hall.

"Who's that?" Verne asked, glancing up at the staircase.

Anne, the new chambermaid, was hurrying upstairs, encouraging-ly neat and fresh in appearance.

"That is our new chambermaid," Cecily replied with pride. "Cour-tesy of Mrs. Longstone, who recommended her."

Verne smiled crookedly. "Then I shall watch my back. She's prob-ably a spy."

"You are ridiculous," Cecily observed. "If Mrs. Longstone wants to know how many pairs of sheets we have, she has only to ask me."

Verne laughed and kissed her, but it sounded somewhat mechani-cal to her ears. He cast another glance upstairs as he strode toward the front door.

THE PRESENCE OF the Longstone maid in his home caused Verne unease. So much so, that he was reluctant to leave the house. In truth, he doubted that Henry was responsible for the attacks on him, but he knew damned well Henry wanted to succeed him and he did not trust the girl. Discovering James in the stables, he told him to go to the house and keep an eye on the new chambermaid. Then, frowning, he added that if her ladyship went out, he was to go with her and forget the chambermaid.

As he rode over to the Hart, he wondered if his reaction was un-reasonable. He was only going to be away for a couple of hours, and if he was so worried about the wretched chambermaid, he should merely dismiss her. Wanting Cecily to build the household she chose warred with his powerful protective instincts which were, he thought ruefully, becoming ridiculous. He had not been married a month, and yet life without her had become unimaginable.

The Hart was quiet at this time of day, so he chose to enjoy Mrs. Villin's breakfast in the empty coffee room. As he sat down, he could hear her and her daughter singing in the kitchen while they cooked.

The sound, cheerful and unexpectedly sweet, made him smile.

Villin ambled in. "Morning, my lord," he greeted him, and, taking a rather grubby letter from his apron, he dropped it on the table in front of Verne.

"Good morning, Villin," Verne replied. "When did this arrive?"

"About a week ago."

Verne glanced at the name scrawled on the front of it. *N. Potter, Esquire.* As he'd assumed, it was not urgent. If it had been, the smuggler captain would have signaled with a light on the marsh.

"It's all that's come since you've been gone," Villin volunteered.

"Anyone else sniffing around?" Verne asked casually.

"No, sir, not a one."

"Thanks." Verne unsealed the letter and scanned the two sentences within. They were in the code he knew and he easily understood it to mean the new spy was in place and well. He stuffed it in his pocket and returned to his own problem.

The solution might be to go and see Henry and scare the wits out of him, just in case he was contemplating anything underhand…

The innkeeper's daughter, Lily, bustled in with a heaped tray of ham, eggs, and toast, with various side dishes of fish and beef and a large pot of coffee.

"Good morning, my lord!" she said cheerfully, unloading it all in front of him. "How was your wedding trip?"

"Most enjoyable, thank you," he said distractedly, before her satisfied smile caught his attention.

He gave her a quick, sardonic smile. "You needn't pretend you're pleased she married me. I know for a fact you told her I was a dangerous man not to be trusted."

Lily only laughed. "Don't hold it against me, sir. For some women, a warning is enough to intrigue."

He blinked. "And you imagined Lady Cecily to be such a woman?"

"She married you, didn't she?"

He regarded her with surprised fascination. "Why do you even care? Why throw her at a man like me?"

"You're not really a bad man, my lord."

"You don't know that."

She laughed, as though such a possibility was preposterous. "More to the point, you needed her. And she needed you."

"Then you know more about Lady Cecily than I ever will."

"No. But I had met her a couple of times before you did. The first time she came here was to find Miss Charlotte Maybury and try to make her brother happy. She has a kind spirit and a strong one."

Verne picked up his fork. "If it weren't for your occasional word of wisdom among the fustian, I'd complain of you to your father as an idle, interfering chatterbox."

She curtseyed with bold exaggeration. "My lord."

He laughed. "Go away, Lily."

He returned home via Finsborough, to make sure the plasterer would come tomorrow as instructed, to begin work on the ceiling moldings in the north wing. As he stepped out of the workshop to untie Jupiter, he glimpsed two men on horseback riding away from him. Although they had their backs to him, he was sure they were Henry Longstone and Lord Torbridge.

What the devil was Torbridge doing back here again? He frowned over that all the way home, for the combination of Torbridge with his heir made him uneasy. Why did these people keep congregating around him?

He got home in time for a late luncheon. Cecily looked pleased to see him and told him proudly that she had engaged two more maids and a first footman who would teach James and George about their new roles.

"And where have they all come from?"

"The footman and one of the maids are from Audley Park, alt-hough they've been without a position since the Overtons let them go last year. They were economizing. The other maid has worked for the vicar but wants a step up. Shilton found them."

Verne nodded approval. "Excellent. You can probably let the Longstones' maid go then."

She blinked. "Why would I do that? You are not serious about the spying nonsense, are you?"

"Not exactly, but I don't like her being here."

She put down her fork. "Patrick, you are being unreasonable. You insist on keeping Shilton here although she has nothing to do since the fire, and yet you would have me dismiss a useful new member of the staff who works hard and has done nothing wrong."

He scowled. "Is this about being rid of Shilton?"

"Of course not," she retorted, the light of battle in her eyes, which both aroused and worried him. "In fact, I am thinking about making her our new housekeeper. She knows this house like the back of her hand and she is unexpectedly good at directing the new staff. I had been going to discuss the matter with you, but I shall leave it until you are in a better mood."

"My mood is not ill," he said after a long silence. "Although I am most likely unreasonable. It is your mood that is out of sorts, I think. What has happened?"

"Nothing has happened." She picked up her fork and stabbed her fish as though it had unforgivably offended her.

Verne caught her eye and she smiled reluctantly, relaxing her shoulders.

"Nothing has happened," she repeated. "Just… no one has called. I would have expected at least one bride visit by now."

"I expect everyone is giving you time to settle in," he said. But he did not like to lie. She should have understood how it would be from the beginning. He thought she *had* understood. He shoved his chair back from the table. "What did you expect?" he asked. "It's one of the many downsides of marrying me. I thought you would not care." And that she did hurt unbearably. He walked out before she could see.

He had estate business to attend to, but the matter of the chambermaid played on his mind all the time he was out. When he returned to the house, he went in search of her, and found her cleaning one of the bedchambers that had not been used since his impromptu house party for Cecily.

She was a pretty little thing, somewhere under five-and-twenty summers, he guessed, and at least she appeared to be industrious. On her hands and knees, she was sweeping under the bed. He leaned against the door frame and watched her for a moment or two before she became aware of him and jumped to her feet in order to bob a respectful curtsey.

"So, you're the new chambermaid," he observed.

"Yes, my lord," she breathed, risking a glance up at him that was half curious and half coquettish. He wondered if the latter came naturally, or if it was deliberate. "Anne Wilson, my lord."

"I hear Mrs. Longstone was forced to let you go."

"She is economizing, my lord."

"I never heard they were in such straights. Was it Mrs. Longstone's idea? Or Mr. Longstone's?"

"I'm sure I couldn't say, my lord." And there it was again, one of those seductive upward glances, almost like looking through her fluttering eyelashes.

Curling his lip, he strolled toward her. "What *can* you say, little bird?"

She did not back away but met his gaze boldly. There may have been a hint of fear in her bright eyes, but mostly they were welcoming, teasing. It was an interesting mixture of expressions, and he was fairly sure he understood it.

Deliberately, he placed one finger under her chin and tilted up her face for his examination.

"Whatever you want me to say, my lord," she breathed.

"What did they tell you say?"

Her caught breath and the flash of intensified fear in her eyes told him all he needed to know. He was right.

"I don't understand, my lord," she said desperately.

A movement at the door caused him to look beyond her. Over the chambermaid's head he met the shocked gaze of his wife.

CHAPTER SEVENTEEN

*H*OW DID IT *all go so wrong so quickly? How has it come to this?* From a couple of trivial quarrels, easily mended, and a silly suspicion, hastily discounted, Cecily now found her husband flirting with the chambermaid he'd been so eager to dismiss only a few hours ago. Was it revenge? Had he wanted the temptation removed? Even now, she couldn't believe he was so crass or so shallow.

And yet, there he stood, close enough to kiss the maid who was in his power, his careless finger under the girl's chin. He showed no shame. Instead, his lips quirked upward into a half-smile, as though she was meant to understand. Confused, she stared back.

It was Anne who moved first. With a gasp, she whisked herself out of Verne's hold, grabbing clumsily at her dustpan and brush and dusters. "My lord," she mumbled. "Sorry, my lady."

Cecily turned and walked away. She could not bring herself to speak. Instead, she hurried along the passage and downstairs. By the time she reached the bottom, his footsteps were clattering after her. She could not bear his company right now, and yet, she had nowhere to go that was not his, no room of her own. Her only hope was to reach the bedchamber and lock the door before he caught up. Surely, he would not make a figure of them both by demanding entry or breaking down the door?

She could not put either past him, and as it turned out, she never had the chance to put him to the test, for by the time she had crossed the library, he reached over her and held the door to the bedchamber shut.

"Stop."

"I cannot speak to you right now."

"You would rather live in ignorance?"

She closed her eyes. "Is that what I have been doing?"

"God help us both, I don't know." The flat of his hand struck the door hard, making her jump. "Damn it, Cecily!" he exploded. "Without any evidence whatsoever, in the teeth of everyone else's accusations, you insist on believing me innocent of all guilt in the matter of the fire that killed my brother and his wife. And yet you suddenly assume I'm guilty of such paltry, squalid little acts as making love to that same sister-in-law and seducing the maids? I suppose you believe the same of Shilton, too?"

Anger soared, heating her face as she swung around to face him. "Oh no, Verne, you will not make this my fault! You were all over that poor girl like a rash."

His furious gaze clashed with hers. She had never provoked his temper before and now that she had, a fierce, perverse triumph took hold of her, urging to push him further and further.

"Yes, I was, wasn't I?" he said, curling his lip with a contempt she had never imagined she would inspire in him. "Now why do you suppose that was?"

Her anger vanished so suddenly she felt dizzy. Stricken, wordless, she stared at her husband's cruel face while her world crumbled.

And then a soft knock at the library door heralded the entry of Will, the new footman.

"Your pardon, my lady," he said woodenly. "Lord and Lady Overton have called. I've shown them into the drawing room."

"Thank you," Cecily managed, and as soon as the door was closed, she ducked under Verne's imprisoning arm.

"Cecily," he said, and suddenly his voice wasn't harsh at all, but she couldn't turn, couldn't wait or she would break in pieces. She knew enough not to do that.

She walked on blindly to the library door.

"Of course." His mocking voice followed her. "A bride visit at last. You had better go before they change their minds."

She kept walking. It seemed to be all she could do. In the hall, she drew a deep, shuddering breath, and straightened her shoulders. She had always excelled at the game of manners and social graces. At this moment, it seemed her only salvation, so as she climbed the stairs to the drawing room, she summoned up a smile and metaphorically pinned it in place.

"How lovely to see you," she greeted Lord and Lady Overton. "How do you do?"

"You look wonderful," Lord Overton beamed.

"We just heard you were back and had to come and welcome you!" Lady Overton said. "Henrietta is in London with Thomasina, but I had to come home since the children are ill. Your rebuilding has gone apace, I see!"

"Indeed. We are still a little at sixes and sevens, but I'm so glad you came. Do sit down and I'll ring for tea. How are the children?"

"Oh, I think they are on the mend. I suspect the boys brought something nasty home from school and kindly passed it to their sister!"

By the time tea was brought in, Cecily had been brought up to date with local gossip, including the fact that the Longstones were back home and that Lord Torbridge and the Renardees were both staying there.

What an odd time to economize, Cecily thought. Her stomach twisted as she wondered if Patrick could possibly be right about Anne Wilson. Why would you get rid of a chambermaid when you were entertaining guests? She thrust the thought aside to concentrate on her own guests, while waiting in vain for Verne to join them.

"So, are you happy to receive visits now?" Lady Overton inquired as she stood to take her leave. "If you are, I shall spread the word! But don't feel obliged, for everyone understands you are in the middle of building and decorating."

"Oh, everyone is welcome," Cecily assured her.

Only this morning, this visit and the prospect of others would have delighted her. Not so much for her own sake as for Verne's. She had assumed, perhaps too optimistically, that marriage to her would somehow make him more acceptable, absorbing him into the community that had shunned him for years. She had been annoyed that such hadn't so far been the case. Now, the whole matter seemed trivial, for something she couldn't quite grasp had gone wrong in her marriage and that was so huge it blotted out everything else.

When the Overtons had gone, she plucked up her courage and did what she should have done earlier—went to talk to her husband. But he wasn't in the library or the bedchamber. She found Daniel in the dressing room, sorting out laundered shirts and freshly brushed coats. For some reason it was odd to see him actually carrying out the duties of a mere valet.

"Where is his lordship, Daniel?" she asked.

"Riding, my lady," Daniel replied. He hung up his master's best evening coat and turned to face her. "He'll come back in a better mood."

Cecily regarded him carefully. Had he been in the bedchamber and overheard their quarrel? She could not ask him that. Instead, she said lightly, "Were you on the receiving end of his temper?"

Daniel grinned. "Don't worry, my lady. I'm used to it."

And he was still here. As Cecily would be.

Daniel threw a pile of stockings onto a shelf. "He's quick tempered but as quick to forgive. And apologize where it's due."

"Of course," she murmured and went out before his information became any more obviously advice for her.

She remembered something Alvan had said to her about Verne,

perhaps trying to talk her out of the engagement. *He is quite disastrously self-destructive and liable to swallow everyone around him in the explosion.* When she'd married him, she had convinced herself she would prevent such calamities, as Charlotte kept Alvan's melancholy at bay.

Yet, here she was fanning the flames, accusing him of things in the heat of the moment, through her own insecurity. The truth was, she had never been sure of Verne. She had pursued him, given him ideas, perhaps, which he would never have considered left to himself. *Was she good for him?*

In an agony of self-doubt and need of his presence, she waited for him to come home.

She changed for dinner with a heavy heart, for there was still no sign of him. And then, as Cranston pinned her hair, she heard the thud of galloping hooves in the yard. Relief washed over her.

As soon as Cranston released her, she went to meet him, and found him already striding into the dining room. Instructing the servants to bring dinner in, she followed him.

He was gazing out of the window but turned as she entered. "Hope you'll excuse the dress," he said, indicating his mud-spattered breeches, "but I'm starving and I'd only hold you up if I stop to change."

"I don't mind in the slightest," she said civilly, taking her place which was set close to his as always. At first, despite their almost oppressive politeness to each other, Cecily merely reveled in his return, his safety, his presence, but gradually, since there was no opportunity to talk privately, with servants going in and out all the time, she grew frustrated and impatient.

Patrick, on the other hand, seemed in no hurry. He responded to whatever she chose to talk about, and despite his absence during the Overtons' visit, looked interested in their news and the fact that the Renardees and Lord Torbridge were both staying with the Longstones.

"I knew Torbridge was there," he observed. "I saw him with Henry in Finsborough this morning. I'm sure they'll all be beating a path to your door now that the Overtons have shown the way."

Unlike this afternoon, there was no sarcasm in his tone or expression, just a profound distance that made Cecily miserable.

"Shall we go to the library?" she suggested when the interminable meal was finally finished. "Bring your wine with you, if you want to."

His hesitation made her heart ache. *Have I truly ruined this already?* No, she would not *let* it be ruined. She would talk to him, explain…

At least he followed her down to the library and closed the door. The long summer evening was coming to a close and the fringes of dusk were beginning to darken the sky and the marshes in the distance.

She turned to face him. "When I think, I do not doubt you," she blurted. "But my own weakness, my self-doubts make me jealous and then I no longer think. You have such power to hurt me that I'm frightened. I don't want to quarrel, Patrick."

She could not read his turbulent gaze, but just for an instant it was no longer cold or distant.

"Neither do I," he said. "But since you live with me, we *will* quarrel. That does not mean…" His gaze shifted beyond her, growing more distant once more. "You must understand…"

"What?" she urged, almost despairing.

"We'll talk," he promised. "But not now. I have to go out."

Her mouth fell open. "Now? You have to go out *now*?"

A sound escaped his lips, half groan and half laughter. "Oh, my dear, you should never have married me! Don't wait up."

And with that, he was gone. No kiss, no soft word. Slowly, she sat down on the sofa and gave way to tears.

IT HAD NEVER entered Verne's head that Cecily would feel insecure in his love. It was he who had never been good enough for her and never would be. That *he* had won *her* love would never cease to amaze him. But suddenly understanding that she feared she was unable to keep him—chaotic and wicked as he undoubtedly was—floored him. He meant to stay, to make things right between them again, only the light in the marsh caught his eye. Eerie and unnoticeable to most among the weird, natural lights that often appeared there, this steady light was undoubtedly the signal of a most urgent message from France, or even a most urgent need of his presence, and he had to put that first.

When he came home, he would show her how much he cared. As he galloped hard across the country, picking his way through the familiar marshes, he could not help dwelling on all the many ways he would show her. Until he pulled himself up short.

According to Jerome, the traitor knew everything, which must surely include the signal. Verne could be riding straight into a trap.

He could be, but he couldn't take the chance of ignoring it. He had to get to the Hart, keeping his wits about him at all times.

It was fully dark by the time he reached the inn, fortunately without incident. He found the taproom busy and Captain Cromarty glaring at anyone who tried to sit at his table. He glared at Verne, too, though more for effect, and in any case, Verne was immune. He'd known Cromarty since he was sixteen-years-old and the smuggler had fished him out of the sea and away from the excisemen pursuing his comrades. Those same comrades who had fed him to the wolves to escape themselves. "You're a gentleman," they'd said with contempt. "No one will lock *you* up."

Cromarty, on the other hand, hadn't cared what kind of family he came from. He treated everyone the same, cabin boy and prince. He was, in many ways, a deeply flawed man, but he had his own rough honor and Verne had never quite lost his boyish admiration.

"There are no other places," he said, mildly, sitting on the bench opposite the smuggler captain and waving at Villin for ale. Then, he focused his gaze on Cromarty. "Your light?"

Cromarty nodded. He dropped his palm on the table next to Verne's, and a folded paper passed between them. "For Hobbs," Cromarty said grimly.

The name on the letter always indicated its urgency, and S. Hobbs demanded speed. With an inward groan, Verne knew he would have to ride to London tonight, which meant not seeing Cecily until tomorrow. All he could do was have Villin send a note to her. He just wished he could send Villin or Cromarty to London in his place.

He sighed and pocketed the letter. "No trouble?" he asked the captain.

Cromarty shook his head. "What about you? I hear you are a married man."

Verne couldn't help grinning. "I am. I'll bring her to meet you one day."

"I doubt she'll be wanting to number me among her acquaintances," Cromarty said wryly. "I shan't be offended."

"Neither will she. You'll like her."

Cromarty cast a searching glance at him and then laughed. "Caught, by God. You treat her well, then. None of your nonsense."

A pretty maid set a mug of ale before each of them and swayed away with an inviting smile over her shoulder.

"None of my nonsense," Verne agreed, and turned back, raising his mug to the captain in a silent toast.

Cromarty returned the gesture and they drank.

"I'd best be off," Verne said, rising to his feet. The sooner he left, the sooner he'd be back to Cecily. "Take care, Captain."

"And you," Cromarty said with a quick frown that spoke of genuine anxiety. "Is your man with you?"

Verne shook his head.

"Then perhaps I—"

"No," Verne interrupted. He gave a crooked smile. "Against the rules. Good night, Captain!"

"Patrick."

HE SET OUT across country by the quickest route toward the main London road. But he had not gone far before he realized he was being followed. To begin with, it was merely a feeling he could have put down to mere anxiety, but he had learned to trust his instincts in such matters, at least when he was sober. And so, all his senses were on high alert. The faint sound of distant hoofbeats, of moving branches in the forest.

Someone else had seen the light. Someone who knew what it had meant. They must have waited for him at the Hart—hiding *outside* the inn, for he had scanned the patrons inside quite carefully. They had waited until he had taken possession of the message and now meant to take out both at once.

It could only be the traitor he had been looking for. And by coincidence, both Torbridge and Renarde were in the area. As was Henry, of course, but this was a crime Verne was inclined to acquit him of.

Again, his mind balked at the aristocratic and apparently proper Torbridge taking money from a foreign government to do its dirty work, but in Torbridge's case, there was no doubt, personal animosity, because Verne had won Cecily.

On the other hand, few hated revolutionary France more than the émigrés forced to leave their country and wealth behind for exile and poverty. He could not imagine Renarde getting into bed with Bonaparte, and for Isabelle's sake, he hoped to God he hadn't.

Not for the first time, he thought fleetingly of Isabelle herself in the role of traitor. She had the courage, and the stomach to do just about anything through boredom. It could even be why she had returned to

Renarde. But would she really hurt *him*?

He slowed, more irritated than anything by this new impediment to his swift return to Cecily. Again, he heard the faint snort of a horse behind him on the track. More worrying, something moved in a different direction, as if someone rode parallel with him in the forest.

There were two of them.

His plan of confrontation no longer seemed quite such a good idea. He could ride on, wait for them to attack him… or lead them straight to S. Or at least the office of S whom he had never actually met. Verne liked neither alternative, so, sticking with his original intention, he chose a place at the edge of the wood where he had the cover of trees, and yet the moonlight could shine down on those who came after him.

Quickly, he led Jupiter out of the way of stray shots—although a dagger seemed to be the preferred weapon of the traitor—and tied the reins to a tree branch. From his saddle bag, he took the double-barreled pistol which had been a gift from his brother Arthur. With that, he could get off two shots, which at least evened the odds.

Walking back as silently as he could, he carefully cocked his pistol and waited behind a thick tree for his enemies to reveal themselves. He strained to hear every sound, but they must have worked out that he'd stopped, that he could be waiting for them. In any case, it was hard to distinguish those slight movements he did hear from the normal passage of the nocturnal creatures in the wood. Verne's gaze darted constantly from the path to the forest, while his whole body tingled with awareness.

A low branch whispered against the forest floor. Immediately, Verne snapped his attention in that direction. A man stepped out of the trees, and just as he'd hoped, the moonlight illuminated his face.

Lord Torbridge.

He wore no hat, but otherwise looked as elegant as ever, a dueling pistol held in his right hand. Those things were on hair triggers, but it was not in Verne's nature to shoot unseen. He stepped out from behind his tree.

"Torbridge," he said quietly and prepared to shoot.

Before he could, a gunshot cracked the air and something thudded into Verne's tree from quite a different angle. Not from the path, either. His second assailant—unless there were three of them—had slipped into the woods and had fired from the darkness.

Verne leapt forward, swerving both to avoid Torbridge's shot and to run straight at the unseen gunman. Or at least as straight as he could judge from the hole in his tree. He had several moments before the gunman could reload, and if only Torbridge missed, he might just make it.

He crashed into a body at speed, falling to the ground with him. Something winked in the sliver of moonlight through the trees. Spectacles.

Pierre de Renarde.

CHAPTER EIGHTEEN

L ONG BEFORE THE banging on the front door, Cecily had pulled herself together, at least outwardly. After washing her face in the bedchamber, she returned to the library and rang for tea and went through the motions of enjoying a quiet evening in the comfort of her own home. She sat by the lamp with a novel while she drank her soothing tea, but after a while she realized she had turned at least ten pages and retained not one word.

Sighing, she dropped the book and considered her embroidery work, but her fingers were always so much slower than her mind wished them to be that she could summon up no enthusiasm. She was just considering moving to the drawing room and playing the piano, which at least she enjoyed, when the banging started at the front door—loud, impatient, continuous.

Her heart sank in fear and she jumped to her feet. Had something happened to Patrick? He treated the very real danger as if it threatened everyone *but* him, and she knew Daniel was still in the house, as were James and George.

The outraged remarks of the servants in the entrance hall drifted in to her while she remained rooted to the same spot in front of the sofa. Bad news would reach her soon enough. While she stayed here, everything was still fine.

But the commanding voice she heard cutting through the protests of her servants was a woman's. And the woman had clearly baffled them by barging straight past them, for the library door flew open and Isabelle de Renarde strode into the room, slamming the door shut behind her.

Her gaze darted furiously around the room before clashing with Cecily's.

"Where is he?" Isabelle demanded.

The library door opened again. The new footman, William, entered while James and George bulged behind him in the doorway.

"My lady," James said. "Is your visitor leaving?"

Cecily easily recognized this as an offer to eject said visitor. And she was tempted. How dare the woman barge in demanding to see Cecily's husband? She even knew the likeliest place to find him. It would have done Cecily's battered nerves no end of good to see her husband's lover marched out of the house between the burly footman. But the hint of despair in Isabelle's eyes stayed her. As did the sudden realization that she hadn't stated the name of the man she sought.

"Not yet," Cecily said. "Thank you, William, that will be all for now."

The footmen left reluctantly, and Cecily doubted they retreated very far from the door. Had the visitor not been a lady, and no doubt one well known to James and George, she would never have got past them.

"Where is he?" Isabelle repeated. "Cecily, where is Patrick?"

"He is not here," Cecily replied coldly.

"And my husband?"

Cecily blinked. "Your husband? I'm afraid his whereabouts are even more of a mystery."

Isabelle pounced. "Then Pierre has not been here?"

"Most assuredly, he has not. Isabelle, what is the matter with you? Why are you in such a state?"

Without invitation, Isabelle sank onto the sofa, holding one shaking hand to her head. "He said he was going after Patrick."

Cecily frowned. "Your husband did?"

Isabelle nodded. "You see, I have recently learned... rather more than I would have liked to about my husband. Going back to him was a mistake. There is more to him than he shows the world, but I wish to God I had not discovered what it was." She lowered her hand. Abject misery stood out in her face.

But it all began to make sense to Cecily. "You discovered," she suggested carefully, "that his loyalties are, perhaps, more *to* his country than *against* the regime which rules it?"

Isabelle's lips twitched. "What a kind way of saying treachery."

Cecily brushed that aside. "And he is looking for Patrick? Why now?"

"I don't know. He said something about some light on the marsh. He thinks my fortunes are now so tied to his that I will not try to stop him, but I have to! If Patrick truly is not here, where did he go?"

Cecily frowned. Before his sudden departure, just when she had thought they were going to talk and reach a better understanding, his gaze had moved over her head, fixing, perhaps, on something in the window. Had he seen the same light as Renarde?

"I don't know," Cecily admitted, hurrying to the door. "But I can find out. Wait here."

As she had suspected, James and George were hovering in the hallway.

"Where did his lordship go?" she demanded.

"I'm sorry, my lady, I don't know," James replied. "He took Jupiter. That's all I know. Maybe—"

"Where is Daniel?" she interrupted.

"In the kitchen, my lady. I'll fetch him."

"Don't bother. I'll go myself." It would be quicker. Brushing past the footmen, she rushed through the baize door to the servants' sanctum.

Daniel sat in the servants' hall, his feet stretched out under the table, as he drank a cup of tea with Cook and Shilton. They all leapt to their feet, staggering in their haste as they caught sight of her.

"My lady," Daniel began, but she cut him off without apology.

"Where did his lordship go?"

"He didn't say, my lady."

"But you know," she insisted. "You always know."

He swallowed.

"Daniel, he's in danger!" Cecily said urgently. "There was, I think, a light showing in the marsh. Where would that have sent him?"

Daniel reached for his coat on the back of his chair. "To the Hart, my lady. I'll go after him."

"Bring James and George," Cecily commanded. "I'm coming with you. One of you send word to the stables. We need to hurry."

She had never changed so quickly in her life as she did into her riding habit that evening, with Cranston's help. And it was not just Isabelle whom she swept out of the library with her, but Shilton, too.

"My place is with you," Shilton said stubbornly, and Cecily, with no time to waste on argument, merely shrugged. Shilton, too, had her demons.

"You need to let us lead the way," James told her. "The quickest path is through the marsh, but it's dangerous. You have to watch your feet."

She nodded impatiently. He was telling her nothing she did not already know. "Then lead. Quickly."

THERE WAS NO time to bandy words with Renarde. The émigré's pistol, which had dropped in the fall, might be harmless, but Torbridge's wasn't. Verne had raised his own high as he landed on Renarde, pointing it in the air with his finger off the trigger. He still had two shots.

He jerked himself into a sitting position on Renarde's chest and brought down his pistol arm, peering out of the trees.

Lord Torbridge advanced upon him, his weapon stretched out in front of him while his eyes found Verne's. Somewhere it bothered Verne that Torbridge hadn't already fired. But the failure had saved his life and he wasn't about to quarrel with it. He curled his finger around the trigger and took aim.

"Halt," he commanded.

But, unforgivably, he had assumed Renarde beaten and removed all his attention to Torbridge. He was taken by surprise when Renarde bucked powerfully beneath him. Dislodged, Verne lost his balance, rolling on the ground.

And then at last Torbridge fired.

And missed. Missed? At that close range? For a heartbeat, Verne held his breath, waiting for the pain to strike. It didn't. But no, Torbridge hadn't missed.

He'd shot Renarde. Smoke drifted up from his chest in the moonlight.

Verne leapt to his feet, staring at Torbridge.

"Apologies, my lord," that gentleman said mildly. "I'm afraid I had to be sure."

"Sure?" Verne repeated stupidly.

"Of the traitor. It could have been you, after all."

A hiss of laughter escaped Verne. He lowered his pistol, letting it hang by his side. "Well, my instincts have been very unreliable recently. I admit I couldn't quite see you as a French spy but neither did I see..." He waved his dipped pistol in Torbridge's direction.

"The British spy-master?" Torbridge suggested. "I'm very glad to hear it."

"S?" Verne hazarded.

"At your service," Torbridge said politely. "But don't spread it around. I have no desire to have my identity reaching to Fouche and

Talleyrand in France."

"You're good," Verne said generously. A faint movement from the wounded Renarde caused him to jerk his head around.

The spent pistol lay on the ground between them, but Renarde had another. Half-sitting, he pointed it straight at Verne.

Torbridge cried out a warning, just as Verne hurled himself to the ground and fired. His lust for life, his longing to live it with Cecily, fell into his fear of leaving her alone and unprotected.

Two shots fired in rapid succession. Renarde lay unmoving on his back. And he, Verne, appeared to be still alive.

"Dear God, Verne," Torbridge uttered, falling to his knees beside him.

"What?" Verne demanded, puzzled. He tried to sit up, but his arm would not obey him. Instead, massive pain overwhelmed him. When he grasped his arm, he felt wetness and swore.

"It seems both our instincts are off," Torbridge said shakily.

"He was always such a weasel. I should have known he'd have two weapons. Actually, you'd better make sure he's dead, because the chances are he as at least one dagger on his person, too."

While Torbridge went to Renarde, Verne managed to sit up.

"He's dead," Torbridge reported. "But you were right about the dagger. Let's see to that wound and then I'll take you home and find a quack to take care of you."

"The Hart is nearer," Verne said. He felt dizzy with pain but the last thing he wanted was to scare Cecily with his wound. "Lily... Lily will help. And send to my wife when I'm... decent."

Torbridge hauled him to his feet. "Perhaps you do deserve her after all."

"No," Verne said. "No, I don't. But I shall do my best to keep her as long as I live."

"Then where's your damned horse, so we can make sure that is longer than this one night?"

SOME OF THE locals spilled out the taproom at the Hart to see the spectacle of the grand ladies and their servants who had arrived on horseback at such an unlikely time of the night. Then Villin pushed his way through them, ordering them in no uncertain terms to go back inside or go home.

"My lady," he greeted Cecily with a bow. "Please, come into the parlor and tell me how I may serve you."

Daniel and James walked in first, despite the innkeeper's filthy looks, presumably looking for any threats.

"Is my husband here?" Cecily asked Villin in low tones.

"No, my lady." He glanced wryly at Daniel and James who had thrown open the parlor door and were peering inside. "Feel free to light the candles," he called to them before returning his attention to Cecily. "As you see, the parlor is empty."

Cecily stalked inside and waited for him to follow. Isabelle and Shilton stood on either side of her. Daniel entered with Villin and closed the door.

"No games, Mr. Villin," Cecily commanded, summoning the spirits of all her ducal ancestors to give her the imperiousness she needed. "My husband's life is in danger and we need to find him."

Villin's eyes widened. "Dear God!" he exclaimed, reading the truth, perhaps, in her desperate eyes. "I don't know where he went. He was here but left about an hour ago now. I presumed he had gone home."

"Via the marshes?" Cecily asked.

"He always goes that way so far as I know, but I did not see him."

"Neither did we," Daniel put in. "And we came that way. Who did he speak to?"

"Only the captain."

"Cromarty?" asked Daniel, straightening and reaching for the door.

"Is he in the taproom?"

"No, he left not half an hour after his lordship." Villin scowled. "We'll get up a search party, search all the roads but the path to Finmarsh—"

"Dad!" called a female voice from outside the parlor. "Dad, you need to come at once!"

Villin muttered something under his breath, but the parlor door flew open before he could reach it. Lily Villin's gaze sought her father's, widening when she saw Cecily.

"Oh, thank God," Lily said shakily. "Come with me, my lady."

But Cecily was already out of the parlor, flying across the hall to the stairs where Lord Torbridge, of all unlikely people, was supporting a semi-lolling figure who looked alarmingly like her husband.

James and George following behind them, fell back to let Cecily through, and then she reached for him in terrible fear.

"Patrick," she whispered brokenly. "Oh, Patrick…"

His head jerked up and he smiled, though his lips, his whole face, were livid. "Cecily, my sweet," he said with surprising strength. "What are you doing here? Were you looking out of your window *again*?"

Her laugh came out as a sob as he kissed her lips, and then his head lolled against her shoulder as he lost consciousness completely.

CHAPTER NINETEEN

V ERNE REMAINED UNCONSCIOUS only long enough for them to get him to a bedchamber and into bed with all his clothes removed except for his drawers.

"We need a surgeon, or a physician," Isabelle said from the doorway, white-faced.

"One is sent for already," Lord Torbridge said. "My lady, excuse me. Madame de Renarde, might I have a word?"

Cecily, more concerned that Verne's eyelids were fluttering open, was vaguely aware that Isabelle stared at Torbridge with a sort of tragic resignation.

"Is it my husband?" Isabelle asked. "Is he dead?"

"I'm afraid he is," Torbridge said.

"Did he shoot Verne?" Isabelle asked.

"I'm afraid he did."

"But Verne killed him?" Isabelle asked.

"The honors are divided there," Verne said hoarsely. "I'm sorry, Izzy."

"It's best," Isabelle got out. "I think it's best." She turned blindly away and left the room.

Cecily, examining the wound beneath Verne's bloody bandages, swallowed hard. "How bad is it?"

"A scratch," Verne said, smiling at her.

"It will need the ball taken out," Torbridge said briskly. "I managed to slow the bleeding, so with care and luck and a decent physician, I daresay he will survive."

Lily came in and placed a glass of water in Cecily's hands. She helped Verne to take a drink and eased him back onto the pillows.

"Come, everyone," Lily ordered. "Her ladyship will sit with his lordship until the doctor comes. He doesn't need us all gawping at him."

"Quite right," Torbridge murmured, preparing to obey.

"Wait," Cecily called after him. "I don't understand. How did you even come into this?"

"He was just passing," Verne said, taking her hand. "Fortunately."

Torbridge cast him a faint smile and bowed to Cecily with incomparable grace. "My lady."

With the room cleared, it was so silent that at first Cecily did not notice Shilton, perched on the edge of the chair in the corner. Then the maid stood up and walked toward the bed looking unusually decisive.

"Shilton, go with the others, please," Cecily ordered, for she wanted, *needed* to say at least one thing to her husband in private.

"I will, my lady," Shilton assured her, "but there's something you both need to know first. I wasn't going to tell, for I'd given her ladyship—the late Lady Verne—my loyalty and I always felt she was watching over me. Maybe that was my madness, I don't know, but I see more clearly these days, and *you* are my lady now."

Touched, in spite of everything, Cecily inclined her head. "Thank you, Shilton."

"And he is my lord and has been these five years I kept my silence. Forgive me."

Verne frowned. "Silence about what?"

"About the fire," Shilton said. "I know you took the blame of it, to take it away from his late lordship, and I thought—I *assumed*—you'd want to do it for her late ladyship, too."

Verne shifted, his fingers tightening on Cecily's. "We don't need to talk about this now—"

"Yes, we do," Shilton interrupted. "Because you've imprisoned yourself in guilt and it's spoiling things for you. I was in the bedchamber when you quarreled this afternoon."

Cecily glanced at Patrick, but didn't speak.

Shilton was looking at him, too. "We all know his late lordship wasn't right, wasn't responsible at the end, and you thought you should have known what he would do, should have been able to stop it. That's the guilt that eats you up, isn't it?"

Verne closed his eyes.

"Stop, Shilton," Cecily said uneasily at last. "His lordship isn't strong enough for this conversation right now."

"It will *give* him strength," Shilton insisted. "Because the guilt isn't his. It wasn't even his late lordship's, so it *can't* be his."

Verne opened his eyes, frowning. "What do you mean?"

"I mean I saw *her* do it," Shilton said. "Your brother didn't set the house on fire. His wife did, quite deliberately. She thought it would kill him, and that you and I and everyone else would save her. No thought for her daughter or for you. Only herself."

Verne stared at her, his lips falling open.

She nodded once to him, curtseyed to Cecily, and walked out of the room.

Slowly, Verne turned his eyes from the door and looked at his wife, baffled. "That was a large secret. Why tell us now?"

"Because it's coming between us, your belief that you are too guilty to deserve love." She brushed his hair back from his face with tender fingertips. "You are not a bad man, Patrick. Like everyone else, you only behave badly sometimes. But do you know the funny thing? It never mattered to me if you were bad or not. Because love isn't about what you deserve. It just is. And I love you."

She kissed his lips. After a surprised moment they responded, opening and taking control, kissing her back until she was breathless.

"And I love you," he whispered against her lips. "With everything I am and could be. I didn't mean to. I didn't think I was capable of it, but God help me, I do. I don't want anyone or anything else. Just you. Always you." He drew her on to the pillow, his kiss more urgent as her tears flowed with happiness, dampening her face and his. "Let me love you before the doctor comes," he whispered.

And suddenly, she didn't know whether to laugh or cry some more. In the end, she did both at once, but the huge strength of her emotion, like his, seemed to need more of an outlet, and so she surrendered to his loving, with gladness and joy.

"But your poor arm," she whispered once, in distress.

"I can make love with one arm," he insisted. "See?"

She gasped, holding him closer. "Oh, yes. I see!"

AFTER THE DOCTOR'S excruciating ministrations, Patrick fell into exhausted sleep.

When he woke, he sensed another presence in the room. But it was not Cecily who now occupied the chair by his bed. It was Torbridge. Perhaps he'd dreamed Cecily and their stolen moments of sweet delights.

"What are you doing here?" he demanded of Torbridge.

"I've nowhere else to be since I retrieved the letter to Hobbes from your coat." Torbridge smiled faintly. "I sent your wife to eat breakfast and rest, but I imagine she will be back at any moment. How are you?"

"My arm throbs like a steam engine, so I suspect the laudanum has worn off. Which means I can at least think. What does the letter say?"

"Among other things, that it was Renarde who betrayed Jerome and is in the pay of the French government. And that Bonaparte will never defeat the Russians. He is not equipped or supplied for a Russian winter."

Verne absorbed that while Torbridge poured him some fresh water and handed him the glass.

"Then Renarde tried to kill Jerome when he escaped back to England," Verne said. "But he had left the Hart before someone shot at us the next day."

"Only officially. He must have been hiding, waiting for you in case Jerome had recognized him. For he didn't reach London until very late that night."

Verne nodded thoughtfully. "And it was he who attacked me near Mooreton Hall."

"Ill-judged. He was half drunk."

"And not wearing his spectacles," Verne guessed. "What a fine fellow I am to have scared off a blind and intoxicated man in a fist fight."

Torbridge grinned. "He was a slippery villain, drunk or sober. We are well shot of him." He rose to his feet. "And here, if I am not mistaken, is your wife returning. I shall take my leave and return to London. A speedy recovery to you, Verne."

Verne held out his good hand. "Did I say thank you for saving my life?"

Torbridge took his hand. "You are welcome." His lips curved, half rueful. "Thank you for your invaluable service."

And then the door opened and Cecily came in, smiling with delight when she saw that he was awake and talking. Torbridge bowed to her and was included in her smile, but she didn't seem to notice that he left the room.

"You look better," she said warmly, perching on the end of the bed, and smoothing his forehead with her cool palm. "We are to watch for fever and keep you in bed for the rest of the day and tomorrow."

"Dashed quack," Verne said ungratefully.

"Are you so anxious to get home?"

"I like home better now you are there." He took her hand. "You know I would not have left last night had it not been urgent. There were so many things I meant to say, to try and make things right between us again."

Her fingers squeezed his. "I know. The light on the marsh. Isabelle came. She told me Renarde was looking for you, that he was the traitor. So we all came flying over here to find you. I was afraid we were too late. Compared to that, silly suspicions, chambermaids, dreams, none of that matters."

He lifted her hand to his lips and kissed it. "For what it is worth, you have no need to be suspicious. The chambermaid had been sent by the Longstones to seduce me and sour things between us so that we were less likely to produce an heir. They were clutching at straws. What you saw, was me proving the point. I would not have touched her with more than one finger."

"I know. And I know you are right. For one thing, Mrs. Longstone would never have dismissed a chambermaid when she has guests staying."

"And Marjorie," he said.

Cecily flushed. "Don't. I had no business saying what I did."

"You had every right to ask. It is my fault for keeping secrets from you. You're my wife, my love, and I want you to understand." He held her hand to his chest. "Marjorie had a difficult life which she made worse by refusing to admit the problem. Instead, she convinced herself she loved me and all would be well if only we were lovers. Only I did not love her and I wouldn't have touched her if I did. She was Arthur's *wife*, the mother of his child. If you sense some guilt in me, if I speak her name at odd times, that is the reason. Because my brother's wife wanted me, because just occasionally I was so low I was almost tempted. But I never, ever let anything happen between us."

She tugged their joined hands to her cheek. He felt the drop of a tear, but she was smiling.

"Thank you," she whispered.

TWO DAYS LATER, their carriage pulled up at Finmarsh House. Verne, looking very dashing with his arm in a sling, stepped down from the carriage unaided, and held out his hand to his wife.

The servants, old and new, came out to welcome them back. From the open windows of the north wing, the plasterers cheered and waved their knives and brushes.

Verne and Cecily walked in together.

"Mrs. Shilton," Cecily greeted her newly promoted housekeeper, who smiled at her with pride.

"Mrs. Longstone is here to welcome you home," William murmured at the front door. "With Mr. Longstone."

"Excellent," Verne said at once. "Would you like me to see them off?" he asked Cecily.

"No. I believe I would like the privilege."

Mrs. Longstone came rushing downstairs to greet them, Henry at her heels. "How wonderful to see you both home," she exclaimed. "You could have knocked me down with a feather when I heard the news! Thank God your injury is no worse, Verne. Poor Renarde has disappeared altogether, so there are clearly some shocking footpads in the area."

"Shocking," Verne agreed.

"Don't worry, we aren't staying," Henry said with a quick smile to Cecily. "We only called to inquire, and when we heard you were expected home, stopped only to give you our best wishes."

"How very thoughtful," Cecily said politely. "Thank you. As you see, Verne is still very tired. He lost a lot of blood."

"Of course. Well, we shall hope to see you soon. What an eventful start to your marriage, Lady Cecily! Lady Verne, I should say."

"Oh, we need not stand on ceremony," Cecily said. "I'm sure we understand each other very well."

Henry cast her a quick, uncertain glance, though his mother seemed oblivious.

"We shall leave you now to look after your patient," Mrs. Longstone said, patting her hand kindly.

"Thank you," Cecily said, and looked around the still congregated servants until she found the chambermaid and beckoned to her. "Anne Wilson will be going with you."

Mrs. Longstone blinked in surprise, looking more than a little flustered. "Anne? My old chambermaid? Does she not give satisfaction?"

"No," Cecily said baldly. "I believe it is perfectly clear where her loyalties lie. We'll send her things on, along with the pay she has earned."

"Oh. Well, whatever you like, my dear," Mrs. Longstone said, faintly. "Perhaps we can afford her after all."

Anne, flushing scarlet to the roots of her hair, followed her employers from the house. Cecily accompanied them as far as the front steps.

"It was all in vain, you know," she murmured, "as I have just discovered, I was already with child when we returned from Scotland. And if," she continued relentlessly through the false congratulations of both Longstones, "if anything happens to either me or my child, whether or not your machinations have anything to do with it, Verne will undoubtedly kill you. And trust me, my brother will see that no jury of his peers will convict. Goodbye, Mrs. Longstone. Mr. Longstone."

While they gawped at her in a jumbled mix of fear and guilt, she strolled back into the house, resisting the temptation to dust off her hands.

"I doubt they will be back," she said with satisfaction to Verne who grinned, and ushered her toward the library door.

"Then I suggest we shove all the recent nonsense aside and enjoy the beginning of our married life," Verne said. He opened the library door, then paused, laying his good hand on her flat stomach. "I heard every word. Is it true?"

She flushed, smiling because she couldn't contain her delight any longer. "Yes, it's true," she whispered. "Are you pleased?"

"Oh, my dear, I could not be happier," he breathed.

Cecily laughed and drew him inside. "Let us see if that is true…"

Printed in Great Britain
by Amazon

61782230R00133